Love & Order

Holidays in Hallbrook

Elsie Davis

Sweet Romance Publishing

Sweet Romance Publishing

POB 778

Liberty, NC 27298

Cassie – At least you don't have an Italian leather sofa Tricia –Our conversations helped this story come to life – thank you!

Ecclesiastes 3:1
There is a time for everything, and a season for every activity under the heavens.

Chapter One

♥

GARRETT CLICKED THE BUCKLE of his harness into place and pulled tightly on the ends of the straps. "Ready for takeoff." He gave the helicopter pilot a thumbs-up in case he couldn't hear him over the low hum of the spinning blades and the motor propelling them. Normally, he would just take his own plane for such a short flight, but he wasn't in the right frame of mind to be piloting anything, making this chartered flight an easy decision.

The pilot went through a series of checks with the control tower, and it wasn't long before the whirring sound increased and the helicopter began to vibrate with the increased power, blocking out any chance of regular conversation. The huge metal bird lifted off from a private section of the airfield. The ground below faded away until New York City became an aerial view of rooftops and skyscrapers all blended together. Garrett let out a deep breath.

The flight from La Guardia to Glen Haven, New Hampshire, the closest private airport with a helipad to Hallbrook, was ninety minutes by helicopter and then a fifteen-minute drive north to the town where he'd spent most of his childhood. It was a trip he would always regret not making more often. The news of his mother's death had come as a shock, and now, days later, the ache he felt had deepened, spurred on by guilt. He hadn't even known she was having heart troubles, but then according to Charlie, her friend and solicitor, she hadn't either. Her heart attack had taken everyone by surprise. It was hard to believe she was gone.

He tamped down on the emotions trying to emerge, finding it easier to focus on what needed to be done. Once he settled his mother's estate, there would be no reason to return to his hometown, a place he'd left long ago and only manage to visit once or twice a year, much to his mother's consternation. Work had been his priority for as long as he could remember, and the corporate law offices of Bradley & West were proof of the success he and his best friend and partner, Jim, had achieved as a result of their dedication.

But being rated as the top law firm in Manhattan and in the top twenty nationwide didn't do a thing to ease the pain of knowing his mother was gone forever, especially since he'd disappointed her by canceling his visit this past summer. The Baden-Hamilton merger had derailed, and the multimillion-dollar deal was his baby, and therefore his responsibility to save. And then one thing after another had popped up, and before he knew it, September was fast rolling in. But for his mother, there would be no September.

Angelica, his sister, had been notified of their mother's passing through official Naval communication, but as a U.S. Naval officer on a submarine somewhere in the Pacific, there was no telling when she'd be home. Charlie was taking care of their mother's arrangements per her wishes, and a woman by the name of April St. James was taking care of the house. Charlie had insisted Garrett arrive as soon as possible to deal with some legal issues. Garrett had cleared his schedule, making sure he could be at the celebration of life to honor his mother on Saturday and could stick around for the reading of her will on Monday.

Luckily, his partner would be able to help Garrett with his caseload while he was out of town. Garrett wasn't sure where to begin with his mother's estate. Until he talked to the solicitor and his sister, his hands were tied. He'd have to close up the house until he could sell it. Neither he nor his sister were in a position to live in or manage a country estate. Finding a buyer would be the easy part, selling it...not so much.

The place was filled with mixed memories for him and his sister, mostly because it had been the start of their new life without their father after a bitter divorce. His mother had poured her heart into the place after purchasing it, her love of the land filling her with the determination to make a success of the place. Garrett's love, however, was for the city. His sister's love of the sea drove her career in the Navy. They'd been three completely different people on different courses in life.

In no time at all, the pilot landed the chopper in Glen Haven, the closest town to Hallbrook that had a private airstrip. Garrett removed his seatbelt, pushed open the heavy door, and waved his thanks to the pilot. He crouched low as he jogged out from under the air current of the blades and made his way to the waiting limousine.

"Good afternoon, Mr. Bradley. Sorry to hear about your mother. Sarah was a fine lady." George Bowman owned the limousine service, and he still operated some of the bookings for select customers. He was used to Garrett coming and going, although the visits had been few and far between the past few years.

"Thank you. It came as quite a shock." His mother had been an integral part of putting Hallbrook on the map. She'd not only managed to raise him and Angelica on her own, but she'd found the time to create a niche for the small town by attracting tourists to the area in search of artisan crafts made by the locals. She'd given up everything for him and his sister, including her marriage and home. And in return, he'd been a horrible son, making business more important than visiting her more often.

"If you'll drop me at the house, that would be great. It sounds as though I've got a lot to do." Garrett's guilt factor ramped up another notch.

"Ain't that the truth." The man shook his head, putting the car in drive and raising the privacy window. But not before Garrett caught the odd expression peering back at him through the rearview mirror.

Garrett made a mental note of their progress as they got closer to the house.

They passed by several farms, including the largest dairy farm in the state. Old man Peterson's place. His mother used to treat him to the delicious handmade ice cream for excellent grades as a reward. His reward, of course, had been getting into Yale and eventually out of Hallbrook.

It wasn't that he hadn't appreciated the town, but he'd loved the action of the city. It was the land of opportunity, a place where you could make your mark, other than by winning first prize for the fattest cow at the 4-H fair.

He spotted his old high school, Turlington High. The place where he'd gotten into his first fight with a bully, protecting a girl. They'd dated on and off the first couple of years of high school, but then her interest had turned more toward the high school quarterback and less on the geeky guy who'd preferred to study.

George turned right onto East Main Street as he made his way through town. The closer they got to the center of Hallbrook, the bigger the houses got. Many of the stately Victorian and Colonial homes had been restored to their former glory by the families who'd inherited them. The place hadn't changed much in the twenty-five years since they'd first moved there, other than the slow growth and addition of businesses and a few more homes. He spotted Sally's Diner and smiled, remembering the place fondly. For Garrett, the diner was where he had his first date, his first kiss, and the best peach pie in the county.

When they'd moved here, he'd been bored out of his eight-year-old mind and hated the hard labor and dirty chores that had come with living in the country and his mother owning farmland.

He'd dreamed of escaping back to the city. It had driven him to study harder to make that happen. His success as an attorney was proof of the determination, but each time he returned to Hallbrook, he felt a tug in the region of the heart.

They reached the outskirts of town, passing Angie's corner grocery and gas that had long since closed the gas pumps, the place now a convenience store for many of the locals. Fresh fruits and vegetables were readily available from farms nearby, but hodgepodge of other endless items crammed into the place.

George slowed, turning right at his mother's driveway, passing under the stone archway and through the wrought iron gates. The dirt road had been recently recoated with a fresh load of gravel. He spotted the two-story white house seconds before he noticed an unfamiliar dark blue sedan parked out front. It was an older car that had seen better days, and one Garrett assumed belonged to the woman staying here and taking care of things until he arrived.

George slid the dividing window down. "Here you are, sir. Hope things go well for you."

"Thanks. Don't bother to get out. I can handle everything." He grabbed his travel bag off the seat in front of him, looped his briefcase over his shoulder, and slid out of the car. He stopped to glance around and took a deep breath, inhaling the fresh country air and the scent of blossoming roses. There was no shortage of rose bushes strategically placed all around the house, another of his mother's passions.

The sun would be setting soon, and the front porch looked inviting as a viewing place for a glorious sunset. His mother had loved the orange-red colors that illuminated the sky with the setting sun, and she'd tried to capture the elusive perfect picture on her favorite camera so many times he'd lost count. Tonight, in honor of his mother, he'd do the same. Sunsets like this didn't happen in New York City, at least not with rolling farmland as far as the eye could see. His sunsets came complete with skyscrapers, and he'd be back to those in four days. Four short days to take care of business. It was all the time he could afford to be away from the office.

Garrett approached the house, climbing the three wooden steps that led to the front door. He wasn't sure whether to knock to announce his presence or to simply use his house key. The last thing he wanted to do was scare the poor woman watching over the place. Maybe a combination of both was in order.

Knock. Knock. Knock.

He tried the door handle and discovered it unlocked. Garrett started to push the door open, but it slammed shut, a loud bark coming from inside. He took a step back, unsure of what to do. He wasn't a fan of dogs, not by any means. The dog's bark was deep. *Big dog deep.* Garrett swallowed hard, his hand automatically going to the scars on his arm, a reminder of a run-in with a not-so-nice canine.

He heard voices on the other side of the door but couldn't make out what the words were over the barking dog. The decision was made for him when the door started to open, and he came face-to-face with three young kids. The boy, who appeared to be the oldest of the three, had a hold on the dog's collar, keeping the huge brown and white Saint

Bernard barely in check as he danced, trying to break free from the restraint, slobber dripping to the ground.

"Hi, I'm Garrett Bradley. This is my mother's house. Are you all here with April St. James?" He addressed the boy, thinking he was the best option for reasonable answers.

"Yup. She's cooking dinner. Do you need to talk to her?" The young boy stood straight and tall, answering his question as if he were in charge.

"Yes, that would be perfect." It would be a whole lot better than trying to talk to three kids, something he had zero experience doing as an adult. He was quite surprised Ms. St. James had brought her children and an oversized beast of a dog with her while she watched the house. It was a little unorthodox.

"Melanie, go get her. I've got to hold the dog 'cause you're too puny to handle him." The boy spoke to the oldest of the two girls who couldn't be much more than seven or eight. "Am not. You get her." Garrett couldn't believe this. He shook his head, trying to figure out what to do.

"Hey there, kids. Why are you hanging half in and half out the front door? This isn't a barn. Shut the door and come back inside." A feminine voice called out from somewhere behind the children.

"There's a man here to see you." The older girl spoke up.

"A man? Oh, good heavens, let him in. It must be Mr. Bradley." The woman's voice was soft and yet persuasive.

"That's what he said. But the dog won't budge," the boy spoke up, trying to pull the dog back.

"Come on, Rufus." The brunette came to his rescue, all barely-over-five feet of her. She wasn't much of match for the hairy beast, but she did manage to wrestle him back from the door enough for Garrett to step into the foyer.

"Sorry about that." She beamed at him, her eyes a striking shade of sapphire. She kept hold of the dog, much to his relief.

He nodded. "Thanks. I'm Garrett—"

"Bradley. Yes, we've been expecting you. I'm so sorry about your mother." She glanced at the kids and winced. "Kids, why don't you head into the kitchen, and I'll be right in. I need to talk to Mr. Bradley alone for a second."

The older boy shrugged and left; the others close on his heels. Apparently, they didn't care who Garrett was.

"Sorry, I don't like to talk about your mother in front of them. They loved her like a grandmother, and it's been so upsetting to them. I'm sure you understand."

"I do. It's been a shock for everyone, I imagine. I appreciate you stepping in to help keep the house in order and taking care of her horses." April shot him an odd look, one that disappeared just as quickly as it happened. It was the same look he'd seen on George's face.

She extended her hand, "April St. James. It's nice to meet you, although the circumstances could have been better."

He shook hands with her, holding on a tiny bit longer than necessary. The strength of her grip took him by surprise. So did the warmth.

"I know you just got here, and I hate to do this, but I've gotten behind at work and need to head to the office."

"I'll be fine. I'll make arrangements for everything before I leave so you won't need to worry about a thing." Garrett hoped it would be as easy as he made it sound.

April shrugged as she bit her lower lip, her head tilted to one side. "I hope you enjoy spaghetti because I made a huge pot of it. I thought it would be easier than you needing to find something to cook soon as you got here tonight."

She pulled the dog toward the front room. "Stay, boy." April closed the door behind her, locking him in the room. "If he isn't put up, he thinks he's one of the family and should be able to eat at the table accordingly." She laughed. "I don't usually him let back out until after dinner."

"Sounds like a handful. Looks like a handful. Must be a handful." Garrett forced a smile. April was insane to add a giant dog to her already chaotic mix of responsibility. He followed her down the hall and into the kitchen, the aroma of tomatoes and garlic greeting him. His stomach rumbled. He hadn't had a thing to eat since this morning on his way to the office.

"You have no idea." She grinned. "But you'll get a chance to find out." Her soft laughter was like music. Garrett frowned, unsure of what she meant. He was almost afraid to ask, but he sure hoped his mother hadn't taken in a dog—especially not one the size of Godzilla. He wouldn't have a clue what to do with it, especially considering his dislike of dogs. He may not have visited his mother often, but they talked at least once every two weeks, and she never mentioned getting a dog.

"Let me introduce you to the kids properly. This is Bryan, and he's nine." She tapped the top of his head and then moved on down the row of children, almost like a game of duck-duck-goose. "This is Melanie, and she's seven. And this is Sandy, and she's three. Sandy doesn't talk much, but the doctors say she'll be fine in no time. They've all had a lot to deal with over the past few months, and her way of dealing with the emotions has been silence."

"I'll take your word for it." It sounded as though the kids had gone through more trauma than a child should have to deal with, and it made him wonder about their story. When he was Bryan's age, the impact of his parents splitting up had been monumental, especially given the divorce was his fault.

April lifted the lid off the first pot. "Just stir this occasionally until you're ready to eat. The noodles get dropped in the water, stir them frequently, and they'll be ready in ten minutes if you prefer them al dente, otherwise, let them cook a minute or two longer. Easy enough, right?" April looked at him with confidence in her eyes, a confidence he didn't deserve.

"Smells awesome. Looks as though you made enough to feed an army."

"That'll last you two days, tops, but I'm sure your mother's friends will be stopping by with lots of food to help out. Here's my card if you need anything. You can call, and I'll help any way I can. I know this is going to be a tough transition for you—" she reached out to touch his arm, "—but you'll be fine. I'm sure of it."

"Thanks. I appreciate that. And don't worry, I'll be okay. I've handled this sort of thing before."

"If you say so." April crossed the kitchen to where a wheeled suitcase was parked in the corner. She pulled up the handle and started toward the front door. Garrett and the kids followed, Melanie stopping to let the dog out.

"Here, let me get this for you." He picked it up and hauled it to her car. He would have expected a much bigger suitcase considering all the children.

"Thanks. Don't forget, call me if you need me." She leaned down and hugged each of the kids. "I'll see you three soon, I promise. Be good for Mr. Bradley."

April wasn't making any sense. And why weren't the kids getting in the car with her? And for that matter, why wasn't she getting the dog? Something was seriously wrong with this picture.

She slid in the driver's seat and started the car before manually rolling down her window. "Take care." April waved, put the car in reverse and started to back up.

The motion of the vehicle snapped him out of his trance. "Wait. Where are you going? You can't leave your kids here." Normally calm under fire, Garrett couldn't keep the panic out of his voice.

She stopped the car and leaned toward the window. "They're not my children, they're yours." April seemed confused. Which was far better than stupefied, and exactly how he felt. She had this all wrong.

"I don't have any kids." The children looked as though they were about to cry, and he felt awful, but he couldn't let April drive off without them and the dog.

"Should have known he wouldn't want us." The boy grumbled in a low voice, grabbing his younger sister's hand, and taking off for the house. Melanie glanced at April and then glared at him before running to catch up with her brother and sister.

"What's the meaning of this?" Garrett demanded. He could handle a lot of things, but this wasn't in his wheelhouse and his patience was running out.

April got back out of the car and faced off with him. "Your mother adopted these children three months ago. Haven't you talked to her solicitor yet? I would have thought—"

Garrett winced. "You thought wrong." *Adopted*. As in legally hers. Why would his mother adopt kids at this stage of her life? She hadn't even consulted him about such an important issue. And she'd had three months to tell him. *You haven't been home in over six months.* "What am I supposed to do with them? I don't know the first thing about children. I have a job. A penthouse apartment in the city. What am I supposed to do?"

"Step up." Her answer was short and to the point, the thin set of her lips driving the point home. She was serious.

He swallowed hard and turned back to the house where three kids and the dog were waiting and watching.

"I'm sure Charlie will explain everything." The compassion in her voice was genuine, making him feel slightly better.

"Our meeting isn't until Monday, and the celebration of life is tomorrow. Don't you think you could provide me with a few more details? You seem to know a thing or two about the situation." He was desperate, and he couldn't let her leave without a better understanding.

"The children lost their parents four months ago, and your mother didn't want the kids to end up in the foster care system, so she adopted them with a promise to always do what was in their best interests. Their mother was a friend of hers from church. I was the assistant caseworker assigned to them, which is why I volunteered to stay with the children until you arrived. They know me. They are sweet kids, and it's been hard for them to lose their parents and now their Grams."

"Grams?" There was so much he needed to ask her, the meaning of Grams the least of them, but that's what came out.

"It's the name they called your mother, short for grandma."

April got back in her car. "I'm a sucker for these kids and will do anything I can to help, but right now, I've got to make sure I can keep my job. I've missed a lot of work and need to catch up on my caseload."

"Fine. I'll figure a way through this situation for the next few days until my sister can get leave and decide what she wants to do. Clearly, she's the better option to handle this unexpected situation." He didn't feel as confident as he tried to sound. There were two problems. He didn't know when his sister would be home, and he didn't know a thing about taking care of kids, not even temporarily.

Chapter Two

♥

GARRETT RETURNED TO THE front porch; four sets of eyes trained on him. He didn't even know where to begin. "I didn't mean what I said, the way it sounded. I had no idea you were living here or that my mother was your grams." It wasn't a word he'd ever heard associated with his mother, and it didn't come naturally. "What do you say we start over?" He had a suspicion the next few days depended on making peace with the trio. His fate hung in the balance as he waited for them to answer.

"I guess that depends what you intend to do with us." Bryan stood with his arms crossed, his feet slightly apart as he drew a line in the proverbial sand.

"Well, the first thing we should do is eat the food April fixed. Seeing as my mother adopted you, something I didn't know, by the way, we're family. I think we should talk and get to know one another. Maybe things will look a little better." Garrett could eat his way through an all-you-can-eat buffet and things wouldn't look better. This entire situation was like something out of a nightmare, only it seemed things wouldn't return to the way they were when he woke up in the morning.

"I meant after that. Are you going to put us in a foster home? We're not going let anyone split us up. There's a girl at school they did that to, and she hasn't seen her brother in three years. Grams promised to take care of us. Are you giving us the same promise?" The boy was way beyond his years, and Garrett didn't have the slightest clue how to answer. *How did you reason with a nine-year-old going on fourteen?*

Garrett ran his hands through his hair, needing a few seconds to find the right words. "I don't have a crystal ball, and I haven't had a chance to go over the legalities, but I can give you the same promise my mother did."

The kid's faces lit up with hope. "Yes!" The two older kids exclaimed, giving each other high five.

"Now wait a minute, just so we're on the same page, the promise that I'll do what's best for you." He didn't want to add to the long list of disappointments they'd been through the past few months.

"Figures. I'm going inside to play on my tablet." Melanie shrugged away from her brother, a pout on her face. "Come on, Rufus." The dog followed her inside.

"Dinner will be in about fifteen minutes," Garrett hollered after her. Wonderful. In charge less than five minutes, and he already had one of them mad enough to flee the scene, her faithful dog not far behind. "Any chance you know how to cook spaghetti?" He directed the question at Bryan. "I don't cook."

Bryan nodded. "Anyone can boil water and stick spaghetti in it. I learned that when I was like seven."

Having a nine-year-old cook dinner didn't seem right. "If you say so. Your grams did all my cooking, so I didn't get many opportunities in the kitchen. I guess we'll find out if you're right. Can you keep an eye on Sandy while I'm inside trying not to burn the house down?"

Garrett caught the hint of a smile as it creased Bryan's face, but it was gone just as quickly. "Sure. I usually do. She is *my* little sister." Bryan's emphasis on the word was a sharp reminder of the problem they faced. These kids might all belong together, but not with him.

Bryan turned, pulling his sister toward the house, but she resisted, looking up at him, a question in her eyes.

Garrett felt a tug in the region of his heart as he stared down into her expressive baby-blue eyes. Eyes that held far more sadness than a young child deserved. He took a step toward her and knelt. "It will be all right, I promise." He reached out to ruffle her hair.

"Come on, Sandy." Bryan led the little girl inside, but Sandy's eyes didn't leave him until the door closed.

Garrett shook his head. He was considered one of the toughest attorneys in the business for a reason. He didn't back down. And he wasn't going to shy away from this challenge. How hard could it be to take care of them until he talked to Charlie, and Angelica got home? Except for the idea of taking them to New York, even if only for a few days, scared the heck out of him.

He entered the house and made his way to the kitchen. The garlic aroma was stronger now than before, his stomach reminding him yet again how long it had been since he'd had something to eat.

Picking up the ladle, he stirred the sauce the way April had instructed. If it tasted like it smelled, it would be the best part of his night. He turned on the burner under the pan of water and dumped in the box of spaghetti and covered it with the lid.

Ten minutes for al dente—a cooking term he actually recognized. After setting the alarm on his phone, he watched and waited. Bryan was right—there was no way he would screw this up. Garrett leaned back against the counter and used his phone to check his emails.

There was a sizzling noise behind him, and he glanced at the stove, shocked to see a bubbly liquid dripping down the sides of the pan. He pushed off from the counter, shoved his phone in his pocket, and grabbed the potholder to shove the pan to the back burner. Cloudy water flooded the stovetop making a huge mess, but at least he saved the spaghetti. He turned down the burner and put the pan back on it to let it finish cooking.

His alarm sounded off a few minutes later. April had already set the table in her infinite wisdom, so now all he had to do was serve the food. The woman was an expert with kids and cooking. Efficiency was a highly admirable trait, but the kitchen wasn't exactly at the same level as the boardroom. It would seem even he could handle the learning curve of kitchen duty.

"Kids," he hollered, "dinner!"

Melanie and Sandy wandered in and sat. Bryan, on the other hand, was noticeably absent.

Garret navigated his way down the hall, stepping over toys. He reached the living room and discovered the boy completely absorbed in a game on his tablet. *So much for keeping an eye on his sister.* Garrett pulled an earplug out of the boy's ear. "What happened to watching Sandy?"

"Mel said she would do it." The boy shrugged.

Garrett shoved back the reprimand that popped into mind. "Dinner is ready. You need to come to the table and eat." Dealing with a child not willing to listen wouldn't be the same as dealing with an employee who didn't listen. It wasn't as if he could fire the kid. They were stuck together—at least for now.

"I'm not hungry." Bryan stuck the earplug back in his ear and resumed playing his game.

Garrett pulled the plug from his ear again. "April went to a lot of trouble to make this dinner, and you will come to the table to eat it. I know you're unhappy with what's going on, but it's her you're hurting if you don't eat the dinner she prepared."

Bryan hesitated for just a minute before powering down his tablet. He headed for the kitchen, and just like that, crisis averted. April had left an impression on these kids in the short time she'd stayed with them.

"You didn't wash your hands," Melanie corrected Bryan as he pulled back his chair and sat down.

"Did too, so mind your own business, little Miss Busybody." Bryan glared at her.

"Did not." Melanie wasn't backing down.

"Kids, please. Bryan, we both know you didn't, so please go wash up, and I'll serve dinner." Garrett jumped into the conversation, surprising the kids. They fell silent, surprising him.

The kid did as he was told—thankfully. Garrett wasn't sure what he would have done if he hadn't. Probably let him eat with dirty hands. He searched the cupboards for a bowl to put the spaghetti in.

"What's that smell?" Melanie asked, scrunching up her nose in distaste.

"What—"

"It smells burnt. Seriously?" Melanie jumped to her feet and hurried to the stove, pushing the pan to a cold side burner.

It was ten minutes, exactly as April told him to do. Or it had been about four minutes ago. The conversation with Bryan had slowed him down.

"*Ummm*, I don't think so." She lifted the lid and peered inside. "There's no water."

Bryan and April had been wrong, he couldn't cook spaghetti. It would seem he'd failed Cooking 10.

"It's ruined," she said.

"I could pour out what's on top and leave the burnt spaghetti in the bottom of the pan. The sauce will cover any burnt taste on the food."

"If you say so." She looked at the spaghetti, a heavy frown on her face.

Garrett took the pan and dumped the pasta into the bowl, the entire mass landing with a thud.

"Didn't you stir it?" Melanie shook her head.

"No one mentioned anything about stirring." He felt like a fool. It was a simple task, at least according to everyone else. Failure was a bitter pill to Garrett.

"Are you for real? Have you been living in the dark ages?" The disbelief in Melanie's childish voice drove home the magnitude of his failure.

"I told your brother that my mother did all the cooking. And in college, I ate fast food. And now, I have people that cook for me or I eat out. It's never been a skill I needed to learn."

"Now what are we supposed to do? We can't eat this." Melanie scrunched up her face. "One thing I am good at is delegating duties. I'll get Bryan to cook some more spaghetti seeing as he knows how." He hated to give up control, but for the sake of dinner and his hunger, he'd do it.

"Bryan?" She rolled her eyes. "He can't cook. But I can."

"Aren't you seven?" Garret asked.

"I am. But I've been cooking mac and cheese and spaghetti since my last birthday."

"Okay, then. If you'd cook a fresh batch of spaghetti noodles, that would be perfect." One thing was for certain, it couldn't be any worse than his attempt.

Bryan moseyed back into the kitchen just as he handed Melanie a new pan. "Smells like burnt crap."

"That's enough from you, young man. Your sister is making a fresh batch."

The next ten minutes were spent in silence, and it was a relief when Melanie announced dinner was ready. She made it all look so easy. Garrett took up the plates and ladled plenty of sauce on the noodles before sliding each plate in front of each of the kids.

"You have to cut up Sandy's food. And that's way too much for her." Melanie picked up her napkin and draped it across her lap.

I can do this. Garrett took half the food off Sandy's plate, cut up the rest and set it in front of her. He took his seat, anxious to eat. The burnt odor still lingered but had lessened considerably.

Rufus bounded into the kitchen and sat next to Bryan.

Garrett remembered April's warning about letting him in the kitchen. He got up and led the dog down the hall and locked him in the front room. By the time he returned, Sandy hadn't touched her food.

"Isn't she hungry?" he asked.

"Umm, it's spaghetti, and you have to feed her. She's only three." Melanie stared at him as if he'd grown another head.

So much for eating his own dinner. Bite after bite, he fed Sandy, minutes ticking by with each forkful. Did kids always eat this slowly? Sandy pushed his hand away, the food spilling from the fork onto her booster seat. She immediately reached for it, smearing her fingers in as she tried to pick it up and put it in her mouth, her face soon covered in sauce.

Garrett got up to get a washcloth to wipe her face and hands. By the time he returned, she'd grabbed an entire handful from the plate he'd left sitting on her tray. The two older kids giggled. *Terrific.*

The last thing he wanted was orange tomato sauce all over his suit. He reached forward to grab one of Sandy's hands and held it out of the way. He reached for a wipe and cleaned up her face. Success. Now all he needed to do was wipe her hands. He reached for her free hand, but just as he did, she reached for his tie.

Garrett pulled free, only to discover bright sauce all over his silk tie.

His dry cleaner would have a fit.

As far as he was concerned, the tie was ruined and belonged in the trash. He reached up and removed it, handing it to Sandy to play with to distract her while he got her cleaned up. After removing her plate, he wiped her tray and finished cleaning her hands.

"Who wants one of April's sugar cookies she baked and left for us?"

"Me," both kids hollered.

"Her cookies rock," Bryan added.

Sandy pulled on his shirt sleeve and pointed at the cookies.

"Here you are. One for each of you. Why don't you take them in the living room and let me clean up the mess?" That is, he'd take care of it after he ate a plate of cold spaghetti.

"You don't have to tell us twice." Bryan smiled. It was a fleeting reaction, but a smile, nonetheless.

A victory in Garrett's book. The kids took off down the hall, Sandy not far behind them.

Garrett rolled up his sleeves and started to clean up the kitchen. He rinsed the dishes and loaded the dishwasher, the same way he'd done a million times. Dishes were a chore he and his sister shared. He might not have had to cook, but there had always been chores to be done.

He'd almost finished wiping off the table when he felt a tug on his pants. Sandy had wandered into the kitchen, her thumb stuck in her mouth.

"What's going on, little one? Do you need anything?" Sandy hadn't spoken a thing since he'd been there, but April had already explained the problem, so he wasn't expecting an answer.

Sandy pointed at a purple cup on the counter.

Another type of communication, but one he understood. She wanted a drink. "Do you want water?"

She shook her head.

"Milk?"

She nodded.

And just like that, they had a two-way conversation going.

He poured milk in the cup. "Can you handle this, or do you need me to hold it for you?"

She held up her chubby little hands and squeezed her fingers.

"I guess that means you want to hold it." He grinned. It was small and similar to the cups he'd seen parents give their kids.

She took the cup from him and pressed it to her mouth. Rufus wandered into the kitchen and sat nearby, watching them, his tail thumping. The dog must be thinking it was his turn for dinner, and he'd be right.

Garrett found the dog food and poured the hard chunks in the dog bowl. He picked up the other bowl and headed for the sink to refill it with water, but before he got that far, Sandy started to cry.

He looked back at her and spotted milk everywhere.

What next?

He picked Sandy up to lift her out of the milky puddle and carried her to the living room. "Hey, Bryan and Melanie, can you watch her for a minute? She spilled her milk everywhere, and I need to clean up."

"Didn't you use her sippy cup?" The girl shook her head. It was something she often did as if she were dealing with a child and not the other way around.

"The purple cup?"

"Yes. Then it couldn't spill. Did you put the lid on it?" she asked.

Garrett winced. Another mistake. "What lid?"

"The orange top sitting at the back of the sink," she quickly pointed out.

He'd seen the contraption but hadn't been sure what to do with it. "Oh. Guess not." He started to head back to the kitchen, but Sandy started to cry louder. She held up her arms to him.

"Guess she wants to go with you. Is that right, Sandy?" Melanie asked her. The little girl nodded.

Garrett headed back to the kitchen, the toddler in his arms. As he rounded the corner, he noticed Rufus licking up the milk. Well, that's one redeeming quality for a dog. The floors probably needed mopping, but at least nobody would play slip and slide with the milk puddle.

He rinsed out her sippy cup, filled it with more milk, and put the lid on this time. He handed it to Sandy, who eagerly took it.

Using her other hand, she tried to push off from him. He put her down, and she took off running, back to her brother and sister.

Garrett pulled a bottle of his mother's favorite wine from the pantry and poured a glass. Five minutes of peace and quiet was heaven. Hoping for answers, he tried calling the solicitor but was forced to leave a voicemail.

He was barely getting through tonight. A few more days would feel like forever. How could anyone expect him to watch three kids, even if only for a few days, and deal with the celebration of life his mother wanted that was set for tomorrow?

Thank goodness, Jessica, his mother's craft boutique manager, had emailed him shortly after he'd received the call from Charlie, letting him know she would handle everything with his mother's business. Jessica was the silver lining he needed to get through the weekend while he waited for Angelica, freeing him up to handle the situation with kids.

Garrett glanced at his watch. A full hour had passed since April had left. He tapped his watch, checking to make sure it was still working. Seven o'clock, and it already felt like midnight-the bewitching hour. He hoped these kids' bedtime was seven-thirty, or he'd never make it. How did anyone survive this kind of madness?

Chapter Three

♥

APRIL HAD NEVER MET Garrett in person, but she'd seen plenty of pictures in his mother's house. They didn't do the man justice. Tall, dark, and handsome had nothing on this guy. He was all that and more. His black hair was cut short and perfectly styled, with a natural waviness across the top. Long lashes and perfectly shaped eyebrows complemented his dark brown eyes. His olive skin was courtesy of his mother's Italian heritage, the two of them the spitting image of one another right down to his sharp, angular jaw. The man deserved to be on the sexiest man alive list put out each year, although he was more businesslike than the easygoing men who usually won.

Garrett's power suit and tie didn't come close to a department store knockoff. One didn't need to see the label to know he wore custom-tailored clothes. Sara Bradley had spoken of both her children with love and pride in her voice with good reason.

But right now, Garrett was floundering. Unfortunately, she had a feeling it would get worse before it got better. She'd struggled with how much to tell him, recalling a conversation she'd had with his mother months ago.

Sarah had wanted her own children to meet the little darlings living with her before they found out she'd adopted them, thinking it would help smooth the way to their acceptance of what she considered a non-negotiable outcome. Garrett obviously hadn't been home, and he was finding out in the worst way possible. It made her sympathetic to his plight, but not enough that she could afford to stay longer.

She hoped Garrett was up to the task of parenthood because the one thing she hadn't told him was going to send him over the edge. Angelica was not the answer Sarah Bradley had in mind when she set up her new will.

It didn't take her long to get to the New Haven County Social Services office. The place was mostly deserted, but a few stragglers were hanging out trying to ease the caseload that never ended. She made her way to her cubicle and sat in her well-worn leather chair, the cracks revealing the white fibers beneath the surface. Government budgets didn't include new chairs, especially not for assistants, even if they were overworked and underpaid. The creaky chair had seen better days.

Her desk was piled high with files and pink message slips. You'd think she'd been gone for weeks, not days. April flipped through the folders and picked out the most urgent ones. Tomorrow was Saturday, and technically her day off, but it had been months since she'd had one of those. Her cases wouldn't resolve themselves and finding people at home on a Saturday was easier than hunting them down during the workweek.

Too bad she didn't get credit for overtime. Instead, it was considered all part of the job, and the powers-to-be had no problem making sure everyone knew it.

"There you are, April. I was beginning to think you weren't coming back." Her boss's voice made her cringe. She turned to face Tammy. The woman enjoyed lording her power over the employees who reported to her, making everyone's life more miserable than it needed to be.

"It was just a few days, and it was client-related." April felt the need to defend her decision.

"Well, I was just telling Teresa we should start looking for your replacement." It had been three days, for crying out loud, and her boss knew exactly what she'd been doing and who she'd been doing it for. Once upon a time, those kids had been her charges, so in a way, she was doing her job. Too bad Tammy didn't see it that way.

"Mr. Bradley just got in tonight. I couldn't leave the kids. I came straight here to get some of my work to take home." Her chin rose a notch, but only as much as she dared to make herself feel better, unwilling to push Tammy too far.

"Well, see that you get caught up. There are more than a dozen applicants waiting for the chance to get a job here."

"I understand." She also understood most of them wouldn't last a month here with the long hours, long weeks, and never-ending workload.

"I will have to write this up as a warning. It wasn't calendared for vacation, and it's not personal leave for a family emergency or death, so those three days count as unexcused absences. Four total and you're history." Tammy pushed her glasses back, her haughty stare daring April to contradict her statement. The woman was a walking human resource handbook waiting to catch employees in the wrong.

April bit back the reply that popped into her head, knowing she couldn't afford to lose this job. "Yes, ma'am."

Tammy turned on her high heels and sashayed away like a queen holding court. Formal and stiff. One day, things would be different. One day, April would get the satisfaction of having the last word with that woman.

April's dream had been to teach elementary school, not only to help kids learn the fundamentals of reading and math but also to help them learn life skills. Teaching them to grow as individuals and deal with the curves life threw you when you least expected them. Something no one ever did for her as a kid while she drifted in and out of foster homes.

She loved kids, and they were one of the main reasons she hadn't quit this job. That, and her bills, of course. Once she'd save enough money to return to college, finish her degree, and could teach—she'd quit, but until then, she was stuck right here.

Throughout the night, April had pored over her files, making notes. By morning, she was bleary-eyed and tired but felt more in control of her workload. She got ready in record time and headed out the door, intent on stopping at the Sweeter Side of Life bakery for donuts to take the kids before she started her workday. She spent half the morning convincing herself it had nothing to do with seeing the man, and everything to do with checking up on the kids, but the truth landed somewhere in between, and there was no sense denying it.

April knocked on the door of the Bradley residence. Rufus barked, letting everyone in the house know someone was at the front door whether they'd heard the knock or not. The dog was a handful, and not always the best behaved, having been treated like an equal in the kid's family and then with Sarah. Sometimes it was as though he forgot he was a dog.

The door opened, and Rufus rushed out to greet her, almost knocking the coffee out of her hand. She spun away from him to protect the treats she'd bought.

"Down, boy," she scolded. The dog sat down, his tail wagging and slobber dripping down on the porch. She hazarded a gaze back at Garrett as he stood in the door watching the fiasco but unmoving. The poor guy looked like heck compared to his normal professional business image.

He still managed to get dressed in a shirt and a pair of slacks, even at this hour of the morning, not to mention on a day off. But that's where the similarities ended. His tie hung loosely around his neck, and his shirt was untucked. He sported bags under his eyes and a worn-out, haggard look on his face as though he hadn't slept a wink.

"Rufus, inside," she commanded in the most authoritative voice she could muster. It seemed to surprise them both when he did what he was told.

"Wow. Well done. You're like a dog and kid whisperer." Garrett's compliment pleased her, and she flushed under his gaze.

"I wish. Sorry for stopping by so early, but I felt terrible leaving you in the lurch yesterday and thought I should stop in and see how things were going. I've got a few minutes and brought some coffee and donuts." She held out a cup of coffee as a peace offering.

Garrett pushed the door open wide, gesturing for her to come inside and taking the bag from her. "Thanks. Are you a fairy godmother or something?"

"Or something." She beamed, not willing to share her personal life with someone she didn't know. She started down the hall toward the kitchen but made the mistake of glancing right to check on Rufus, but it wasn't the dog who'd jumped up on the couch to make himself comfortable that caught and held her attention. The living room was a disaster. There were pillows on the floor, toys scattered everywhere, cups and bowls of popcorn on the coffee table and what looked like half the popcorn on the floor. "What happened here? A tornado?"

"A tornado would've done less damage than those kids." His voice was a mixture of teasing and seriousness, causing her to shoot him a look of concern.

"What you mean?"

"I mean the kids were nonstop balls of energy last night. Is it always like this? A cage full of monkeys at a zoo would have been easier to control." The lines across his forehead deepened.

"How much trouble could they have been after dinner? Sandy goes to bed at eight, and the other two at nine." She shook her head, fighting back the grin threatening to escape.

"Interesting. I think I've been had." Garrett shook his head and let out a sigh born of frustration. The man was a rookie when it came to kids, but then he'd told her as much right before she drove away.

"Let me guess, that's not what they told you." She couldn't hold back her grin any more than she could have stopped the dawn of a new day.

"Bingo. And it's not funny. The version I got was *whenever we want to because it's not a school night.* They stayed up to watch movies, eat popcorn, and have pillow fights. There was nothing I could do to stop it, so I just hung out in the corner to make sure no one got hurt."

"They got you good. I know it's not funny, but they're just kids being kids. They sense you're a newbie at this and will test your authority. I'll have a talk with them." Not that it would be of any use when she wasn't around. It was up to Garrett to establish the ground rules and his authority. She hoped he'd figure it out quick, for his sake.

"I'd appreciate that. Do you have time to share your cup of coffee with me? Adult conversation would go a long way to making my morning brighter."

She glanced at her watch. "Sure, I've got about thirty minutes before I have to leave for my appointment."

Garret led the way, using his foot to push a couple of toys out of their path.

"Where are the little darlings?"

"Fast asleep, thank God." He shook his head.

April was stunned when she got a glimpse of the kitchen. She expected another war zone, but that wasn't the case. "What happened here?"

"I happened. By the way, you were wrong. Cooking spaghetti was not a simple affair. It boiled over, then I burned it, and what was left was a huge lump that was inedible. Melanie saved the night by cooking a new batch. Between that and Sandy's spilled milk, last night can only be termed a disaster." *Ouch.* "I'm sorry." Her shoulders shook as she tried to contain her laughter. "It sounds as though you had the heat too high. It boiled over and lost too much water. And it sounds as though you didn't stir. A dab of oil in the water helps also." She couldn't imagine what it felt to be bested by a seven-year-old.

"None of which you mentioned." He frowned.

"I assumed you had basic cooking skills. You do live alone." It wasn't her fault she'd overestimated him. How did the son of a woman who had been a fantastic cook end up not knowing the fundamentals?

"I never needed to cook. Mom didn't let anyone in the kitchen when she was cooking, then came college and fast food, and now an upscale version of take-out is available from several local restaurants near where I live."

"So how did you get from all that—" she pointed back to the living room, "—to this?" She indicated the clean kitchen with her hand.

"I sent them to the living room and cleaned up the kitchen. I might not be able to cook, but growing up, mother had Angelica and me cleaning and doing chores. A large part of that was kitchen duty. I learned to enjoy my spaces neat, clean, and uncluttered. Last night, I made this my sanctuary and posted it as off-limits. I even moved the dog's water bowl to the front room and kept him out." Garrett pulled a serving platter from the cupboard and set it on the table.

April busied her hands by laying out napkins. Anything to keep from watching Garrett and thinking about him as anything other than the children's new guardian. Handsome and smart made it difficult. "Great idea. Wish I'd thought of something like that. At least the cleaning would've been more centralized."

Garrett looked at her with interest. "You mean you're not perfect at this? I was beginning to wonder."

"Hardly. Let's just say, I had to do a lot of cleaning when I was growing up, and I didn't have much control over what people did."

"Want to elaborate?" Garrett lifted his left eyebrow slightly and cocked his head to the side.

"Not really. The past is in the past, and I prefer to keep it that way." She pulled the donuts from the bag and laid them on the plate for when the kids woke up. Nothing like starting them off with a sugar rush, but it would score some points for Garrett. "Hope black coffee was okay?"

"It's perfect. The stronger, the better as far as I'm concerned." His mouth curled up, tiny crow's feet appearing at the corners of his eyes. He might look a little rough, but his smile was the only thing she noticed when he turned on his charm.

"The Sweeter Side of Life has some of the best coffee and donuts around, or at least, that's the way the locals tell it." April took the lid off her Hazelnut coffee and blew on it, trying to cool it off.

"Right now, I'd take generic week-old coffee over the weak chai tea my mother keeps in the house."

April laughed, remembering his mother with fondness. "Sarah was definitely an avid tea drinker, and she was forever trying to get others to switch from coffee to tea, claiming it was better for their bodies. I don't remember her having much success. I do know, however, there is some coffee hidden away here for the non-converts. Your mother wasn't a barbarian." She shot him one of her famous *be-real* looks, took a bite of her powdered jelly donut, and then wiped at her mouth with a napkin, all without batting an eye.

"Then please, point me to it." He leaned forward and brushed her cheek with the pad of his thumb.

The move caught her unawares, and she drew in a deep breath, trying to remember what he'd asked, the tingling she felt all the way down to her toes befuddling her brain.

"You had sugar on your face," he teased, the devilish twinkle in his eyes telling. "The coffee?" he repeated.

Yes, that's it. Coffee.

April slid one of the chairs toward the refrigerator and stood on it. She reached into the cupboard over the top and pulled out the coffee pot, the filters, and the bag of coffee, placing them on the counter. "Here you are. I didn't think to get it out because I'm not much of a coffee drinker, myself. Ramps me up too much."

"You're naturally this energetic in the morning?" The way he asked the question sounded as though he was paying her a compliment, and she couldn't help the warmth that flooded her face and throat.

"I guess you could say that. This morning's coffee is a treat. Hazelnut with cream. It's more like a coffee beverage than coffee." She'd learned long ago that coffee agitated her more than it ever woke her up. Her job kept her on edge enough with adding to it.

"I would tend to agree." He chuckled.

A cry echoed from upstairs. *Sandy.* "Sounds as though your day is about to begin. Want me to get her?" April had fallen in love with the little girl, her heart breaking for all three of the Williams children, but especially Sandy, who seemed to be having a tough time of adjusting. April's maternal instinct had gone into overdrive as she tried to draw the girl back into the real world and help ease her fears.

"Sure. Maybe I should follow along and see how you do it. At the office, I learn by staying on top of everything, diving right in, and taking control. But here, when it comes to kids, I think watching someone else might be time better spent."

"Excellent idea." Garrett followed her up the stairs. As she passed the bathroom, April noticed it hadn't fared any better than the living room.

"Don't forget the celebration of life is this afternoon at one. Give the kids lots of extra time to get ready." She had to work, and he was on his own, but it didn't stop her from wanting to give him helpful information to pave the way.

"Okay, thanks for the heads up. Jessica, my mother's boutique manager and friend, made all the arrangements and let me know she'd be over to set everything up later. I'm glad she didn't accept my offer to let me handle it now that I'm responsible for the kids."

Sandy stopped crying the second they opened her door and entered.

April crossed the room to her toddler bed. "Morning, sunshine. Did you have a good night's sleep?"

Sandy nodded as she sucked her thumb. It was another toddler behavior she'd reverted to after her parents' deaths. April reached for her, but Sandy crawled to the end of the bed and held her arms and squeezed her fingers at Garrett. "Well, it would seem she wants you instead, so you're on duty. You must have done better than you thought last night. I've got to leave soon anyway." For as much as it gave her a twinge of jealousy to have the little girl prefer Garrett, it made her heart swell to know Sandy was reaching out to an adult, learning to trust again.

"But what do I do?" Garrett asked, looking unsure of himself.

"Pick her up to start with." April couldn't help but laugh.

Garrett shot her one of those I-knew-that-much looks. "I was referring to what needs to be done afterward. Last night, you failed to tell me all the particulars about feeding her, and I had to learn from Miss Know-It-All, Melanie." He shook his head. "Think about how foolish I felt having a seven-year-old telling me how to do things."

Probably the same way he'd felt when Melanie had to cook the spaghetti. "Melanie's a huge help, but, yes, sometimes she goes too far. As for Sandy, it's easy. She can dress on her own, but she needs help in the matching department, so I pick out her clothes."

Garrett reached for Sandy. She clung to him, wrapping her arms around his neck. Whether Garrett realized it or not, he'd taken to holding her like a natural, positioning her on his hip and freeing up one hand.

"Good morning, Sandy. April tells me you can get dressed all by yourself like a big girl."

Sandy nodded.

"Let's make this happen, then we can head downstairs for a donut. April brought a lot of yummy choices." Sandy smiled, her eyes becoming wide saucers at the mention of a donut.

Bribery wasn't Garrett's best option, but she'd leave that lesson for another time. If there was another time, that is. He opened each of the drawers, pulling out socks, underwear, a blue and white striped shirt, and black pants covered with pink glitter stars.

"Not the most coordinated outfit I've seen, but it will do," April joked.

He looked surprised. "What? Pink, black, blue, and white all go together."

"It's a stretch, but my main concern is the stripes and stars. There's a lot going on." She pressed her lips together to fight back from saying anything more on the subject. It wouldn't do to discourage Garrett.

"Well, then you pick out another pair of pants." Garrett helped Sandy pull the shirt over her head when it got stuck at her chin.

April handed him a pair of blue jeans, exchanging them for the others. Sandy took them from Garrett and finished getting dressed.

"The others should probably wake up no later than nine. You can get them to help you clean up their own messes in the living room. They are old enough for that. Don't let them push you around. You're the parent."

Sandy pulled him toward the door.

"Gotcha. Thanks for the tip. A bit late, but I'll take it." He glanced up at her and winked.

A warm, fuzzy feeling shot through her again. His sexy charm had an effect on her she seemed unable to control. Luckily, they'd headed down the hall, and Garrett couldn't see her reaction.

He paused at the top of the stairway and turned back. "Any chance I can get you to stay and help with the kids this weekend? I'm out of my league here and could use your expertise. Especially since I'm not sure when my sister is coming home."

"I wish I could, but as much as I love these kids, I can't. I already got in trouble at work for taking off three days. They threatened to fire me if it happens again, and I can't afford to lose my job." She frowned, remembering her run-in with Tammy.

"I'm sorry. It doesn't sound as though it's an enjoyable place to work. Don't worry about us. I'm handy at problem-solving, and I'll figure this out, too." He swung Sandy up into his arms and headed down the stairs.

"I'm sure you will. It gets easier, I promise." Kids just needed love and to know someone cared, something April missed out on with the ever-changing foster homes she'd found herself assigned in.

"Let's just hope you're right. Ready for your donut, little lady?" He addressed Sandy with his last question, loving it as her face lit up. Garrett headed toward the kitchen, and April followed, knowing she should get going.

He sat Sandy in her booster seat and glanced over at her. "If my sister's not here by Monday, I'll have no choice but to take them to New York with me until she arrives, and even then, I'm not sure how this will work with her getting out of the military. But my place isn't set up for kids, not to mention I have a business to run and clients depending on me." Garrett might be stressed out about the possibility of moving the kids, but April was more than stressed out by the idea. Garrett was an adult, but these were kids, and more change was the last thing they needed.

"New York? Are you kidding me? You can't rip these kids from their home so soon. And what about school? They start after Labor Day. You can't take them to New York City for an undetermined amount of time and not do something about their schooling. That's called truancy." She had to get him to see reason.

"I don't know what to do. This has all come as a shock." Garrett rubbed his hands through his hair. "I tried calling Charlie last night, but I haven't heard back. I'm hoping he'll show up today because I need answers before I can figure out what to do next."

Whatever answers Garrett thought he would get, wouldn't be the ones he wanted to hear.

April had known changes were inevitable for the kids, but even she hadn't foreseen them being uprooted to the city. Her best friend Maddison had always warned her against getting too involved in her cases but watching these kids over the past few days was involved, and there was no turning back her feelings for them.

Chapter Four

♥

GARRETT APPRECIATED APRIL'S GENEROSITY but wished it could've extended at least through the weekend. He handed Sandy a donut and then set out to see what else he could find for breakfast. Cheerios was the easiest, and something he couldn't mess up. After pouring Sandy a bowl and adding milk, he sat down to help her eat, remembering to pull off the tie he still hadn't managed to put on correctly and keep it out of her sticky-finger reach. One ruined tie was enough.

Sandy watched his every move, not saying a word, but taking bite after bite. Her appetite was nothing short of amazing, considering how small she was. Garrett poured her glass of orange juice in her sippy cup, this time getting the lid on before handing it to her. He scooped her up from her booster seat, carried her into the living room, and set her down by the toybox.

"I'll be back in a second," he told her. He wasn't sure what to expect, because for some reason, she'd become attached to him and didn't want him going anywhere without her. She was a lot of work, but she was adorable, her blonde curls in complete disarray.

He grabbed his briefcase off the kitchen counter where he'd stashed it yesterday, hoping to get a few hours work in before the other kids woke up. With only one kid to keep track of, it would be much easier. Garrett watched Sandy for a moment, pleased she was happily playing in the corner with some toy that spun around making animal noises. Whatever it was, she seemed to enjoy it.

He flipped open the top of his computer and keyed in his password to pull up his office email account. Thirty-three new emails, and he'd only been gone a day. It would take more than a couple of hours to wade through these. Time he was positive he wouldn't get. He fully intended to heed April's warning to give the kids extra time to get ready for the celebration well before everyone was expected to start arriving. Garrett managed to get through two emails before a Barbie doll found its way to his laptop.

Sandy had plunked the doll's bottom right down on his keyboard, using the screen like the back of a chair. Her smile tempered his initial reaction when the screen turned black. It was hard to be irritated with such innocent cuteness. "Here you are, honey." He handed the doll back to her. "This is a computer, not a toy. Take Barbie and play in the corner."

Sandy shook her head.

"I've got to do some work. Can't you have a tea party or something?" It was the first thing that came to mind. He wasn't overly in tune with little-girl playtime. It was a pleasant surprise when she nodded her head, turned, and ran back to the corner. "Thank goodness." Garrett hit the power button of the computer again, hoping the email reply he'd been working had saved as a draft.

The account was loading when Sandy returned, this time, with her doll and a teacup. After dumping both in his lap, she returned to the toybox and grabbed another doll, teacup, and two plates, and brought them all back and dumped them in his lap.

"Sandy, I've got to work." Garrett let out a deep breath. Instead of leaving, Sandy climbed up on the sofa next to him as if he hadn't spoken. She watched him closely, her baby blue eyes imploring him to play with her. Those eyes got him every time.

Not exactly what he had in mind when he suggested it.

He didn't know the first thing about tea parties, but it appeared he was about to find out. Jim wouldn't believe it if he saw it with his own eyes. His partner had once commented that Garrett wouldn't know what to do with anything that didn't come attached with a legal document. It would seem Jim was right.

Step by step, Sandy showed him what to do. How to position the doll. How to pour tea. How to sip tea from his miniature cup. How to help the doll drink. Garrett couldn't remember the last time he'd played, especially something so silly.

But Sandy was content, her smile proof he was doing something right, and one that melted a place in Garrett's heart he hadn't even known existed. And for a man who never wanted kids, that was saying a lot. The tea party ended, and Sandy wandered off, leaving her toys right where she left them, Garrett watching her closely to see what she would do next.

Even the dog was on his best behavior, currently curled up at Garrett's feet after Garrett had made him get off the couch. He could only hope he'd find a sticky roller to get the hair off his slacks. Garrett glanced at his watch and let out a sigh. It was time to wake the other two kids.

A knock at the door got his attention. Rufus sat up and barked, beating Garrett to the door. "I know someone's here. Try not to jump on whoever it is. It's not good manners." He pulled open the door, ready to welcome any other adult into his new crazy world.

Jessica stood there, her arms overload with bags. "Good morning, Garrett."

"Morning. It's nice to see you again. It looks as though you could use some help." He reached to take a couple of the bags to help her before she dropped anything.

"Yes, thanks. It's good to see you, too. We've missed you these past few months."

Garrett winced, not needing a reminder of his failure. "Work has been in overload mode," he explained. But then it was always in overload. They hadn't become a top firm in the country by working a regular workweek, and now that they'd achieved that status, there were dozens of upcoming law firms eager to take the spot from them.

"I'm sorry about your mother. It was quite a shock, and I feel so bad for the children." Jessica's eyes glistened with tears. His mother and Jessica had been close friends even though Jessica was his age.

"It would seem she took on more than she could handle." Garrett voiced the thought he'd been harboring since he'd learned about the children. This had been too much for his mother.

Jessica seemed shocked by his comment. "I don't know what you mean. They were the light of her life."

He wasn't blaming the kids. More like the energy it took to keep up with them. He'd barely survived the first night. "And now she's gone. She never mentioned having heart trouble, so what else am I to think?"

"She took heart medicine for years and never had any problems. Lots of people take heart medicine. I'm surprised you didn't know." She shook her head and shrugged.

"It would seem there were a few things she didn't bother to mention." Garrett walked back into the house, carrying the bags to the kitchen.

Jessica followed. "Your mother loved having kids to fuss over again. She had a huge heart and tremendous amounts of love to give."

"Apparently, it was a defective one." He grimaced. "Is there any way you can keep an eye on Sandy for a few minutes? I've got to get the other kids up and moving." It was no use talking to Jessica, she wouldn't understand.

"Sure. I don't have much to do except setting up, and I'd love to help you. I've put together some pictures of your mother from what I have and some of her albums. I hope you don't mind.

Maybe we could go over them together?" Jessica stood close, her hand on his arm as she looked up at him.

"That won't be necessary. I trust whatever you picked out. I appreciate everything you're doing to help arrange this." She hadn't removed her hand, and Garrett stepped away, intent on emptying the bags to put some space between them. An attractive woman, Jessica had been married for as long as he could remember, but he recalled his mother mentioning she'd gotten a divorce. Garrett wasn't interested in anything more than the same friend- ship they'd always shared, and he certainly didn't want to give her the wrong signals.

April was another story entirely. From the beginning, he'd been interested. Her sweet, pixie face was a breath of fresh air. But he also knew he was headed back to the city, and didn't want to give her the wrong idea, and he was pretty sure she wasn't into casual relationships. At least based on the impression she'd given him with her down-to-earth approach to life.

"Mine was the easy job. Everyone else is bringing the food. You'll have more than you know what to do with for weeks on end. The people of Hallbrook loved your mother, and if there's anything you need, I'm sure they'll be there to help. And I'll be here if you need me, all you have to do is ask."

"That sounds awesome." It would be hard for the residents of Hallbrook to help once Garrett was back in the city, but after April's reaction about him taking the kids there, he wasn't about to say a word to anyone else.

He started for the stairs, but Sandy cried out and chased after him as fast as her short legs would let her as she tried to catchup. She raised her arms, her fingers clenching together, a signal he'd come to recognize. He lifted her up in his arms, resigned to the fact he'd have to deal with her and the others at the same time.

"Never mind. I'll take her with me." He stopped at Melanie's room first and entered. "Melanie, you need to wake up. You need to get ready for the celebration today, and we still need to clean the house." Garrett still couldn't get used to calling today's get together a celebration. He understood, but it was different. His mother's life would be celebrated, not mourned.

Melanie groaned and rolled over away from him. "I'm tired," she muttered, pulling the covers over her head.

"If you'd gone to bed at your proper bedtime, we wouldn't have this problem."

She rolled over and stared back at him, a guilty expression on her face. "But it's Saturday. Grams let us sleep in."

"I'm not Grams, and we have stuff to do." Garrett remembered April's advice. "You need to do what you're told." There, that ought to do it. Firm and in control.

"Fine."

Mission accomplished. One down, and one to go. He knocked on Bryan's door and entered. When he pushed the door open, however, it was to discover Bryan in his beanbag chair in the corner. The kid looked up and then went straight back to what he was doing.

"I didn't know you were awake. You need to get dressed and come downstairs. Get some breakfast, and then we need to clean before people start showing up today." Bryan didn't budge or give him the courtesy of a response. He just kept playing his game.

"There are donuts downstairs courtesy of April." It worked. Well, somewhat. He had the kid's attention, but the boy still didn't budge. "Unless you want me to take your tablet away for the rest of the day, I suggest you do as you're told."

A look of shock crossed Bryan's face. But he did toss his tablet to the side and push himself up off the beanbag. Garrett decided it was safe to leave him to get dressed alone, having made his point. He didn't want to be hard on the kid, but he didn't know what else to do. Garrett remembered the tactic his own mother had used on him frequently to make sure chores got done. Only back when he was a kid, his Achilles heel wasn't a tablet, it was hanging with his friends and playing outside.

He stopped at Melanie's room and knocked. No answer. He poked his head in the door to discover she hadn't moved. *Didn't anybody around here do what they were told?*

"Melanie, get moving." He hadn't found anything to use for leverage with her yet, and short of calling April for advice, had no idea what to do next.

"Fine," she grumbled from across the room, but this time she shoved back the covers, swung her legs over the edge of the bed, and rubbed her eyes.

He let out a breath of relief and closed the door. "I'm glad you're not as difficult as the others," he said, knowing Sandy probably wouldn't understand.

She reached out to touch his face, her finger poking his eye.

"*Hmmm*, try to miss the eyes. I rather enjoy being able to see. Thank you." He grinned and headed down the stairs.

Ten minutes past before the kids managed to drag themselves downstairs. Much to their credit, they were dressed, their hair was combed, and they were presentable. It was a favorable start to the day and encouraging.

His positive attitude changed by the time people started arriving for the celebration. The children did what they were told but had no problem expressing their displeasure in the form of silence. Sandy, on the other hand, didn't speak anyway, but she also wouldn't let him out of her sight. Jessica was in and around, using every opportunity to flirt.

And he still hadn't heard from his sister. The uncertainty of knowing how long things would remain the way they were was unsettling. Garrett was used to his employees following his orders, but these children didn't have the same motivated desire.

Ever since Charlie had called him with the news of his mother's death, Garrett hadn't had a chance to slow down and absorb the impact. At first, he was too busy at the office getting ready to leave, and then from the second he'd gotten to Hallbrook, it had been a nuthouse. What he wanted to do was take a stroll and escape to his mother's favorite spot just to breathe. But with kids, even that wasn't possible.

People started arriving, and soon, the driveway was filled with cars all the way back to the street. They brought casseroles, desserts, and salads, filling every inch of counter space in the kitchen and on the table. Jessica had been right about the food. It was more than he could possibly imagine needing in a month.

Everyone either stopped to say hello or introduce themselves. They were all cheerful—not something he'd expected. His mother had been firm in her wishes, at least according to the pastor when Garrett had called him about funeral arrangements. No crying. No tears. No sadness. A celebration of her life was her wish. She'd planned for everything, right down to how she wanted her ashes spread on her favorite spot of the estate. The place overlooked miles and miles of countryside, frequently capturing the beauty of an evening sunset, her favorite time of the day.

Garrett continued to mingle; in awe of the footprint his mother had left on the community. He waved at the mayor when he spotted him across the room. His mother and Mr. Tucker had spent lots of time together in the name of research, his mother determined to keep the town's traditions and history alive.

His mother had been loved by the entire town and everyone she'd met. Everyone, it would seem, except his own father. A man more dedicated to his work than his family. When he had focused on family, it always ended badly. He hadn't even bothered coming to the celebration of life or to acknowledge the loss.

The man was a savvy attorney, and Garrett had chosen to follow in his footsteps, with the sole purpose of being better than him. They talked about once a month because some things never changed—he still wasn't a family man. He hadn't even bothered to contact Garrett to acknowledge their recent loss.

Garrett spotted Rufus running in the front yard as he gazed out the window. One of the kids must have let the dog out because he'd personally seen to locking the beast up for today's celebration. The oversized four-legged dog who thought he was a human would wreak havoc if turned loose inside the house with everyone, not to mention in the kitchen with all the food.

He headed outside, hoping to find a way to round the dog up. He was more than a little surprised to see the kids out front. Garrett had forgotten about them—proof he was terrible at being responsible for kids. Monday morning, he wouldn't be sending his sister a regular message, it would be more like a SOS signal.

"What are you kids doing out here? You should be inside talking to people," Garrett said, his voice coming out harsher than he liked.

"It's boring inside. And I'm keeping an eye on them," Bryan scoffed.

"But I'm the one in charge. No one asked me, and I didn't even know you were outside."

"Chill. Grams let me watch them all the time. I'm nine and quite responsible, you know." Bryan talked to him as if he were the child.

"Yeah, well, I'm thirty-three and have my own share of responsibilities. And right now, that includes you three. I want you inside, therefore, you should do it. End of discussion." April told him to take control and being direct was the only way he knew how to communicate.

"You're no fun." Bryan scowled.

"Welcome to my world, kid." Sandy ran up to him and took his hand. Together, they returned to the house, Garrett expecting the other two to follow.

He took Sandy over to the toybox in the living room. "Why don't you play here for a minute." She nodded. At least she didn't give him a hard time.

Garrett stood next to the fireplace, finding the only spot in the room where there wasn't a body. A place for him to stop and breathe. He gazed at his mother's photograph perched on the mantel, remembering the time it was taken. She had just opened her boutique and they'd had a grand-opening party. His mother had been in her element as people from all over New Hampshire stopped in to check out the artisan arts and crafts, handmade furniture, and housewares she proudly displayed in the boutique. It had been the beginning of what turned out to be a huge success.

Sarah Bradley had been a beautiful woman. The smile she wore in the photograph was one of his favorites. Her special-occasion smile as he liked to think of it. One he and Angelica would see whenever they did something noteworthy while growing up. Always proud and full of praise, that was his mother. But it was a smile that only started to happen after his parent's divorce. The divorce he'd caused. Him and his big mouth, begging for a dog.

It was the last fight they'd had before they'd called it quits, and it was a night he'd never forgotten. He'd been a handful as a kid, and apparently, more than his parents could deal with. Angelica, on the other hand, followed true to her name and was the angel of the family. But in the end, even the angel had had to deal with the split-up of her parents. Just one more thing for him to feel guilty about.

"Hey, Garrett, it's good to see you. I wish it were under better circumstances." Fred Kritzer clapped him on the back. His high school science teacher had been a fixture at Turlington High for well over thirty years.

"Me, too. Thanks for coming."

"Wouldn't miss it for the world. I rather enjoy this new thing of a celebration. Wakes are so somber, and your mother wanted no part in that tradition. She was always so full of joy." Years of well-worn lines deepened on the old man's face as he recalled his friend with fondness.

"I agree. She loved it when family and friends found any reason to get together." His mother believed relationships required time and effort if one wanted to enjoy the fruit. Something he'd lost sight of when it came to visiting his mother.

"Are you staying in town for long? With the kids? It's a shame those kids lost their folks in a car crash. They were a wonderful couple and filled with love for their children. Your mother was a saint taking the kids in, giving them a chance to stay together. The whole community was relieved. Not many people would take in three kids and a dog."

You could say that again. "I'm not sure what's happening quite yet. There's sure to be an adjustment period. The kids are doing okay, but they are still up and down emotionally, which is understandable. Each one's reaction is so different, so it's hard to say." Reminded of what they'd been through, it made him feel more guilty for not being more understanding.

Charlie Wilcox approached him. The two men shook hands. "Charlie."

"Sorry about your mom. Lovely lady. Biggest heart I know." The older man's eyes glistened, leaving Garrett to wonder if the solicitor might have had a soft spot for his mom.

"Big heart, but apparently not in working order from what I understand." Garrett couldn't help but keep the harshness out of his voice.

"Hey, Fred, if you'll excuse us. I need to talk to Garrett for a couple of minutes." Charlie wasn't hinting. His direct comment showed he expected his request to be honored.

"Sure thing." Fred left to join another group of people nearby that were deep in conversation.

"This may not be the best time, but I got your message last night. It was too late to call you back. I knew you'd have questions, and I decided it would be better for a man in your position to have those answers right away. No reason to wait for Monday."

"I appreciate that. So, what is going on? April tells me my mother adopted these children. Is that true? And what does that mean to Angelica and me? Have you heard from her?"

Charlie reached out and lightly touched the photo of Sarah, letting out a deep sigh. "Slow down, and I'll explain. First, your mom was friends with the kids' mom, Carrie Williams. They attended church together and were in a Bible study group together. Carrie was also a crafter and did a lot of business with your mom. Your mother loved those children and watched them grow and play for years. She was even at the hospital when Sandy was born.

It nearly broke her heart when Carrie and Alex died. The kids were immediately placed in foster care, which is when April St. James entered the picture. Your mother couldn't stand the idea of the children being separated or sent away, knowing not many people around here would be able to take in three kids. Or the dog for that matter."

Garrett winced. He wasn't planning on separating the children, but he was planning on taking them away from here. He couldn't help but think his mother wouldn't approve. "I thought as much myself. Continue." Her compassion for the Williams family was understandable. But it was still crazy for an older, single woman in her golden years to adopt. That's the part he was struggling with, more so, because his mother hadn't thought to include him or Angelica in on the decision making.

"That's where I come in. And you, for that matter. Your mom approached me and told me she wanted to adopt the kids. Her heart was in the right place, and she insisted you and your sister not be told what she was doing until it was a done deal. She knew you'd try and stop her and considered herself quite capable of making her own decisions. She figured when you came to visit, you'd meet the kids and fall in love with them the same way she did. That was three months ago. But then the unthinkable happened." Charlie looked uncomfortable delivering the news.

"So not telling us was intentional? Of course, because it was a crazy idea. Why didn't you try to talk her out of it?" Garrett tried to calm down. Letting his emotions overrule common sense wouldn't help him, and emotions were something he'd long-ago put on lockdown. After years of running on common sense, any emotion left in him couldn't be trusted.

"Because your mom had a lot of love to give, and those kids needed her. But there's more to this you need to know. Your mother had clear ideas about the children's future. She loved you and your sister more than anything, and she was extremely proud of you both. She also knew there was nothing you needed from her if anything ever happened to her, but the kids are a different story. They were left with nothing after their parents passed away. Sarah was determined to provide for their futures. At the time of the adoption, she had me draw up a new will and make several changes." Charlie's voice had dropped as he delivered the shocking news.

"A new will? This just keeps getting better and better. I can't believe I wasn't called, or that she didn't discuss any of this with the family beforehand." Garrett stared hard at his mother's picture, willing her to give him the answers he needed to help him understand.

"Your mother was a determined woman. There's no easy way to tell you this, so I'm just going to come right out and say it. She made you their sole legal guardian in the event anything happened to her."

"That's ludicrous. You're telling me *I'm* the legal guardian of these three kids? I've never even met them before. How is this possible? What about Angelica?" He spun away and stared out the window, trying to maintain control.

"It's what your mother wanted." Charlie delivered the final strike as if it explained everything. What about what he wanted?

He turned back to Charlie. "What happened to feminine nurturing and motherly instincts? Clearly, Angelica's the better choice for this responsibility." There had to be some mistake.

"Your sister is in the Navy and gone on deployment for extended periods of time. Your mother didn't want to ask her to give up her entire career and life to take on the children."

"But my mother was aware I never wanted a family or children."

"Maybe this is a case of *mother knows best,* or she thought she did anyway. You can provide stability, which is what they need most. You must realize, she never actually intended for this happen. It was a back-up plan."

"What about the will? You mentioned she made changes to care of the kids. What kind of changes?" He might as well know it all now.

"As you know, the settlement from your father when they divorced was quite considerable. Since then she's been quite successful with her financial growth. We decided on a plan of action for the children's futures if anything were to happen to her. Otherwise, she would have seen to it personally."

"What exactly are the terms of the will?"

"The estate can't be sold until the youngest turns twenty-five. If at that time, if any of them want to live here and continue to operate the shop, they can, and it will be shared. If not, it will be sold and divided three ways. She's tasked you with keeping it running and in the family, to keep it safe for them. She's provided trust funds for the operation of the estate with you as executor over the business and her affairs going forward outside of the reading of her will. She's also set aside a large trust fund for each child's college fund. She wanted to make sure each one was provided for."

His mother had never been prone to such wild and nonsensical ideas, and he'd give anything to figure out why she would do such a thing. He didn't care about the money. He had plenty of his own. But keeping the estate running until Sandy was twenty-five? That was another story. Twenty-two years was a long time.

"This wasn't thought through completely. I live in a high-rise apartment in Manhattan and work eighty hours a week. What kind of a life is that for kids, especially ones used to the freedom associated with living in the country? I can't just quit my business and become a daddy."

"That's something you'll have to decide for yourself. I can't advise you on what to do next, but I can tell you they are your responsibility, and it's up to you to provide for their care. Your mother knew you could provide them with stability. She always held out hope one day you'd get tired of city life and return to Hallbrook."

Garrett shook his head, still trying to absorb the information. He didn't know the first thing about kids or raising them. What was his mother thinking?

"I'm sorry to be the one to have to tell you all this. They are wonderful kids. Give them a chance, and you'll find that out for yourself."

"Well, so far, I beg to differ with you. It's been more of a nightmare." Not all of it, he qualified the statement in his head, remembering Sandy and the bond they'd started to share.

"It'll get better, trust me." Charlie sounded sure of himself.

A loud scream resonated through the house, the sound coming from out front. Seconds later, the door burst open, Melanie charging into the house, a look of terror on her face. Crocodile tears ran down her cheeks as she cradled one arm. He didn't have to know a thing about kids to see what was wrong. Her wrist was bowed up like a V.

He glanced at Charlie and frowned. "Trust you? I don't think so." He crossed the room in no time and knelt next to Melanie, several women in the room clustering around them both.

"We've got to get you to the emergency room. The doctor will fix you up and make the pain go away, I promise." Garrett tried to reassure Melanie. Her frightened look kicked him in the gut, making him wish he could do more to help. "Keep holding your arm steady, just the way you're doing."

She nodded her head in understanding.

One woman brushed Melanie's hair back from her face. Another wiped the tears off her cheeks.

"Can someone take us to the ER?" Garrett asked. Without a vehicle, he needed help to follow through on his promise to get her help. At least Hallbrook had a medical center, and they wouldn't have to make the thirty-minute trek to Lancaster, for help.

"I'll be out front in just a minute," Mabel Tucker, the mayor's wife spoke up first. She was gone before he could answer.

"Bryan, what happened?" Garrett questioned him, knowing the doctor would need the information, something the newly ordained parent in Garrett didn't have.

"She fell out of the tree we climbed. I'm sorry. I know you told us to come inside, but we didn't listen. This is my fault." Bryan was scared, his lower lip trembling as he spoke. The child in him didn't come out often, and this wasn't the way Garrett wanted to experience it. *Poor kid.*

"Stop. It'll be fine. We can talk about what you were doing or not doing later. Right now, I've got to get her to the doctor. Melanie will be okay, I promise." He was making a lot of promises for a guy who'd just found he was now a fulltime parent.

"Really?" the boy asked, his voice filled with hope.

"Really." Garrett ruffled the boy's hair before he and Melanie headed outside.

Iris Parker followed them. "I'll take care of the other two until you get back. The kids are safe with me."

It's not as if he had a choice, and he welcomed the help. "Thanks, Iris, I appreciate that."

Jessica rushed up to him as he was helping Melanie into the back seat of Mabel's old Chevy Malibu. "Garrett, I'll take care of everything here at the house and clean up. Between Iris and me, everything here will be under control. Don't you worry about a thing. That's what friends and family are for."

"Thanks, Jessica." Garrett climbed in the back seat, preferring to sit next to Melanie in case she needed him and hoping to keep her calm.

The mayor's wife drove them into town. Mabel was one of the town's gossips, only surpassed by Bertha Higgins, but at least Mabel meant well with her meddling. As they hurried toward the emergency room, Garrett realized he didn't know the first thing about the Melanie. At least, not the kinds of things he needed to know to check her into the medical center. Hopefully, the doctor already had all the information, because Garrett couldn't even tell the man the kid's middle name or birthday, even though he was now the legal guardian and the one filling out the forms.

Looking at the unnatural angle of Melanie's wrist made him cringe, but he tried not to show any visible reaction. It had to hurt a lot, but she was quiet, with only the tears running down her face as evidence of the pain she was in. Mabel, on the other hand, talked nonstop, making up for everyone.

The woman glanced into the rearview mirror, exchanging a knowing look with Garrett. "They are sweet kids, but kids are kids, and three is a lot to handle for anybody, especially a single guy. You're going to have your hands full, that's for certain. Might want to consider getting yourself a wife. Any prospects?"

Garrett coughed, her suggestion taking him by surprise. "Hardly. My current schedule doesn't allow for a wife *or* kids." Right after he spoke the words, he regretted them. It was one thing to think the truth, quite another to say it out loud in front of Melanie.

"Well, I guess it does now. The kid part anyway. If you don't aim to take wife, what you need is a full-time nanny. Someone to cook and clean. I'm sure New York City has plenty of those. I don't figure you're sticking around here. It'd be a shame to have the kids uprooted, but I guess nothing can be done about that, your business being in the city and all." Mabel was digging for information, and Garrett understood any response would make the Hallbrook gossip line by midnight.

"That would be correct." Clearly, the old woman knew a lot more than she was letting on. *A nanny.* The idea of some woman living in his home on a regular basis didn't sit well. But then neither did three kids and a dog. Maybe Mabel was right, and a nanny was just what he needed. Someone to take care of the kids and leave him to get on with his job.

"That's a great idea, Mabel. Thanks. I might just do that." In fact, it was an outstanding idea. And he knew just who to ask to fill the position.

Chapter Five

❤

IT HAD BEEN A long day, and April was looking forward to a quiet evening. A couple of clients hadn't been home when she arrived, and others hadn't wanted to talk to her. Only one client seemed genuinely interested in working with her, and she believed the woman had the child's best interest at heart.

Sometimes people fell on hard times and made wrong choices, but the child's mother was determined to prove she could be a worthy parent, and April was inclined to give her a chance. The bond between the child and mother was strong, something important to April when making recommendations that could affect the child's entire future.

April pulled in her driveway just as her cell phone rang. She didn't recognize the number and was tempted not to answer, figuring it was a telemarketer. But in her line of work, she didn't have a choice whether to answer or not. She never knew when an important call regarding a child's welfare might come in. "Hello?"

"April? This is Garrett." His somber tone sounded ominous.

"Is everything okay? Are the kids okay?" She couldn't help the anxiousness in her rapid-fire questions. Her concern for the children was on high alert.

"Relax, I'm at the hospital with Melanie." *Relax* and *hospital* didn't belong in the same sentence. "What's wrong?"

"She fell out of a tree and broke her wrist. The doctor's setting it now, and it's going to be fine. He's given her something for the pain, and she's doing well."

"Poor baby. Thank goodness she's okay. Give her a hug for me." She let out a sigh of relief. "I thought you had the celebration of life today. What happened?"

"We did. As to what happened, that would be a question for the kids. They weren't supposed to be outside, but…"

"Say no more. I get it." She couldn't help but feel sorry for him and Melanie. "Do you need me to meet you there at the hospital?"

"No. That's not why I'm calling." He hesitated, making her more curious about the reason for his call.

"Then what do you need?" She pressed the phone tightly between her ear and her shoulder to hold it in place while she grabbed her purse and opened the car door.

"You said to call if I ever needed help, and I do. I'm in over my head. You and I both know that. Charlie's been here, and he explained everything. I know now what you meant when you told me I was responsible for the kids." Even over the phone, she could hear the distress in his voice.

"I would have told you, but I didn't think I was the right person to break the news. Hallbrook is a small town, and your mother wasn't quiet about her intentions."

"Other than with me, you mean." He was rightfully bent out of shape being broadsided by the situation, but she hoped he'd come to accept it in time—for everyone concerned. Especially the children.

"She wanted to tell you in person. What's wrong with that? Think about it. And there's no way she could have foreseen this coming." April pressed him to try and understand his mother's reasoning.

"True." She could almost see him let out a deep breath, the silence telling.

But he had yet to get to the point, and she needed to jump in the shower, grab a glass of wine, and decompress from her day. "So, what can I do to help you?" She unlocked the door and pushed it open, grateful to be home.

"I want you to be my nanny. Just temporarily, that is. You love the kids, and you're the perfect person to help me." She hadn't seen that coming.

She tossed her purse onto the chair in the living room, put the phone on speaker, and headed for the kitchen. Wine before the shower was starting to sound like a wonderful idea. "For the weekend? I've already told you I'm behind on work and can't take any time off." She'd like to help, but it wasn't possible.

"No, not just the weekend. Come to New York with me. Take an extended leave of absence from your job and come stay with the kids. Make this easy on them and me. I know how much they care about you. It's just until I can find a new nanny-housekeeper type person. Mabel suggested it, and I think it's the perfect solution. You can help me find someone. I wouldn't even know what kind of questions to ask in an interview. Besides, you did offer your help." He was serious.

April closed her eyes and drew in a deep breath. This was a familiar story—but one she hadn't heard since she'd turned eighteen and aged out of the foster care system. Foster parents wanted the older girls for the unpaid services they could provide. Services like cooking, cleaning, and childcare. Services April vowed not to do for anyone again unless it was for her own family. Not that she didn't love the children—she did, but there was also her job to consider, and her boss had made it quite clear last night, one more misstep, and she'd be fired.

"You don't know what you're asking. I mean, I'd love to, but I can't. When I offered help, I meant stopping at a grocery store for you, or taking them to school, or helping you fix something for dinner, or even taking them to the doctor. Not move to New York." Garrett's offer sounded like a man in panic mode, desperate for help. Once he got through the current crisis, he'd understand why it wouldn't work.

"Well, you weren't here to take Melanie to the doctor, so I think this is the next best option. What if I offered you ten thousand dollars to come to New York for one month? All expenses paid." He wasn't just serious. He was *dead serious.*

Ten grand. His offer just moved into a whole new arena. Before, in another situation, when she'd done the childcare and cooking and cleaning, she hadn't received a dime. Garrett was offering money for her services—a lot of money. It was enough to pay for her last year of college and put her one step closer to her teaching job, something would take years and years to save for at the rate she was going.

"I don't know. I'd have to quit my job. What happens when the month is up?" She could get a part-time job, but the idea was overwhelming, and it wasn't something she could decide in a split second.

"If you find the perfect person as a nanny-housekeeper for the kids and stay the month to help them transition, I'll give you another ten-thousand as a bonus. No strings attached. Plenty of money to give you time to find another job. You can have my room, we can put the girls in one room, Bryan in the other, and I'll sleep on the couch. It's a three-bedroom suite." Garrett presented the idea as though he'd thought it through carefully, but it still sounded insane.

"I don't know what to say. That's a lot of money. What's the catch?" There had to be a flaw somewhere in his plan.

"No catch. Come to New York, find me a nanny, get everything worked out, and you earn twenty grand. I'm sure you can find another job. You can even take a vacation. Both of us win in this situation."

April was blown away. She hadn't been holding out for more money, and now the offer had grown into a once-in-a-lifetime opportunity. She'd be crazy to tell him no. The man clearly had the money to pay top dollar for whatever he wanted, and right now, he wanted her. Well, not her, her services. For the children.

Living with Garrett would be odd, but it might not be so awkward with the kids there. They would be chaperones. The idea of giving up her job was scary, but there was no doubt she'd love to do it. She could forget a reference if she didn't give two weeks' notice, but then it's not as though her boss approved of her anyway.

April tried to rationalize all the details. It would more than pay for her college and living expenses if she was careful with her finances for the next year. And once she graduated, she'd be able to apply for her dream job as a kindergarten teacher.

Take the chance and reach for your dream.

"Okay." She let the word slip before she chickened out. "But on one condition. It's for two weeks tops. I need to be back before the school semester at Plymouth University."

"You drive a hard bargain. That's an expensive two weeks."

"Then cut the bonus in half. Do the math. I'd say that's an excellent deal considering it's full-time, twenty-four-seven. Three kids. A dog. And you. Nanny, housekeeper, cook, and interviewer. That's four jobs." She held her breath, waiting to see if he would agree. Wanting him to say yes.

"You have yourself a deal."

"Really?" Giddy with excitement, she raised both hands in the air and did a half dance in the kitchen. *Goodbye social service office and hello college.*

April could hardly wait to call Maddison, but she had to finish out the details with Garrett. She tried to refocus, just for a minute. There would be time to celebrate later after she met up with Maddison at O'Malley's to toast her good luck.

"Yes. And for the record, you could've named your price. You weren't here last night, but I'd give anything not to fly solo through that again." Garrett chuckled.

"I'll remember that in the future." April took a deep calming breath to calm her nerves. "When do you want me to start?"

"Be here at seven." Garrett's quick answer caught her off guard as she glanced at the clock.

"But that only gives me thirteen hours to get cleaned up and packed, close up my apartment, and put my mail on hold." She shook her head, thinking of all that needed to be done to make it happen.

"No. Seven p.m. Tonight."

No way. Garrett's terms bordered on insanity. "But that's in one hour." She couldn't possibly be ready in an hour.

"Yes, it is. I figure I'll be back at the house by then, and I prefer reinforcements when it comes to handling the situation with the kids and dealing with their disobedience. Maybe you can even handle it for me."

There was no arguing with Garrett. "Make it an hour and a half. I need a shower."

"Seven-thirty it is. See you soon. And, April, thanks. You won't regret this."

So much for celebrating. She dialed Maddison's number. The news was too fantastic, not to share.

"Hey, stranger. What's up?" Maddison answered on the first ring, which meant she was having a slow day at work.

"I've got news. Big, big news. And I don't know when I'll get another chance to update you." April would have preferred to see her friend's face in person when she told her, but this would have to do.

"Spill it. I'm going outside to take a break."

"I'm quitting my job." Words she'd dreamed of saying but didn't see happening for a long while, if ever. All that changed with a single phone call. Well, and with two weeks of her life.

"What? You can't be serious. What happened?" Maddison's voice rose a notch, concern evident in every question.

"I got another job offer. One that's going to bankroll my last year of college."

"Tell me more. This sounds too good to be true."

"It is too good, but it is true. You know I've been watching the William's children at the Bradley place until Garrett Bradley arrived. He arrived yesterday and has no clue what to do with the children. He offered me a temporary nanny job, and I accepted."

Something made easier by Tammy's threats issued yesterday.

"But to give up your job? That sounds rash. And how will it bankroll college? This doesn't sound like you."

"I know. I'm going to New York City with Garrett and the kids for two weeks. There's a bonus involved if I locate a nanny for him while I'm there. He needs help transitioning into parenthood." How hard could it be to find a nanny in the city? There were probably as many agencies in New York City as there were in all of New Hampshire.

"Are you sure about this? When do you leave?"

"I better be sure because I start tonight." April let out a deep breath.

"Oh, honey. I hope you know what you're doing. This wouldn't have anything to do with the hunky prodigal son returned home, would it? I've seen Garrett. The man is totally drool-worthy."

"You know me better than that. This is about the kids and my checking account."

"If you say so. Take care of yourself and call me if you need anything. And stay safe, New York City isn't Hallbrook, not by a long shot."

April shook her head, her friend's concerned warning touching, but unnecessary. "I can handle it. Trust me. I'll keep you posted." They hung up, April aware her clock was ticking, and she didn't have much time to get ready to leave. Garrett was about to make all her dreams come true. Well, Garrett's money, she corrected. The city slicker was not her idea of a forever kind of guy for any- thing else, no matter how handsome or how much she hadn't been able to get him out of her head all day. Something she wasn't about to tell Maddison, or she'd never hear the end of it.

April would have preferred to see Tammy's face in person when she delivered the news she was quit- ting, but an email was all she had time for. Starting Monday morning, April's caseload would be Tammy's problem, and all the candidates sup- posedly lined up for the job were welcome to it. Her biggest regret was handing off the file for the young girl and her mother that she was recommending the courts leave together. She hoped Tammy would heed the comments April had made on the file, but she realized it was out of her hands. When she returned to Hallbrook, she'd check up on the pair to see how they were doing.

An hour and a half later, on the dot, she pulled up to the Bradley house. Knowing what she would need was almost impossible, so she'd thrown together some outfits that could be mixed and matched and last a few days. She'd have to swing by later to get more of what she needed before they headed to the city.

She knocked on the door and waited. The sound of raised voices coming from inside was not a good sign, and the dog's barking only made it more chaotic.

The front door opened, and Garrett reached for her bag and pulled her inside. "Thank goodness, you're here."

"What's with all the shouting?" April asked.

Garrett pointed toward the two older kids who stood glaring at him as if he were the devil. Her arrival was clearly none too soon.

"Melanie heard me talking about New York, and she told Bryan, and they aren't thrilled about it. And I'm not getting anywhere trying to make them understand I don't have a choice but to return to the city, and they have to go back with me." Garrett ground out his frustration in each word as he tried to explain. *Maybe she should reconsider.* There was still time to change her mind. *No.* Her education and future depended on her seeing this through, not to mention the children's well-being was at stake.

"What seems to be the problem?" She directed the question at the kids. Better to dive in and get straight to the source. Both kids launched into a diatribe, and April caught bits and pieces. She held up her hand. "One at a time, please. This needs to be a civilized conversation if anyone is going to listen and come to some sort of agreement."

Bryan huffed. "Fine. He," he said, pointing at Garrett, "—expects us to move to New York City with him. To leave our friends and our school. And we don't want to go. It's not fair."

"Yeah, we don't want to go." Melanie echoed his words, her lower lip in a full, drooping pout.

April's gaze landed on her casted arm, and she felt a momentary rush of sympathy. Now wasn't the time. She had to get this situation under control and fast. "I totally understand." April nodded, moving farther into the room, and stopping six feet away, blocking Garrett out of the conversation with strategic positioning.

"You do?" Bryan was shocked, his voice dropping a few decibels.

"I do. You have school and friends here. It's all you ever known. It would be scary to live somewhere else." With kids, sometimes you needed to nudge them to the right conclusion, not bulldoze them. Garrett apparently was a heavy-equipment operator.

"I didn't say I was scared. I'm not scared of anything, except when maybe dummy here fell out the tree. I just don't want to, and he can't make me." Bryan crossed his arms and took a defensive stance—but at least they were talking and not yelling.

"I'm not a dummy, and I'm not scared either. That's dumb." Melanie chimed in.

April chose her next words carefully. "No one said anyone was dumb. Melanie falling from the tree was an accident. There's a huge difference. I think you're both afraid and won't admit it."

"No—" Bryan interjected.

"Wait. Hear me out. We need to listen to each other. It's not a one-sided conversation."

"Fine," he huffed again, plopping down on the sofa to listen.

"Thank you. As I was saying, fear makes us not do things, and sometimes we don't even realize our fears are being driven by fear. Here's what I see on the other side of what you see. I see kids who have wonderful friends here in Hallbrook, and that won't change. But here's what else I see. I see kids who have an opportunity for an adventure. It's like a vacation to a new place, to try it on and see how it fits. Kids love adventure, so to say no to that would tell me you might be afraid." She'd come a full circle, and she could see the two of them trying to make sense of what she just explained. April also knew this was the most critical part and kept quiet.

"Adventures are fun." Bryan shrugged. "But what if we don't like it?"

He'd thought of the one question she wasn't prepared to answer. She hoped, for everyone's sake, Garrett didn't correct her answer. "We can discuss it then. Make decisions together. It's easier to cross that bridge and make decisions after you've had a taste of the adventure and know all the facts. Let me put it this way. If you could have vanilla ice cream, which you know you like because it's familiar, or you could have some secret flavor that could be amazing or not, which would you choose?"

"The secret flavor. Vanilla is boring." Melanie's answer gave her hope this would work.

"Bryan?" April waited for him to get on board with the direction she was taking the discussion.

"Vanilla is for girls." Bryan scrunched up his nose. "I want something different. Like green and chocolate."

"Exactly. Think of the city like green and chocolate ice cream. Something to try, so the next time you're asked vanilla or mint chocolate chip, you will know exactly what to answer." The light clicked on for both children. It was evident in the way they stood looking at each other, more relaxed now.

"Okay, but if we hate the mint, I don't want to be forced to eat it." The kid was quick-witted for his young age, making her even more grateful they were on board for the adventure.

"Sometimes, we don't have a choice what's served, and we just say no to dessert." April had no idea where the last thought came from, and it was over their heads, but it helped her to fully understand what she was trying to explain. A life lesson about trying new things, but also about understanding that sometimes decisions were made for you, but sooner or later you could make the decision for yourself. Exactly the lesson she'd learned as a foster kid stuck in the system.

"What's that supposed to mean. Who says no to dessert?" Melanie chimed in.

"It means, give the city a chance. Maybe you'll like it, maybe you won't. But in the end, it becomes a part of growing up, and it helps you to figure out what you like and don't like. It'll help you know what you want to do with your own life when you grow up and get to make your own choices."

"Okay. So, when does this adventure start?" Bryan asked the question, but all three of them turned to face Garrett for the answer.

He stood staring at April in amazement with Sandy fast asleep in his arms.

April shot him one of those I-got-this-looks and shrugged.

"Monday. April, if you can put together some of their things, I'll take care of my mom's affairs and call for a ride to the airport and book us a charter flight to La Guardia." Garrett was in a take-charge mode now that the kids were settled. Except Monday was the day after tomorrow, and not at all what she expected.

"I didn't see that coming." There were loads of problems associated with leaving that soon, but she tamped down her response, not wanting to give the children any wiggle room. "Okay, then. I'll get everything ready. I'm sure the kids will help pack their own clothes for our adventure." She smiled for the sake of the children, but her mind was racing with all that needed to be done. This was insane.

"But what about Rufus?" Bryan asked, stroking the dog's back. "He has to come with us. Can he ride in a plane? And not in the cargo area. I've heard awful things about that from the other kids at school." Bryan was well-informed.

"Not a plane. We're going by helicopter. And the dog can fly with us in the main area. It's a huge chopper," Garrett replied.

"A helicopter? A real helicopter. Yes!" Bryan exclaimed. "I mean, *ummm*, cool." Caught between a boy and a young man, the kid wasn't sure how to react.

April shot Garrett a secret wink, accompanied by a grin she couldn't hold back. *Score a point for Garrett.*

Chapter Six

♥

GARRETT HAD TURNED THE entire household over to April the minute she arrived. Best decision ever. He still couldn't believe how she'd been able to diffuse the volatile conversation that had been going on for over ten minutes by the time she arrived. Melanie had been sullen and withdrawn all the way home from the doctor's office, and not even Mabel had been able to draw her out.

At first, Garrett had worried her wrist was bothering her, but when they got closer to home, he knew there was more to her attitude. It didn't take long to find out what. The second they entered the house, Melanie told Bryan what she'd heard about them going to New York City. It was as if a bomb had been dropped. His negotiating skills were some of the best in the country, but they were useless when it came to dealing with children.

Luckily, April's tactic had worked, because he was at the end of his rope dealing with them and had no idea what to do next. He wasn't sure what would happen when the kids found out they might be eating mint chocolate chip ice cream for a long time to come, but he'd decided to follow her suggestion and cross that bridge when the time came. Anything to bring peace to the household, even if it was temporary.

He couldn't even begin to imagine how this would all work out. His penthouse suite was his personal space. A place of his own created exactly as he wanted—a haven of perfection. Which was ironic, considering he'd moved to the city for the lights and excitement. In the end, he preferred the lights from his balcony overlooking Manhattan and the Hudson River over an exciting nightlife. He got enough of that with all the client dinners and parties he had to attend.

And now he had to share it with three kids, a dog, and a nanny. He let out a deep breath and shook his head. Everything would change, and it was up to him to figure out how to make it work. He needed to take a page out of April's playbook to watch and learn. She'd come in and systematically begun organizing everything last night. Dinner was reheated leftovers from the home-cooked meals, salads, and desserts the neighbors had dropped off. The children picked up their toys, had their baths, and like magic, they were all in bed on time. Sandy at eight, and the other two at nine.

Not to mention the smooth, efficient way she'd handled the kids on Sunday, getting them packed and prepared for the move to the city. It was most impressive and confirmed the money he'd offered her was well spent. For the past two nights, Garrett had felt guilty sleeping in his own bed, knowing she was on the couch. He'd offered her his mother's room that he was currently using, but she'd turned him down, insisting it would be easier to get a jump on things in the mornings if she was in the living room. This morning, however, when he came downstairs, he was surprised to find her sound asleep, considering they needed to be out the door by eight a.m. Although judging by the suitcases piled high at the front door, she'd worked late last night.

He watched her sleep, appreciating the soft look on her face, her hair cascading across the pillow. She was a beautiful woman, inside and out. Garrett noticed a golden butterfly birthmark on her throat that he hadn't seen before. An image of him kissing it crossed his still half-asleep brain. He snapped out of the no-go zone he'd traveled into and headed for the kitchen.

He flipped the coffee pot switch to on. April had set it up the night before, and it wasn't long before the warm aroma of chicory percolated throughout the kitchen. Way better than the plastic instant cups he'd used every day. It made a nice change.

It wasn't long before April entered the kitchen, brightening the place considerably and energizing him in a way no cup of coffee would ever do. And all while still dressed her in pajamas.

"Good morning. I totally overslept." She yawned and headed for the coffee pot, the long beep signaling it was ready drawing her attention.

"Good morning." He started to rise, intent on getting his own cup of coffee.

"Sit down. I'll get yours." She waved him off, and he complied, finding it oddly comforting to watch her in action.

She handed him a cup of steaming coffee. He took a sip; the flavor was bold and daring. "Thanks, this is perfect."

"I'll jot that down in my memory notebook. Two cups of water and three tablespoons of Graystone Dark Magic coffee per cup." She tapped her temple.

"Memory notebook?"

"Yes. It's something I learned to do a long time ago. It helps me to remember things. Someday it'll come in handy when I'm trying to keep up with twenty-plus kids in a classroom." Her laughter filled the kitchen with warmth.

"You want to teach?" There was a lot to learn about April, and everything about her interested him. Maybe she'd used the same magic she used on the kids on him. He was definitely a fan of hers.

"Yes. Kindergarten, to be exact. That's why I want to finish my schooling and agreed to your offer." April fixed a sippy cup with milk and screwed on the lid. Of course, she wouldn't forget the top. That was for amateurs like him.

"Now why doesn't that surprise me?" He pictured her presiding over a classroom of little beasts like she was the queen of the jungle.

"I love kids. What can I say?" She shrugged. "Why didn't you finish your schooling before? I'm guessing you've been out a few years."

"Do I look that old?" She smoothed back her hair, frowning.

"I didn't mean it that way. You don't look like a fresh-face college girl. Is that better?" He winked.

"*Ummm*, maybe." April shook her head and rolled her eyes. "I made it through three years of college, but then I got sick and missed too much school and had to drop out. One thing led to another, life changed, and I couldn't afford to finish. I've been trying to put money every week into a fund so that one day I could finish."

"And that explains why you jumped at this opportunity—for which I'm grateful." His mother trusted him to make this work, and for her, he'd try to make things right for the kids. He still didn't have all the answers but getting April to help was an excellent start.

"That makes two of us. We'll make it work."

"You mean, you'll make it work. I'll be at the office escaping the madness," he teased.

"So that's how it's going to be. At least I know ahead of time what to expect. By the way, I called the principal of the elementary school in your neighborhood and explained the situation. They agreed as long as the kids are enrolled in school by Labor Day, you'll be fine, and they won't miss much." April picked up the coffee carafe and filled his cup.

"Thanks. And I appreciate you taking care that. It's not something I would've thought of, at least not right away." He'd have to find out what school district he was in. Or maybe a private school would be better. That would be an excellent task to assign his secretary, Brooke, once he got back to the office. She was a New Yorker through and through and was well-versed on all the ins and outs. Better to trust someone citified who knew the ropes than to lay that on April's plate.

"Trust me, if you had forgotten for long, you'd be reminded. It's called truancy. The truancy police would come knocking on your door looking for the kids. The law requires them to attend school unless you've arranged for homeschooling." April laid out three bowls, spoons, napkins, small plates, and a juice glass. She was a master at time management.

"I'm expecting there's a lot to learn along the way, which is another great reason to have you to help guide me through this. What are you feeding them for breakfast? A smorgasbord?"

Her sassy grin was endearing, the dimple on her chin more pronounced when she was fighting back a laugh.

"The dishes are for cereal and a piece of toast. A balanced breakfast." April added the peanut butter and jelly to the table. "And don't worry, you'll get the hang of it. Kids are resilient, and they'll come around. They just need to get to know and trust you."

"By the way, nice pajamas." He'd almost been able to resist the temptation to tease her about the kitty-cat flannel bottoms and matching T-shirt top, but not quite.

"What? I love cats. And they're comfortable." There wasn't a trace of discomfort in her voice. Her confidence was admirable. April was a unique woman with special talents when it came to kids and just about everything she did, and he couldn't help but wonder more about her. Her history.

She probably had no shortage of boyfriends, and he wondered if her current boyfriend had any issues with her running off to New York City, knowing a man was part of the package deal. If April and he were an item, no amount of money would make that situation right, and he wouldn't want her traveling with some guy. Not that someone could necessarily stop her. She was fascinating, yes, but also determined.

"Thanks. I woke up early and tried not to disturb you." Garrett took the steaming cup of coffee from her and took a sip.

"Disturb? I barely slept. That couch is the smallest, most uncomfortable bed I've ever slept on. The princess had it made in the fairytale with just peas under her mattress. The lumps under that couch mattress felt more like oranges."

"I did offer you the bed in my mother's room."

"Yes, but when you offered, I didn't feel right about it. But last night made me regret my decision."

"At least in New York, you'll have my king-size bed to get lost in." Garrett grinned.

"It sounds heavenly. The idea of sleeping alone on a king does have a certain appeal." April looked up at him as if for confirmation, the word *alone* a clear message.

"Yes, and it'll be me on the couch." He landed the point nicely, confirming their platonic relationship.

"You can't guilt me into sharing your bed." She quipped, the dimple on her chin a giveaway she was teasing.

"I wouldn't think of it." Garrett sipped his coffee but couldn't hold back the grin threatening to escape.

Sandy started to fuss up in her room. "Guess that's my call button for the next two weeks. Lucky you," April said.

Garrett chuckled as she left the room in a hurry, apparently unwilling to let him see her embarrassment, but she'd been too late. He had seen the attractive pink blush on her cheeks and found it endearing.

He picked up his coffee and headed for his mother's office. The place still held a hint of Jessica's perfume from yesterday when they'd worked together for hours going over his mother's business accounts. Her arrival yesterday had come as a surprise, and her obvious interest in him made it difficult to accept the help she offered, but he needed it, knowing he was leaving in the morning. By the time they were through, he'd arranged for someone to check in on the house, to transfer the craft boutique sales data program to his computer system in the city and worked out a plan with Jessica about how to manage everything going forward.

Garrett still had a few more things to finalize before they could leave. He wanted to visit his mother's favorite spot on the estate. There hadn't been time before today, but now, with him leaving again, he refused to leave without going.

April got dressed quickly, not wanting to linger in her pajamas, especially not after Garrett had made fun of them. It was better than a granny nightgown any day. What did he expect her to wear, some sexy satin boxer shorts and a camisole?

She headed up the stairs to get Sandy and was shocked to find the older kids already up and getting dressed, practically ready to head out the door. They'd had a complete change of attitude since their talk, and it made her morning easy. "Breakfast is on the table. Eat up before it's time to leave."

"Okay." The pair of them raced down the stairs. April shook her head, entered Sandy's room, and made her way to the crib. "Good morning, sunshine. Ready to fly in a helicopter? I bet this is your first flight. I wonder if we can get you wings?" April grabbed Sandy's fingers as she pulled at the butterfly pinned on her shirt, preferring not to lose the one thing she had left of her mother's. She picked out Sandy's clothes, helped her to dress, and threw a few last-minute items into a bag, including Sandy's stuffed bunny she slept with every night.

Holding on to the rail with one hand, April carried Sandy downstairs. The kids were still in the kitchen, wolfing down their breakfast. She put Sandy in her booster seat and gave her a piece of toast and fed her cereal, trying to keep her extra clean for the trip. They talked excitedly about their adventure. It would seem everything had come together nicely despite the rush, with the exception that she hadn't been able to return home and get more clothes. But she was going to New York, home of fashion and clothes galore. When else would she get the chance to splurge on herself, or have the extra money in her pocket to do it?

Rufus barked, letting everyone know someone was at the front door and sending her into a panic. She glanced at her watch. *Yikes*. If it was the chauffeur, the man was early.

Bryan jumped up to leave. "The man's out front, and it's time to go." He was having a hard time holding back his excitement.

"Take a chill pill," Melanie huffed, following close on the heels of her brother, her arm bound in a sling and not bothering her in the least.

"Stop right there." Both kids stopped and spun around.

"Bowls in the sink, please. And do you both have everything you used last night or this morning that you need to take in your backpacks? Chargers. Tablets."

"Yes, ma'am." They both were quick to respond, fidgeting, and glancing down the hall.

"You need to brush your teeth and pack your toothbrush," April reminded them.

"Yes, ma'am." They sprinted out of the room, the thud of their footsteps racing up the stairs sounded like a herd of elephants. Moments later, the herd of elephants raced back down the stairs just as April finished cleaning the dishes and tidying the kitchen.

She carried Sandy into the living room just as Melanie opened the door, letting Rufus charge past her.

"Great. She let the dog out, now what do we do?" Bryan's frustration with his sister was evident.

"I couldn't help it. I've only got one arm to use, thanks to you," Melanie whined.

"Wasn't my fault." Bryan instantly became defensive, and just like that, April knew what was coming. *It was a sibling thing.*

"Was too. You wanted to climb the dumb tree."

"Knock it off you two. Bryan, grab his leash and see if you can call him. I'll be right back down to help."

She would deal with things one at a time. And first on her list was getting Sandy's teeth brushed. Then she'd deal with the dog. It's not as though he'd run off far, the monster dog overly attached to the kids.

When they finished, she pulled open the door and started to drag the luggage out onto the front porch, wondering where Garrett was. It was two minutes to eight.

"Here, ma'am, let me get those." The chauffeur appeared relaxed in his polo shirt and slacks as he picked up the first two bags.

"Oh, thank you. That would be wonderful."

And just like clockwork, Garrett appeared in the hall. "What can I do to help?"

"Little late for that question. Yesterday, help would have been even more appreciated." Teasing with a little truth mixed in. Yesterday, his help would have been great, but she wasn't sure if it was because she'd needed it, or because he'd been closeted away all day with the darling Jessica, whose interest was all too obvious, leaving April a bit jealous and confused about why she should be feeling that way. It would do her no good to start imagining her and Garrett together.

Imagining always led to trouble.

"I'm sorry. I was so tied up in my mom's affairs, I didn't think to see if you needed help. You always seem to have everything under control. I got a lot of work done, so I appreciate it."

"Guess that's why you pay me the big bucks," she teased.

"Do you need any help now?" He glanced around to see what was left.

"The driver already took care of the bags. I think you timed it that way on purpose."

Garrett's smile deepened, but he shook his head. "Not me," he added innocently.

"To answer your question, yes, we need help. You can get the dog. Melanie accidentally let him out, and he's outside running around, which isn't a bad thing before a long trip. I'll get the kids in the car if you can get the dog."

"Or we could just leave him here and let Jessica take care of him. My place isn't cut out for a dog." Garrett's comment didn't sound as if he were joking. She shook her head. "Or not. Pick your battles, mister, and this isn't one of them. You'll learn that soon enough."

"It was worth a try." He shrugged and headed out the door, intent on rounding up Rufus.

Within minutes, kids, adults, and the dog were successfully in the limo. The kids were kept occupied looking out the window and playing car games all the way to the airport. Garrett and April ended up next to each other, and the smell of his cologne lured her into taking deep breaths and savoring the spicy mix.

Garrett looked at her and smiled. The kind of smile that made her heart do a topsy-turvy roll before she turned away. *Don't start getting any ideas. He's just nice because you're doing him a huge favor.*

"Yuck, gross. The dog just drooled on me." Melanie brushed the spit off her arm and wiped it on her pants.

At least she didn't wipe it on her brother. "Just wash your hands when we get to the airport. He's probably hot." April tried to console her.

On the drive, Bryan talked nonstop about the helicopter ride, the kid a fount of information on the subject. His dad had given him a model helicopter for his birthday eight months ago, and it was the last connection he remembered. Bryan treasured the model chopper he and his dad had built together. And now, Garrett was giving him a new treasure—a real ride in one.

April's palms were sweaty, and she rubbed them on her pants, trying to hide her fear of flying. She gripped her purse tighter as they pulled into the airport and drove past the main terminal area toward the heliport and their ride. The helicopter was bigger than she'd imagined and seeing it up this close made it more real.

"Wow, that's huge." Bryan's excitement was the opposite of the gut-clenching nerves April was experiencing.

"That's an Airbus H160. It holds up to twelve passengers. I figured we needed plenty of room for everyone and everything, including the dog. That beast takes up a lot of space." Garrett chuckled, reaching out to pat the beast on the head.

Bryan jumped out of the car the second it stopped.

"Hold up, Bryan," Garrett called out as the kid started toward the helicopter. The blades were turning at a low speed as part of the warm-up process. "You need to hold someone's hand as we make our way to the chopper because the wind force generated by the turning blades is enough to knock you over." Garrett took his hand.

"*Naaa*. I'm tough." Bryan grimaced and tried to pull away, not wanting to be babied.

Garrett didn't let loose his hand. "It's easier if you crouch a bit and stay low." Bryan quit resisting and walked beside him to the chopper door. He lifted Bryan up inside and then returned for Melanie, followed by Rufus, who didn't seem to be a fan of the noise. Garrett took the leash and pulled the dog toward the helicopter.

"Come on, Rufus, don't be afraid." The dog followed but only because Garrett kept pulling to guide him forward.

The chauffeur and another man loaded the luggage. Garrett came back to help April and Sandy. "Here, let me have the baby. I can give you a hand up and then hand her back to you." He spoke loud enough to be heard over the whirring of the blades.

"Thanks." April handed Sandy over, but she was having trouble taking a step forward.

"Are you okay? You seem nervous about this." "I'll be fine." She nodded and started forward, determined not to show her fear. She had to be strong. To show weakness allowed people to take advantage of you.

He climbed in behind her and started to systematically buckle the children in their seats, double-checking everything. Satisfied all was in order, he moved to work on April's safety straps. "Take a couple of deep breaths. You'll be fine." He clicked the buckle in place.

"Is it that obvious?" April asked, her voice still tense.

Garrett pulled tightly on the end of the straps to make it secure. "To me, it is, but your secret is safe. I fly this way all the time, and I swear you'll love it. Just give it a chance. Remember, it's an adventure." He winked at her, chucking her chin with his forefinger.

She took a deep breath and exhaled, trying to heed his advice. The whirring sound got louder, and the helicopter started to vibrate. Seconds later, they were going up. Higher and higher. Bryan and Melanie had their faces pressed to the glass, and even Sandy seemed impressed. Only April remained tense, but even that lessened as the pilot pointed out a few things for them along the way, his voice crack- ling through the headset they all wore. Garrett's constant reassurance went a long way to easing her tension, and by the time they arrived an hour and a half later, even April was enjoying the ride.

"Welcome to New York City." Garrett's warm words were directed at the entire group, but the twinkle in his eyes was just for her.

Chapter Seven

♥

APRIL HAD NEVER BEEN to the city before, and as the chauffeur drove the limo through the streets, she felt like they were just one of the many ants hustling around with what appeared to be total chaos, but each with an agenda. People were everywhere, and everyone seemed to be headed somewhere important, rushing about the way they did. Horns honked. The cars stopped and started on a dime. Street vendors called out, selling their wares. There were even musicians and acrobats performing, looking to make a few bucks. The buildings stretched upward, touching the sky, hundreds of them. Or more like thousands.

The kids were loving every minute. It was a fun place that never rested. The permanently on merry-go-round. Fascinating and daunting all at the same time.

The driver pulled in front of a large building and stopped.

"This is where I live. Sutton Hill. It's on the south side of Manhattan." Garrett grabbed hold of the dog's leash and pushed open the door. He exited the limo and turned back to help her while keeping a firm hold on Rufus.

The older kids piled out, both stopping to look around and then up at the tall buildings. April took Sandy's hand and held on tightly to keep her safe. A man dressed in uniform met them at the limo.

"Good afternoon, Mr. Bradley. Welcome back." The man was probably in his late twenties and quite fit, judging by the way he began loading their luggage on the elevator cart as if the cases weighed next to nothing.

"Thanks, Ted. It's good to be back." Garrett turned toward her and the kids. "I'd like you to meet April St. James, and this is Bryan, Melanie, and Sandy Williams. They're going to be staying with me for quite a while. If Miss St. James needs any help, I'd appreciate it if you'd help her in any way you can when I'm not around." Garrett handed him some money.

The man smiled his appreciation. "Absolutely, Mr. Bradley. Thank you."

"Oh, and the first order of business, can you call the building dog walker and get him to add Rufus to his schedule? Just text me with the times he has available. Twice a day, I would assume." Garrett looked at her for confirmation.

April nodded.

"Yes, Mr. Bradley. I'll get right on it. The dog walker's name is Wade." Ted reached out and patted Rufus on the head. "You'll approve of him. He understands dogs, and they all take to him like he's their new best friend."

"Perfect." They all headed up the steps and inside the building. The lobby had a white-tiled floor and was nothing April would want to be responsible for cleaning considering the traffic that would come through here.

They didn't have to wait long for the elevator. Garrett scanned his key card, and the elevator began to climb endlessly, finally coming to a stop.

The kids were still running on high energy, but she could tell they were slowing down. The trip had worn them out. Lucky for her, it would be an early bedtime for them, and she wouldn't be far behind them. Travel had a way of wearing out young and old alike.

"Here we are." Garrett pushed open the door, stepping back to hold it open and let them pass through. Bryan had taken charge of Rufus, the dog minding him quite well, at least for the moment. A new place would likely need to be explored, every inch of it.

"Hold on to him tightly, Bryan. He's got a lot of pent-up energy, and it's a new place he'll want to explore. I'm sure we need to dog-proof and Sandy proof the place."

"I've got him." Bryan waltzed right in, confident in his abilities to handle the dog. Melanie was right behind him, and Sandy stuck close to her sister.

April was stunned by the luxurious appearance of Garrett's home. Everything was crisp, clean, and ultra-contemporary with lots of white, tan, and black. It all perfectly complemented and matched, but it was void of all personal effects. There was no warmth or character to reflect the man who lived here in the design. The place appeared as though it could grace the centerfold of *House Beautiful* magazine and not a place someone actually lived in.

"Whoa," Melanie exclaimed.

"You can say that again," Bryan dittoed the sentiment. "You live here?"

The kids raced into the living room, Bryan tugging on the dog's leash to make him follow. "Look at this." Bryan pointed out the window.

"You gotta see this," Melanie echoed her brother's sentiment.

April was impressed by the view as well, but she was more concerned about Rufus knocking something over. The dog started to bark and pulled at the leash, trying to drag Bryan in the direction of the hall.

Garrett started toward Bryan. "Can't you keep him—"

"Garrett, you're home. I wasn't expecting you this early." They all swung around to check out the newcomer. A beautiful woman stepped into the living room, having come from down the hall where April expected the bedrooms were located.

The woman's dark-blue pencil skirt and light-blue silk blouse fit her shapely figure without more than an inch to spare, emphasizing every curve. Her shirt was unbuttoned just to the point of indiscretion, revealing the swell of her ample bosoms.

"Brooke, what are you doing here?" Garrett obviously knew the woman but hadn't expected her. Not that it meant much if she had a key to his place.

Rufus broke free from Bryan.

"Rufus, no!" April shouted as the dog charged toward the woman, then jumped up, his front paws landing on Brooke's silky blouse, almost knocking her over.

Brooke screamed. "Garrett, get him down."

"Rufus, no." Garrett charged forward, grabbed the dog by the collar and pulled him back. He led him toward one of the bedrooms, pushed him inside, and closed the door.

April knew he was furious but opted to remain silent.

Brooke brushed fur off her blouse, inspecting it for damage. She brushed her hair back from her face, letting her chin rise a notch as she looked them over, disdain written on her face. "What is the meaning of this? Who are these people?"

"I think the question is, what are you doing here?" Garrett countered her questions with one of his own.

"You notified me of your arrival time, and I figured I could turn on some lights and chill some wine to make sure you had a nice welcome home. I know it's been a stressful trip for you based on our conversations." If they'd talked when he was in Hallbrook, it meant they were probably close. Or more than close, considering Brooke had a key to his place.

"I also told you I didn't need anything." Garrett didn't like not having his orders followed, something April filed away for future reference when dealing with the man.

"But it's my job to take care of you. Who are these people?" The woman gestured toward them, her gaze stopping on April.

"This is April St. James. She's here as a temporary nanny to my new charges. This is Bryan, Melanie, and Sandy Williams. And Rufus is their dog. Sorry about the rude introduction to the beast. He gets rambunctious around newcomers," Garrett added by way of explanation.

"What do you mean *new charges*?" The woman's voice had taken on a sharper quality. Not much, but enough for April to notice.

"Exactly what it sounds like." He shrugged.

"And they are *all* going to be living here? Including the nanny?" April could hear the jealousy in her voice. The woman was familiar with Garrett's apartment and clearly assumed she had a right to be here. Of course, a man of Garrett's power and wealth would have a woman waiting for him back in the city. It was a good thing she'd ignored the attraction she felt around him. Knowing he was taken would be the incentive she needed to keep any developing feelings under lock and key.

"April is staying until she can find a replacement nanny and housekeeper."

"I see." The woman's eyes narrowed slightly, leaving April to wonder exactly what she saw. She'd be wrong if she was worried about anything between her and Garrett.

"April, kids, this is my secretary, Brooke Taylor." The secretary sent them a dismissive glance before returning her focus on Garrett. *His secretary*. How stereotypical to be in a relationship with one's secretary.

"I should be going. My blouse is ruined, and I need to change it. I will see you in the office first thing in the morning, Garrett. It's great to have you home." She started toward the door, stopping as an afterthought. "It's nice to meet you...everyone." There wasn't an ounce of welcome in her voice.

"It's nice to meet you, too." Brooke didn't need to worry. April wasn't feeling the sentiment either. As soon as the door closed, April let Rufus out of the bedroom. The sound of him jumping against the door while introductions were being made, had caused her to shudder knowing the damage his large paws would yield as they scratched against the wood.

Rufus bounded into the living room and jumped on the white leather sofa.

"Rufus, down," Garrett shouted. The veins on his forehead were popping out, his anger barely controlled. The dog laid his head down on his front paws and looked up at him with huge, almost puppylike eyes, as if trying to figure out the problem. "No dogs on the couch," Garrett commanded firmly, pulling the dog by the collar to make him move. "I can see we're going to need rules."

Easy for Garrett to say, he'd be gone all day. He could make as many rules as he wanted, and she'd do her best to keep them, but this place wasn't fit for child or beast, the beast being Rufus.

Garrett wasn't pleased to discover Brooke in his home but dealing with the dog was worse. He drew in a deep breath and resisted the urge to inspect the sofa for damage. Fine Italian leather wasn't meant to be clawed. "Listen up, kids. I know this is all new, but can we try to respect that it's my home. That means no food in the living room, no feet on the coffee table or sofa, no dog on the sofa, and keep your things picked up and in your room. Are we clear?"

Bryan shrugged. "I guess. What's there to do here anyway? Where's the fun?"

"I'll see what I can do next weekend, but for now, I've got to work the rest of the week to catch up. You can watch movies or play on your tablets. I'm sure you'll figure something out." He was never a fan of games or clutter, so he was ill-prepared for the sudden change in his life that warranted kid stuff. Maybe Jim's wife could help him pick out some things. Until then, he just wanted things left the way they were. "I'm sure April can find something for you to do." That's why he'd hired her, after all. To keep the kids out of trouble and from destroying his place.

"He's right. I'll find something for us to do, and we'll make our own fun. Don't worry, Garrett, I'll make sure everything goes smoothly."

He shot her a look of gratitude before heading for the front door to start sorting the pile of luggage that needed distribution. "April, if you start a movie for them, we can put away their things and get them settled in. I take it you brought some for them?"

"I did." She nodded. "I'll take care of it. The large lime-green bag is mine. If you just drop it off in my room, I'll take care of it later." They spent the next hour distributing and unpacking, setting up the kids in their rooms and the dog in Bryan's room.

Melanie looked up when Garrett entered the living room. "I'm hungry," she said.

"Me, too." Bryan chimed in.

"I know there's nothing you all would want to eat in my kitchen. Why don't I order a famous New York Sicilian pizza for everyone?" Delivery would be the easiest way to feed this crowd. He noticed April had already fed the dog, which worked well for him considering he wouldn't have a clue what to buy or where to get it. Of course, she had the insight to bring food with her. April's efficiency ranked right up there with the best.

"Yay!" the kids cheered in unison.

"I want pepperoni and mushroom," Bryan added.

"I want ham and pineapple," Melanie put in her own order. Of course, the two were completely different.

"Grams always ordered what you wanted. I think it's time to order what I want," Bryan insisted.

"That's because she liked it my way, and so does Sandy."

"Girls," Bryan huffed. "It's not fair."

Garret pressed his fingertips to his temples and rubbed.

April entered the room. "Kids, calm down. There's no reason that we can't order two."

They looked at Garrett for confirmation. "Two it is." He'd order ten if it quieted the children and restored peace to his home. Sandy crawled up in his lap and smiled, to which there was only one thing he could do—smile back. She was too cute not to.

By the time they finished the movie and the pizza, the kids were more than ready for bed. Garrett picked up the mess while April put them to bed, glad she took Rufus with her. He was looking forward to spending a few quiet minutes talking to April before they retired for the evening. Time alone was something they hadn't had yet. He looked up as she entered the kitchen.

"The kids are in bed." She yawned.

"Care for a glass of wine?" he offered.

April gazed at him as if lost in thought for a moment before she replied. "Tomorrow's going to be a long day trying to adjust and to figure out how to

keep the kids busy. I think I'll pass and turn in for the night. Good evening."

"Goodnight." A sense of disappointment washed over him as he watched her walk away. He wanted to spend time with her, but she clearly didn't feel the same way.

Chapter Eight

♥

APRIL ROLLED OVER AND yawned, glancing at her watch. Seven-thirty. Way later than her normal early-riser routine. By the time she'd gotten the kids settled last night, she'd been exhausted and had crawled into Garrett's bed and fallen asleep, not even bothering to unpack her own belongings.

She glanced around the room, taking in the bedroom suite. A black lacquer dresser extended at least eight feet, the silver handles plain and blocky. The nightstand matched the dresser, with only a glass lamp on it as a decoration. The bed frame matched the entire suite, but the mattress was not at all what she'd expected.

It was like heaven on earth, the padding deep and cool as it molded around her body. The down comforter was white, of course, but more impor-tantly, it was fluffy and soft, the fibers silk against her skin. There was no incentive to leave the plush comfort of his bed this morning, other than the fact she had a job to do.

April slid out from under the covers reluctantly. She wasn't sure what time Garrett left in the morning, but she did want to send him off to work with a fresh cup of coffee. His appreciation of her coffee-brewing skills was nice, and not something she was used to from people.

Last night, she'd wanted to stay and talk with him, but it was for the best she hadn't. She wasn't the type of woman to poach another woman's territory, and Brooke was exactly the type of woman Garrett would want and need. She was businesslike and efficient, always tidy and neatly dressed, all the things April wasn't. By choice.

She would have been fine with her decision if it weren't for the look of disappointment on his face when she left. A look she was still wondering about. She slipped on her robe to cover the kit-ty-cat pajamas he'd teased her about. Once was enough. April headed down the hall, glancing at the sofa in the living room. There was no sign of Garrett or any bed linens to indicate he'd even slept there last night.

Her gaze landed on the note propped up against a book. She crossed the room to pick it up and noticed it was addressed to her.

Gone to work. Ted is delivering some grocery staples at eight-thirty a.m. so you and the kids will have some- thing to eat. If you need anything, call me, or ask Ted. Not sure when I'll be home. Don't wait dinner.

Garrett

So much for making him coffee. There would be no easing into the morning. Her welcome to New York was over. April poured herself a glass of juice and moved to sit in front of the huge picture window, placing a coaster under her drink so it wouldn't leave a mark on the table.

It was an amazing view of the Hudson River, but it didn't hold the appeal of Hallbrook. April knew for certain that mint chocolate chip ice cream would never be her thing. Luckily, it was only for two weeks, and then she'd be back home. But what about the kids? They were young, and she hoped they would adjust well to city life, because for the foreseeable future, this was their new residence.

She snapped a picture and sent it to Maddison.

April: Arrived. View from killer penthouse suite.

Maddison: Wowser. Lucky girl. Nice view inside and outside the penthouse. LOL.

April: Whatever. It's not like that. I mean yes, he's good looking, but not my type. At all.

Cities and city slickers were welcome to each other. She was a country girl through and through, and no matter how attractive or how nice the man was, she wouldn't be foolish enough to fall in love with one of them. She didn't know the first thing about where to go or what to do in the city, and the idea of traipsing around with the kids intimidated her, leaving her trapped in the high-rise until she figured it out.

A knock at the door surprised April. She glanced at her watch. Garrett had mentioned a grocery delivery at eight-thirty, but it was only eight. A country girl through and through, she'd heard about terrible things happening in the city and didn't just want to open the door to anyone.

She looked through the peephole, trying to decide what to do. The man standing outside the door wasn't Ted. Her pulse ramped up a notch.

The man knocked again.

"Who is it?" she called out.

"Wade. The dog walker. I'm here for Rufus."

April let out a deep breath. Wade, the dog walker. *Yes. She remembered now.* Garrett had arranged the man to take Rufus out when they first arrived. She pulled her robe tighter and opened the door.

"Good morning. I'm April St. James. I forgot you were coming this morning."

"Not a problem. But I'm on a tight schedule." Wade smiled apologetically and shrugged.

"Sorry, I'll get him." She peeked in Bryan's room to discover the two of them snuggled together on the bed, sound asleep. Luckily, Garrett hadn't witnessed the dog making free use of the guest bed like a dog bed, completely ignoring the one she'd brought for him. She'd have to talk to Bryan about it when he woke up. "Rufus, come." She called the dog in a low voice, snapping her fingers to get his attention. He looked up at her, paused, and then thankfully decided to obey. He took his sweet time getting up and off the bed, although to be fair, he was close to two hundred pounds.

April grabbed his leash, hooked him up, and handed it to Wade. "Sorry. I'll have him ready tonight. Just let me know what time."

"Six works well. I'll be back in about twenty minutes if all goes well." He winked, chuckling as he headed out the door.

Her morning wasn't off to greatest of starts, but hopefully, it would get better. First thing on her to-do list was to call the Hospitality Placement Center. She'd researched agencies on the ride here yesterday, noting they were the leading business in the area for housekeepers and nannies. There were lots of glowing reviews and they maintained a five-star rating, making them the perfect place to start her search, and if luck was on her side, finish her search. She grabbed her notebook and a pen and called the agency.

"Good morning. Hospitality Placement Center. This is Tanya, how may I help you?" Kind and courteous, the woman's voice personified the general consensus of the reviews.

"Hi, I'm looking to fill a position for a nanny and housekeeper. This would be a full-time position, and it would be nice if both roles were covered by the same person, possibly as a live-in. Can you help me?"

"Certainly. We have several excellent choices available. If you can provide me with the details, I will enter you into the system. I can arrange several interviews as early as Thursday if that's acceptable to you."

"That sounds perfect." April filled her in on all the pertinent information, hoping for some excellent matches. They ended the call after the woman promised to email her tomorrow with the names of several candidates and their appointment times.

Sandy started to fuss in the other room, and April hurried down the hall, not wanting her to disturb Melanie. The older girl hadn't fancied the idea of sharing a room with her sister, but there was nothing they could do about it. The place didn't have enough rooms for everyone to have their own. Once Melanie learned Garrett was relegated to the sofa, all discussions had ended on her part, Melanie bright enough to choose the room-share over a sofa in the middle of the living room.

April held out her arms to Sandy. "Good morning, sunshine," she whispered. The little girl smiled as she picked her up and carried her out of the room. The minute she set her down, Sandy was running toward the glass window, pressing her fingers against the glass.

April winced. "Don't touch the glass."

Sandy ignored her, going from one side of the room to the other, trying to see what was outside, using her hands to slap the window as she played.

April made a mental note to clean it before Garrett got home. She was reluctant to reprimand Sandy, knowing she'd been through so much, and had yet to speak since her parent's deaths. Trauma could mess with a kid's head.

Bryan wandered into the living room, rubbing his eyes.

"Morning, kiddo. Want some breakfast?"

"Sure," he mumbled, putting his arms over his head to stretch.

"Oh, wait. I almost forget. The food should be here any minute. Garrett ordered some groceries, but there's nothing here until then. Sorry." April wasn't ready to suggest the leftover pizza in the refrigerator just yet.

"Fine. I'll just watch cartoons." He picked up the remote and plopped down on the sofa.

"Okay, but just until breakfast. After that, we need to get cleaned up and have some quiet reading time before we decide what else to do today."

"Read? I don't like reading. That's not much of an adventure. Why can't we do something fun?" Bryan grimaced.

"Reading can be fun. It just depends on how you look at it." Growing up, alone time was a rare commodity to be treasured. A time when she'd loved to read to escape the daily grind of being at the beck and call of her foster families. For her, it had been work, work, work. Watching kids. Cleaning houses. Cooking meals. Anything her current foster parent needed her to do, all for the price of a roof over her head and food on the table.

"You mean fun like when Timmy put a frog down Shelly's shirt?" A frown to a grin in seconds, at the expense of poor Shelly. "Timmy thought it was funny, but his mother didn't."

"No. And that wasn't kind of him. I meant like when you get to look up the frog and find out where he lives, why he croaks, how he can change colors. It's like entering a new world and discovering all sorts of neat stuff from the frog's point of view." The world inside of books was a magical place filled with unending knowledge, fantasy, love, or any other endless interests one might have. There were books for everyone, and it was her job to help the children find what they enjoyed.

He shrugged. "I guess. Never thought of that way." Bryan flipped on the TV.

This was the reason she wanted to teach. There had to be a way to make school fun for young kids, to give them back an eagerness to learn and explore. Something beyond the world of technology and the latest tablet or cell phone.

April wanted to find a way to give children a foundation for a positive attitude toward learning and life, something that would stand them in good stead for years to come when faced with adversity. It was her life mission. She never had that chance after her parents died.

Melanie came down the hall and joined them. "Good—" April started to say before the doorbell cut her off. *Fiddlesticks.* "Can you keep an eye on your sister? That's our breakfast arriving."

"Fine. As long as she doesn't cry. I'm so tired. She kicked me a couple times last night in her sleep, and I kept waking up." Melanie ruffled the girl's hair. "Stinker."

"Sorry, honey."

The doorbell buzzed again.

April peeked through the keyhole, spied Ted on the other side, and opened the door to let him in.

"Good morning." The always upbeat and happy guy pushed a cart full of groceries through the door with the energy of someone who'd been up for hours.

"Hey, Ted. Am I ever glad to see you." She helped him unload the bags to the kitchen counter. "You really have a lot of food here. Surely Garrett didn't order all this. The man has limited knowledge of kids, and I can't imagine he would think of half of these things," April said, as she pulled some of the groceries out of the bag. All the essentials plus quite a few kid favorites.

"You're right. His list was about five items." Ted shot her a you've-got-to-be-kidding-me look. "This is the modified list my wife sent me when I explained what was going on and where I was headed."

"Tell her I said thanks. Garrett is clueless at this point." April put the groceries away as they talked, leaving out food for breakfast.

"He'll figure it out. Everyone does." Ted seemed sure of his opinion.

April disagreed. Garrett didn't seem to have any natural paternal instincts, and she wasn't sure that would change, although, for the children's sake, she hoped it would. "You have great faith in him."

Ted nodded. "He's always had faith in me. Got me this job and gave me a chance to prove I was better than I thought I was. Turns out, he was right. I'm not sure where I'd be today if it weren't for him."

Maybe there was hope for Garrett yet.

Ted was leaving as Wade and Rufus stepped off the elevator and headed down the hall toward them. "Not much room on the complex grassy area for Rufus, but he eventually figured things out. He's a big dog for this building." He handed her the leash.

"Tell me about it. He's a big dog no matter where he's at. Thanks for taking care of him. See you at six." April pulled him toward her. "Sit, Rufus." The dog sat, surprising her. Maybe there was hope for more than one overgrown male in the house. The two men discussed a problem with one of the other tenants before Wade left and Ted turned back her way.

"Here, I made you an extra key card for the suite." He handed her a scan card similar to the one Garrett used.

"Perfect. I think Garrett forgot I might actually need to leave this place on occasion." By the end of the day, they probably would want out. There was one gigantic problem with that though, April wasn't comfortable strolling down the streets of the city with three kids without a clue where she was headed. They needed Garrett, but unfortunately, his note said he wouldn't be home until late.

"I'm surprised. He's normally on top of everything and all into details." Ted was a hardcore fan of Garrett's. Much the same as Brooke.

"Well, these are extenuating circumstances, so I'll cut him some slack." Three kids and a giant dog were more than extenuating circumstances. They were like a tornado blowing into his life. Garrett might need help figuring things out, and while she was still in town, April decided it was up to her to make sure it happened.

"Let me know if you need anything else. I can be reached by calling 2616 on the house phone. If I'm not there, Bill should be at the desk covering for me." After he left, April fixed the kids scrambled eggs, toast, and bacon. They were hungry enough that no one objected to turning off the TV to come to the table.

"When you finish, can you put your plates in the sink? And be sure to rinse them out."

"Yes, ma'am," they both answered, their mouths full.

She'd let that slide considering the ma'am part. Everything was peaceful for the moment, making it the perfect time for April to unpack. Even the dog had finished his dish of food and lay quietly by the window. "Bryan, keep an eye on your sister, please. I'm going to unpack and change."

"Okay." He shrugged. Must be a kid thing nowadays, all the shrugging. Kid language for *I will, but I don't want to.*

"Thanks." April headed for Garrett's room and tossed her suitcase on the bed. After pulling everything out, she glanced around, trying to decide where to put her stuff. On top of the dresser would be the easiest, but it would appear messy, and messy wasn't something Garrett handled well.

The solution was to consolidate some of his stuff to make room for hers. She didn't want to overstep her boundaries, but it was the only possible option. He told her to make herself comfortable, and she was going to be here for two weeks.

That decided, she pulled open the top drawer. Neat rows of black socks folded in half lined the bottom of the drawer. She pulled open the next drawer to discover his boxers, again all neatly folded and stacked, and all blue. No spice or excitement whatsoever. It felt odd touching his boxers, almost intimate, but it was just to move them. She stacked them with the socks and pulled open the next three drawers, looking for ways to consolidate his things and make her some room.

She'd have to tell Garrett, or he'd think there was an underwear thief in his house. Or worse, he'd see her undergarments in the drawer. April couldn't fight back the laughter, picturing his face. After she finished and got dressed, she headed down the hall to check on the kids. She fully expected them to be glued to the TV, but they weren't in the living room. She glanced in the kitchen and didn't find them there, either. Picking up her pace, she pushed open Bryan's bedroom door and was relieved when she spotted them, each doing their own thing.

An alert sounded off in April's head. They were too quiet, and they were together yet playing apart. *Odd.* "Is everything okay?" Things had gone well all morning, but this...she had a bad feeling.

The two older kids glanced at each other, a silent look passing between them. "Everything's fine," Bryan said, almost too quickly.

There was something wrong, and it was up to her to figure out what. She'd like to think they were wonderful kids, and this was just the way they were. Perfect. But they were kids, and perfect was nowhere to be found in the definition of a kid in the dictionary. April headed back into the living room and then into the kitchen and then to the bathroom, trying to find something out of place or broken. She breathed a sigh of relief. Her paranoia was a well-developed instinct born of years of experience, but for once, her instinct was wrong.

She was there to find the kids a nanny and a housekeeper, but she'd also made it her personal mission to help Garrett connect with the kids before she left. And that meant keeping the peace *and* keeping his house in one piece.

Chapter Nine

G ARRETT WAS THE FIRST one to the office. Always. And today was no exception. April could take care of the kids, and he got to do his job. It was a perfect setup, and one he wished could continue for at least the tenth time. The kids adored her. A lot. And she had a way with them that seemed to bring out the best in their behavior. Not that they were angels. But somehow, she always managed to bring peace to those around her.

It was a peacefulness he'd looked forward to sharing with her last night, but she'd turned down his offer. It was better this way. She was leaving, and it would better for everyone concerned if they didn't get too attached to having her around. Including him. He shoved aside thoughts of April and the kids and directed his focus on the file he needed to review. The Baden-Hamilton deal was a merger worth close to ten million dollars, and the attorney fees were nothing to blink at, as well as the continued exposure for their partnership. The closing was fast approaching, and everything had to perfect. He'd been hard at it for over two hours when Brooke wandered in his office.

"Good morning, Garrett. I trust you survived the night seeing as you're here." She placed a fresh cup of coffee on his desk.

"I did at that. Barely. Listen, I'm sorry I snapped at you yesterday, but as you can tell, I have a lot going on. I appreciated the extra effort to make me comfortable when I got home. I hope the dog didn't ruin your shirt. Send me a bill if he did." Brooke excelled at what she did when she wasn't overstepping her boundaries, and he didn't want to lose her. Finding a secretary that met his standards hadn't been easy.

Brooke moved around the desk to stand next to him. "You know me better than that. It takes more than that to put me off. It was terrifying at first, but once you took control of the situation, I wasn't worried."

"I'm glad to hear that." Garrett leaned back in his chair, putting more space between them.

"Speaking of control, whatever are you going to do? You always claimed you're not a family man, and here you are with a family. A large family. And a dog." She crossed her arms in front of her chest and settled in, intent on getting the story.

"My mother adopted them and made me their legal guardian in the event anything happened to her. Something happened, and now they are my responsibility. Honestly, I'm not sure what I'm doing, just taking it one day at a time. I'm not exactly in a position to raise three kids full-time."

Brooke nodded, her eyes wide and bright. "There are several top-notch boarding schools in the country, quite a few right here in the North-east. They wouldn't be far away, but they would be taken care of. And as you say, in their situation, it might be best for the kids. Boarding school would offer them stability, something you wouldn't be able to give with the hours you put in at the office every day. Their life would be in turmoil with the constant rush of getting places to make it all work. As would yours." She braced herself against the desk, leaning in toward him.

"Boarding school. I hadn't thought of that as an option." April had mentioned school, but that wasn't until after Labor Day, so he had time to make decisions. Up until now, he'd only considered public and private schools. He also realized that decision would be driven by who April found to help him with the kids, and to what extent they would run them around.

"It's a great idea. Can you do me a favor and check around and find out which school is the best and get me the literature on it. I know this is on the personal side of things, but I'm in a bind and need help. I'd want all the facts before I make any decision regarding their future." The kids might hate it at first, but right now, it was a promising option. Hopefully, April would find him an incredible nanny-housekeeper who didn't mind the role of chauffeur added on. And even then, the idea of coming home to chaos every night wasn't appealing.

Brooke beamed. "I'd be more than happy to help. You and I are way past the just-business side of things."

Her words were yet another red flag he needed to heed. The last thing he wanted to do was give Brooke the wrong impression because although he valued her as an employee, there was nothing else between them, nor would there be. She wasn't his type of woman at all. If he wanted a relationship, which he didn't, April was far more to his liking. Fresh and honest came to mind.

"I'll have something on your desk by the end of today or tomorrow."

"Thanks."

Brooke started for the door but stopped and turned back. "While I'm at it, do you want me to find a home for the dog? He is over-the-top for your place, and no client would be comfortable with that monster in residence."

"He's a Saint Bernard, not a monster." Not that Garrett hadn't secretly thought the same thing on a few prior occasions.

"Either way, he's too big, too hairy, too much. He's got to go." She nodded, emphasizing she was right. It was a technique he used on clients to get them to agree when they were on the fence about something. But he wasn't on the fence.

Garrett frowned and shook his head. "The kids would never forgive me."

"They'll be in boarding school and would never know." She had a point, but the idea didn't sit well.

Something else he would have to think about. But not now. "I'll take your advice under consideration." Brook was a woman and her advice sounded right—*boarding school might be better for the children.* But he wouldn't make any decisions until he found out more about the schools. It was a huge step, no matter which way he decided.

Brooke was suddenly all smiles again. It wasn't as though he was asking her to watch the kids here at the office, so her single-minded intensity to send them and the dog away was confusing. But then women generally were.

She flipped her hair back off her face and reached out to touch his hand. "I'll get right on it and take care of everything, just like I always do."

"Great. Thanks." Garrett pulled back and picked up the file in front of him. "I've got to get back to this file." His message was clear, and Brooke was quick to catch on. He took a deep breath, wondering what to do about her ever-growing and more personal attention without making her mad enough to leave. He forced himself to concentrate on the file. He read each detail, categorizing them. The details were his friend—but only if he could pay attention and didn't keep getting sidetracked when he logged the information into his brain.

Ten minutes later, his office door opened again. "Brooke, I'm really—" He broke off what he was saying when he looked up and noticed it was Jim.

"Last time I checked, I didn't look like a woman." Jim grinned. "Nice to see you back in the office. Everything okay?" He crossed the room to the coffee pot and helped himself to a cup.

By this time, Garrett was on his fourth cup, and Jim was usually just getting started. "It did. And you don't look like a woman. I was knee-deep in the Baden-Hamilton merger. We should be closing on the deal soon."

"Any problems?" Jim stopped tapping the sugar packet to glance over at him.

"None. I'm just going over some last-minute notes to make sure. You know me." Jim was the worrier of the two, and Garrett was into the details. Between the two of them, they covered all the bases.

"I do. We have a lot of hours and money tied up in this deal, so I'm hoping it closes soon."

"Stop worrying. It will be fine." Garrett was quick to reassure him. Jim's worry level would be high right about now since Garrett had been out of the office a couple of days.

"So, Mr. Detail Man, any reason you haven't told your partner you're a new daddy?" Jim crossed the room and sat down in the leather chair in front of his desk.

"Let me guess? Brooke."

Jim nodded. "You guessed it."

"This is the first I've seen you. It's not as though I had a baby and have been passing out cigars and skipped you over." Garrett chuckled. He would have loved to see Jim's face when he heard the news.

"No, you have triplets from what I hear."

Garrett coughed, choking on a sip of coffee and Jim's proclamation.

"You heard wrong. They're three, seven, and nine."

"That's not much different." Jim's matter-of-fact reply was the same thing Garrett had been thinking all along. Three kids were triple trouble no matter ages.

Jim leaned forward in his seat. "Three is three. But having to find out from Brooke, that's not right." His friend shook his head and settled back in the chair.

"Brooke knew because she was at my house when we arrived in New York. Not the best moment in history. The dog jumped on her." It was wrong, but Garrett couldn't fight the grin.

Jim started laughing. "She obviously wasn't hurt, but now I understand why she was talking about the hairy beast you need to get rid of. He obviously scared her."

"A hairy beast is an understatement, and she and Rufus are not on speaking terms. But the dog stays." Garrett joined in the laughter.

"Why was Brooke at your house?" Jim's direct question caught him off guard.

"I don't know. She said to chill some wine or something to that effect." Garrett shrugged, knowing Jim would think he was crazy. His partner had warned him on at least two occasions that his secretary had designs on more than just her secretarial duties.

"Word to the wise—"

"Say no more. Brooke's overstepping her bounds, but there's nothing between us, I promise you."

"Keep it that way. Business ethics. Personal ethics. And common sense." Jim stood and headed for the door.

"I'll get my key back."

"I think that would be best given the circumstances." Jim waved as he left.

The rest of the day, Garrett stayed focused, with only a few interruptions by Brooke, including when she brought him lunch. He was starting to feel caught up on his files and emails. He leaned back in his seat and glanced at his watch, surprised to realize how late it was. Brooke had left hours ago, and he needed to do the same. He couldn't help but wonder if April would wait up, or if she would escape to the safety of her room and avoid him. Because whether they wanted to admit it or not, there was an attraction between them. It just remained to be seen what they did about it.

Garrett arrived back home ready to unwind; hopeful April was still awake. He was pleased when he spotted her on the sofa, a glass of wine in one hand as she flipped through the DVD case with the other. She looked up, the delight on her face when she spotted him not something Garrett remembered experiencing before. This coming home to someone and liking it.

"You're home. It was getting late, and I was beginning to think you were going to sleep at the office." Her dimpled grin kept the comment light and teasing and in no way a reprimand. He hadn't been sure what to expect, all things considered, but her response was more than satisfying.

He left his briefcase by the front door. Morning was just around the corner, and he'd be back at the office soon. "It wouldn't be the first time, but no, not tonight. I'm surprised you're still awake. I was beginning to think you were the early-to-bed, early-to-rise kind of person considering what time you went to bed last night."

"Not me. That was exhaustion from the trip kicking in. With kids around, you get sleep when you can, trust me."

"I'll have to remember that." He slid out of his suit coat and loosened his tie.

"I was just about to start a movie, but only because I was determined to stay up and wait for you. We need to talk." She placed the movie back in the case.

He shot a quick glance around the room, suddenly tense. "What's wrong?"

She frowned. "Nothing close to what you're thinking. Relax."

"Okay." He let out a sigh of relief. If nothing had gone wrong the first day with his new family established in his home, then Garrett considered it a huge success. Cause for celebration, in fact. He poured a glass of wine and joined April in the living room.

"Thanks for all the groceries. Ted's wife added a few things to the list, which was nice right about lunchtime."

"I hadn't thought that far in advance. I'm sorry."

"Can I get you something to eat?" April asked.

"No, thanks. I had food delivered to the office. I've got a deal about to close, and it's important I stay on top of it. After being gone, I had to play a bit of catch-up." He crossed the room to the armchair at the right side of the couch and sat, loving the feel of the soft leather and comfortable cushions at the end of a long day.

Garrett took a sip of wine and glanced around the room. Something didn't feel right. He cocked his head to one side and did another pass, trying to figure out what was different.

"What's wrong? Did one of the kids leave something in the chair?" April got up immediately to help.

"No. It's not that, but the chair's been moved." He nodded. "The question is, why?"

"The kids were probably playing. I don't know." She shrugged, as if it didn't matter, and sat down.

"I don't want things rearranged. I like them exactly as they are," he retorted, his voice sharper than intended. His father had been a drill sergeant when it came to keeping everything neat and orderly, and Garrett had caught on fast. It was either that or punishment, something he'd quickly learned to dislike. To this day when it came to his own personal space, he kept things the same, neat, and orderly.

"Fine. Then move it back. You need to get used to having kids around. This is part of the deal." April shrugged. She didn't understand, and he wasn't about to explain. The kids would have to adapt, it was the only possible solution. If he could do it when he was a kid, so could they.

He set his wineglass down on the coffee table and pushed the chair back where it belonged, anger filling him when he realized why it had been moved in the first place. "Is this part of the deal?" He scowled and pointed at the floor. A bright orange spot marred the light gray carpet. Orange juice was his guess.

April leaned over the edge of the sofa and cringed.

"I'm sorry, that would be my fault. It's my juice. I must have left it out here, and the kids knocked it over. They must have been afraid to tell me and tried to cover it instead. I figured something was up when they were acting strange this morning, but I never figured it out." She looked at him, her blue-green eyes full of remorse, making it hard to remain angry.

He let out a deep breath, biting back any comment he might let slip.

"I'll clean it. Be right back." She practically fled the room to the kitchen in search of cleaning supplies.

He was grateful for the opportunity to get his emotions under control. It was just orange juice...a problem easily fixed.

April returned with paper towels and a bowl of warm water mixed with dish soap. She blotted the liquid stain until it was almost invisible and finished by dabbing at it with some of the water-soap mixture. "It'll dry by tomorrow and be like new."

"Thank you. I'm sorry if I snapped. I understand what you're trying to tell me about kids and messes, but it's not an adjustment that can happen overnight. I'm bound to lose my temper, but I'll try not to let it get to me. It's just that neat and orderly is my way of keeping things under control." Garret tried to apologize but was making a mess of it.

"I didn't say you couldn't get irritated. It's just how you handle it with the kids that counts. Learn to count to ten before you speak when the kids do something to provoke you. Give yourself ten seconds to process and adjust. Like you did just now with me. It worked." Her smile was encouraging.

"I'll try to remember that." Garrett sat back in the chair. "What was it you wanted to talk to me about?"

"The kids and I are going to be bored sitting here day after day. We're used to wide open spaces and going everywhere. I don't know the first thing about the city, and I'm afraid to even attempt to take them anywhere." She got up and walked over to the window. Neon lights lit up the black sky in every direction.

"Manhattan's a fun place, and you'll be fine. Central Park is just down the street from here. There's the Statue of Liberty, the Empire State

Building, an art museum, theaters, a library, restaurants, and shopping galore. You can do an internet search for details. And if you hail a taxi, they'll stop and take you anywhere you want. A lot of people in the city don't have cars." He didn't have time to take them around sightseeing. Maybe after the deal closed, but not now. The situation wasn't ideal, but he hoped she was up to the challenge.

"Well, judging by the traffic out there, there's plenty of people who do."

He chuckled. "That's New York."

"I talked with the agency today, and they are sending several candidates out on Thursday. I've got a good feeling about this place." April pulled her hair into a ponytail with a band from her wrist. The motion revealed the sleek length of her throat. Graceful and elegant came to mind.

"That's wonderful news." If it took her the full two weeks, it was okay by him. He kind of enjoyed coming home and having her here to talk to. "So how were the kids today aside from the orange juice fiasco?"

She shot him a sweet grin, revealing two dimples at the sides of her mouth and one on the chin. "Angels." He'd always heard the one on the chin meant the devil within. Did that mean she meant the opposite of angels, or was she telling the truth?

"Proof you're good at what you do. Are you sure I can't convince you to stay?" He chuckled, determined to find out one way or the other.

"Not really, and no. When kids act strange, they are usually guilty of something. Goes along the line of—if things seem too good, they probably are."

"Another of your rules regarding kids to live by?" She was a wealth of knowledge. The kind of stuff he couldn't possibly learn in years.

"Yes. You should be writing these down," April teased.

They talked for another thirty minutes before April yawned and realized how sleepy she was. "I should head to bed."

"I was thinking the same thing, but you're on my bed, making it hard for me to do." He smirked.

"I'm sorry. It's not fair. Maybe we could—"

"No." He laughed. "On my bed, not in my bed. As in, you're sitting on the sofa. So, unless you plan on sleeping on the sofa with me, you should head for the bedroom. Five a.m. comes early."

"Sorry. I didn't even think about that." April stood and hurried out of the room, but not before he noticed the blush flooding her cheeks and throat.

Chapter Ten

♥

YESTERDAY WAS LIKE A scene out of *Leave It To Beaver*, the old black and white sitcom from the fifties and sixties. April had watched hundreds of episodes of the reruns. Mr. Cleaver arriving home every night after work right on time, June cleaning the house and fixing dinner, and the two kids getting into mischief but always learning something by the end of the day. Except in her case, Sandy made it three kids, and the little girl found more than her fair share of mischief.

April had sent Garrett a text to update him on the employee search, letting him know she had several candidates lined up. Followed by a *'see you at six for dinner'* comment. She'd managed to keep the kids occupied with reading and drawing and movies, and she taught them how to make pancakes, which they loved. Garrett had surprised her by coming home on time, and it had been a pleasant evening watching and eating popcorn. The day had been a success.

They had been like one big happy family.

Wade arrived right on time this morning to take Rufus for his walk, getting the dog out from underfoot so she could set the table for breakfast. She made a pot of coffee, as much for the candidates as for herself. This was one of those mornings she was making another exception. Caffeine was the only antidote to the exhaustion of trying to keep the kids safely entertained in a posh penthouse more suited for a photoshoot than kids. If she wasn't careful, it might actually become a habit.

Sandy woke up right on schedule. April helped her get dressed and then situated for breakfast. Still having to help her with the spoon meant the meal took longer, but she was getting better and better every day. April continued to talk as she fed Sandy, hoping to bring her out of the shell she'd retreated into.

April glanced at her watch. The other kids should have been up by now. And she still needed to get them ready. Sandy pushed her bowl away.

"All done, sweetie?" April washed her hands and face and set her down. "Why don't you play with your dolls while I get Bryan and Melanie up."

Sandy understood everything and nodded.

They walked out of the kitchen to discover Bryan was already awake.

"Hey, I didn't know you were up yet. You've got to get dressed and eat. And I thought we talked about this." April pointed to the coloring book and crayons on the coffee table. "This is only to be done at the kitchen table. You need to pick those up right now and then eat.

"I like coloring here. I can look out the window and pretend Superman is flying by. Or Spiderman comes crawling across the window." The animation on Bryan's face made it hard to stay mad at him for disobeying the rules.

"I understand, I do. But please, pick everything up. I've got to wake your sister. The first candidate for the nanny position will be here in about forty-five minutes."

"We don't need anyone else. You could stay."

"I'm sorry, Bryan. I've got to head back to Hallbrook and start my college classes. I can't teach if I don't graduate. Try to understand, I care about you all, I do, but this is a chance for me to finish school and teach children, something I've always dreamed of doing." She ruffled his hair, trying to let him down gently.

"Okay," he mumbled, the tone of the single word in direct opposition to the word itself.

In his world, April leaving wasn't fine. And she understood. They'd been through a lot of changes. As soon as he started to gather up the crayons and put them in the box, she left to wake Melanie, satisfied to see Sandy playing in the corner. It took a bit of doing, but finally, the two older kids were eating breakfast.

Thirty minutes to go, and she had just enough time to clean up the dishes. As she rounded the bend to the living room to check on Sandy, the sight that greeted her made her stop short. "No!"

Sandy looked up with wide-eyed innocence. April flinched as she drew close enough to assess the damage. Red lines in every direction were haphazardly drawn on the cushions of Garrett's Italian leather sofa that he'd had flown here from Italy.

She raced forward and took the crayon from Sandy. "We don't draw on the furniture, Sandy. This was wrong." Huge crocodile tears formed, and Sandy started to cry.

"Bryan, get out here."

"What's wrong," he asked, his mouth forming a wide O when he spotted Sandy's artwork.

"I thought you picked your crayons up?"

"I did, but I couldn't find the red one. I'm sorry."

"Sorry won't cut it if we can't fix this. We need to work on this together."

Melanie came to see what was going on. "Mr. Garrett is going to kill you."

"That's enough, Melanie. He's not going to kill anybody." At least she hoped he wouldn't. "Bryan and Melanie, take care of cleaning up the kitchen, and I'll see what I can do here." April picked up Sandy, feeling guilty for yelling at her. "I'm sorry I yelled, honey. We don't draw on the furniture. Okay?"

Sandy nodded. April took the crayon from her, relieved to discover it was washable. She set Sandy down and went in search of a rag to clean the cushion. Hopefully, a damp cloth wouldn't ruin the leather, but she had to get the glaring red marks off before the first interviewee showed up. It wouldn't do for the woman to turn tail and run if she thought the kids were out of control. And then there was Garrett. April shuddered to think what he would say if he walked in to discover the mess.

He'd have every reason to be angry—but at her. She was the one who should have been watching Sandy closer. Or making sure Bryan had picked up every color. It was always her fault. Always. It was something she'd grown used to. Garrett would fire her, the same way her foster parents had gotten rid of her.

April rubbed gently, letting out a deep breath as the red wiped off until all except the barest hint of the lines remained. She rubbed harder but was afraid to damage the leather. It appeared the crayon was washable on washable surfaces, but it was clinging to the fibers where it was deeply embedded.

Sandy had gone back to playing with her toys while the older kids finished with the dishes. April tried to search the internet for ways to get crayon out, but she was out of time. The first interviewee was due any minute.

The doorbell buzzed at nine a.m., right on the nose. The woman must've been standing outside in the foyer, waiting for that to happen. Give the woman a mental check for punctuality. She opened the door, pleasantly surprised. Mid-fifties and dressed in a blue suit coat with a matching knee-length skirt and a white blouse, she appeared not only efficient, but kind, and a take-charge type of person.

"Hello. My name is April. And you must be Helena Cordell."

"Yes. It's nice to meet you." The woman took her hand in a firm handshake, exuding a confidence April appreciated.

"Come in, come in." April gestured for her to enter. "Would you like some coffee?"

"That would be nice, thank you."

"Just have a seat, I'll be right out." April direct-ed her to the living room, urging the woman to sit in the armchair.

Helena ignored her suggestion and sat on the sofa. "It will be easier for me to take notes on the coffee table. I think I'll sit right here."

April poured two cups of coffee and made her way back to the living room, hoping the woman hadn't noticed the faint red lines.

"I see you've had a bit of a problem with cray-on. Let me guess, the three-year-old?" Helena smiled.

So much for not noticing. At least the woman was still smiling. "Yes. Her brother accidentally missed a crayon when he was picking up. Luckily, she only managed a few scribbles before I stopped her. Thank goodness, they were washable crayons. But apparently leather doesn't understand the meaning of the word washable." April grimaced, handing Helena her cup of coffee.

"Apparently, neither do quite a few fabrics. I think the box should come with a warning label. But you should try degreasing detergent with a toothbrush. It will get down into the fibers and release the waxy crayon. Just be sure to wipe it clean of the soapy residue and then dry it." Helena came equipped with tips, and April couldn't be more grateful.

"Oh, what a fantastic idea. Thank you. It just happened, and I was searching the internet to come up with a few tips, but none had popped up so far as logical as yours." April couldn't wait to try it out—before Garrett arrived home. It was barely noticeable, but she imagined to a man such as Garrett, it would be like a parakeet repeating the words "not perfect, not perfect" over and over it until it drove him crazy.

"Trust me, it comes with years of experience with children. I just love the darlings, but sometimes they just get into mischief." The woman shot her a half-smile with an odd snort as if remembering other charges prone to a wild side of trouble.

"I'm so glad to hear you say that." The woman just kept checking off all the mental boxes April was looking for in a nanny-housekeeper. If the other two were as suitable as this woman, she'd have a hard time picking one.

By the end of the interview, April was positive Helena was perfect. The children met her and seemed to approve of her well enough, other than the fact they'd both made it perfectly clear they'd rather April stay instead. Bryan, of course, didn't even think he needed a nanny, but Helena had made him realize how her being there would make it easier on him.

The woman was a genius.

"I've got to interview two others today, but I hope to be able to get back to the agency later this evening and let you know."

Woof. Woof.

"What was that?" Helena asked, a frown creasing her face.

"That's Rufus. I left him in the bedroom, but it sounds as though I need to let him out. He won't stop barking otherwise. Besides, you should meet him."

April hurried down the hall and opened the door. Rufus barreled out, eager to check out their guest. It wasn't the best way for the two of them to meet, but meet they would, if the result of today's interviews ended the way she planned.

"Oh my." Helena stood, clutching her purse to her chest. "Nobody mentioned anything about a dog."

Woof. Woof.

"No, Rufus. Lay down. I told the agency there was a dog." April sensed there was a problem. The woman's expression was no longer friendly and warm.

"I'm sorry, there seems to have been some misunderstanding. I take care of children, not dogs." Helena shook her head and started for the door, leaving April to follow.

"Surely we can work something out. I think you would be perfect." April hadn't meant to show her cards too soon, and now she was losing the perfect candidate. The solution was slipping away, and there was nothing she could do about it.

"I don't like dogs. Sorry, but I'm not interested in the position." Helena opened the door, stepped through, and vanished to wherever she'd come from.

Mary Poppins minus a love for animals. *Maybe they could get rid of Rufus.* April was kidding—she loved the hairy beast. Helena didn't know what she was missing. It's not as if the dog needed a lot of care, and the dog walker took care of potty time.

April resigned herself to the reality and scratched Helena off the list. She could only hope the next two interviews were better. At least she'd gotten a tip on how to clean the sofa. That was something.

The next two hours passed by interminably.

Strike three. There was no choice but reject the other two candidates. Neither one had a problem with dogs, go figure. Instead, it would seem one had a penchant for making sure cable TV existed for her daytime soap opera shows and insisted all children needed naps. The other confessed to not being able to cook a lick, but that she was more than willing to try. April might've even considered her if it weren't for her skintight spray-on leather pants and visible cleavage that Bryan hadn't been able to take his eyes off.

Garrett would probably enjoy the view, but then *Brooke* would probably have a thing or two to say about the situation. April pulled out her phone to send Garrett a text, preferring to tell him the disappointing news before he got home.

April: Interviews a bust. Sorry. Have more lined up, don't worry. See you at six for dinner.

Chapter Eleven

♥

G ARRETT FLICKED OFF THE lights of his office, closed the door, and locked it behind him.

"Are you leaving?" Brooke looked up at him, an astonished expression on her face.

"I am. I'll be back in the morning to take care of a few things," he said, not at all concerned with his sudden departure from his normal routine.

"But it's only four. You never leave this early," she said, shaking her head.

"I've never had kids at home waiting to do something fun either." April and the kids had been patient all week, and he'd promised to show them around and let them eat real New York food in the form of a Coney dog from a street vendor.

"I see. Better you than me. I got information back from a couple of boarding schools. One seems perfect."

"Thanks for doing that. Just put it in my mail slot, and I'll review them tomorrow."

"Okay. They did say you'd have to apply right away since the school year is starting right after Labor Day."

"I'm not sure what I'm doing yet, but I'll keep that in mind. Goodnight. See you on Monday."

"Goodnight. I can come in tomorrow if you want help?" There it was again. The too-familiar look in her eyes that intimated there was something between them. Jim was right. Garrett needed to be careful and keep the boundaries in place.

"No, thanks. Enjoy your weekend." He turned and left, aware valuable minutes were ticking away, and he wanted to make an impression on the kids and April to prove he wasn't all business, all the time. *Just mostly.*

He arrived home to four smiling faces and a wagging tail. It was nice.

"Who's ready to leave?" he asked, knowing the answer.

"Me." Bryan and Melanie were quick to respond. Rufus barked.

Sandy held up her arms, and Garrett couldn't resist. Her sweet and innocent smile made his day when she framed his face with her hands to get his attention and then nodded.

"Guess it's unanimous." He grinned at April. "Sorry, Rufus. Not tonight. But I'll get Wade to keep you out extra long." Garrett patted the dog on the head. He was cute in a beastly way, at least he was when there wasn't drool hanging from his mouth.

"They are so wound up. It's been hard keeping them under control." April gathered her purse and the sweaters she'd laid out on the table.

"First stop, Frank's hot dog stand. Then we can walk it off while we explore, and then stop at another stand. You kids can be the judge which you prefer best."

"You mean it? We can eat as many as we want?" Bryan asked, his eyes as big as saucers.

"I do. You can't live in New York and not have a favorite Coney dog." He chuckled.

They headed out, stopping at the concierge desk to arrange to let Wade in to take care of Rufus. It was a nice evening for a stroll, the temperatures perfect.

"This is fun. Thanks, Garrett. I love all the sidewalk cafés and food vendors on every street corner. Not to mention, this is retail heaven." Her excitement was contagious, and Garrett found himself appreciating some of the little things about the city he'd long since stop paying attention to.

"The cars sure do honk a lot," Melanie said.

"Not like in Hallbrook, is it? But it sort of goes with the fast pace of everything here," Garrett said.

April looked up at him, her nose scrunched up prettily. She wasn't much for life in the fast lane. She reached out to touch his arm. "Is that a statue?"

He glanced in the direction she'd pointed. "No. It's a mime. He pretends to be a statue and moves occasionally to confuse or scare people. They do it for money. Notice the plastic bucket in front of him."

"They must get tired," April said, watching in fascination.

"It's a living," he quipped.

"I want to be Spiderman mime," Bryan chimed in.

"We'll see about that buddy." Garrett shook his head and turned away to hide his grin.

"Don't give him any encouragement. He lives and breathes Spiderman now. We don't need him dreaming of a future in it."

"Point taken." He leaned in close to her, the fragrance of her hair filtering through his senses and overriding the smell of car exhaust. *Sweet lilac.* "I hope I figure this parenting thing out without too many mistakes."

"You will. Don't worry."

"I hope you're right. But if I do, it's because I've got you to show me the way. Thanks."

April flushed prettily under his compliment. Something he'd have to do more often because it was a sight he could get used to. At least until she left, he corrected.

Two hours, three hotdog vendors, and an ice cream vendor later, the kids weren't feeling that well. Their appetites had been bigger than their stomachs. Sandy had been the only one smart enough to stop at one hot dog.

"We should head back," April suggested. "My stomach needs to recover from dessert. I must say, the waffle cone drizzled with caramel and rolled in nuts is my new personal favorite."

"Everyone okay with going back, or does anyone want another hotdog?" Garrett was certain of the answer even before he heard their groans but hadn't been able to resist teasing them.

"Can we watch another movie?" Melanie asked. "It's my turn to pick."

"I don't see why not, if it's okay with April. She knows best." He looked at her for confirmation, not wanting to make another parenting mistake.

"A movie sounds perfect. It's a great way to unwind." April put her arm around Melanie and drew her close, walking together as they headed back to his place.

"Miss April, those dolls in the window have on matching clothes. They're so pretty. I love the blue fairy princess skirt and the pink top with shiny beads." Melanie pulled her toward the storefront and pointed at the mannequin.

"It's lovely. Maybe you could wear something like that to school."

"Can I get it? Please?" Melanie looked up at her hopefully.

"That's up to Garrett." April turned back to him. "But that reminds me, they need new school clothes. I can't believe I almost forgot. What they wore in Hallbrook won't work here in the city, and it's important for them to dress right as the new kids in school. You need to take them shopping."

"I wouldn't know the first thing about buying kids' clothes. You'll do it, won't you? I can give you my credit card." He barely took time out to shop for his own clothes, but then that wasn't saying much considering he stuck to traditional suit and ties with mostly blue shirts. They coordinated better with a wide variety of ties. It was the sum total of his fashion sense.

"I'll see if I can squeeze it in. I've got a couple interviews scheduled, and don't forget I'm leaving next weekend."

"Don't remind me. With or without a new nanny." The problem was Garrett wasn't so sure what bothered him most. Her leaving if he didn't have a new nanny, or just her leaving. But one thing was for certain, he couldn't do without someone to help him with the kids. He prayed it wouldn't come to that.

"I could take them tomorrow. Any chance you'd be willing to watch Sandy?"

Garrett looked at her as if she'd lost her mind. "I'm working."

"It's a Saturday. It'll be better for Bryan, Melanie, and me if we shop without her. We'll get a lot more done, and I won't have to worry about her wandering off or getting into things. Please?"

"I can't just take off from work."

"You're the boss, of course, you can. Look at it this way, if I get it done before I leave, you won't have to do it."

She had a valid point.

Not one he liked, but valid. "But I don't have a clue what to do with her." He tried one last time to avoid the inevitable.

"I'll make sure you know what you need to before I leave. It's not that hard. Trust me."

"Fine." He couldn't believe he'd just agreed.

"You won't regret it." April laid her hand on his arm, her touch reassuring.

"I'll hold you to that."

They arrived back at the penthouse, and before long, April had the kids settled down on a blanket in front of the TV, leaving the two of them to share the sofa. It was remarkable how easy she made it seem. But he'd had one night of it before, and it had been a complete disaster.

What made her think he could handle Sandy on his own? She had a whole lot more confidence in him than he did.

Sitting next to April made him forget his rash agreement to watch Sandy as he became more and more aware of the limited distance between them. Her fragrance still lightly teased him, and he wondered what it would be like to kiss her. Not smart, for sure, but he still wondered.

Garrett reached for her hand, the softness of her skin smooth and satiny. "Thanks for tonight.

I haven't had that much fun in a while, and I owe it all to you."

"It was fun, but you made it that way. The kids love spending time with you."

"I just wish there was more time in a day. I love my job, and competition is fierce out there. I can't afford to let up and play parent."

"You don't have a choice. A nanny can only do so much, and they need love. From you."

He pulled away, uncomfortable with the turn the conversation had taken. He only caught bits and pieces of the rest of the movie as his mind wandered, thinking about the future and what it would hold for him and the children.

His children. He was still trying to wrap his head around the idea that this was his life.

Chapter Twelve

G ARRETT FELT OUT OF sorts Saturday morning. He was up early, as always, and entered the kitchen, breathing in the fresh aroma of brewing coffee. *Thank you, April.* It hadn't taken him long to get used to waking up and having it ready every morning. But the idea of not going into the office today, that was a different m a t t e r e n t i r e - ly.

A day off. All he could think of was the work that needed to be done. But a promise was a promise. April kept insisting he needed to find ways to bond with the kids, and that it meant spending more time with them, which included breaking his current cycle of all work and no play.

According to her, he needed to make the children his number one priority, and Garett had resigned himself to the fact she was right. But that didn't make the situation any easier.

At least her suggestion for today would ease him into this parenting thing.

One kid. One dog. It was a simple test, and one he hoped he could pass, but he was as nervous as when he'd sat for the state bar exam. *Failure is not an option.*

"Good morning." April joined him in the kitchen, poured herself a glass of milk, and sat at the table next to him. "Are you excited about today?"

"Good morning to you, too. *Excited* would be a stretch. Let's just say the jury's still out." He frowned, unsure how the morning would play out.

"You'll be fine. Just trust yourself. She's three. It's not as though you're trying to control a willful sixteen-year-old who's determined to skip town with a boyfriend in his twenties," she teased.

"Ha. Easy for you to say. You have a way with kids. And please tell me that's not going to happen with Melanie in a few years."

"It's easy because I've had a lot of experience, but in no time at all, you'll get the hang of being in charge and the ins and outs of how to manage each situation as it arises. As to Melanie, time will tell. Sorry, I don't have a crystal ball. Don't forget I need your credit card for today. I hope you don't mind that I'm taking them shopping."

"Even if I did, it wouldn't matter. You mentioned the kids need school clothes, then school clothes they get. My card is at your disposal. I'm not worried you'll abuse the privilege. You don't seem to be that kind of person."

"Why, thank you for the trust, Mr. Bradley," she announced in as patronizing tone as she could muster. "I promise to only buy them a few outfits each."

"Get them whatever they need."

"Well, in that case...maybe more than a couple. They need something nicer than the jeans and T-shirts they're used to wearing in Hallbrook. I'm hoping it will make them feel like they fit in better. This is going to be a tough adjustment for them, and I can already tell they're starting to miss their friends." April wound her hair in the palm of her hand and pushed it to hang down her back.

It was an innocent gesture, but it made him want to kiss the softness of her neck. "Thank you for taking them shopping. I wouldn't have a clue where to begin. You sure I can't convince you to stay here permanently? You're perfect for the position. No need to find someone to replace you when I already have the best. "The more he thought about it, the more it made sense. And not just for the kids. Garrett enjoyed having her around also.

"Flattery won't help you. My life's aspiration isn't to be a nanny and housekeeper in some posh penthouse suite. As much as I love the kids, my calling is to teach kindergarten. And besides, I'm a country girl through and through. I'm not a fit for here long term. It's probably a good thing I'm leaving next weekend because I wouldn't want to get any more attached to the kids, or for the kids to get any more attached to me. They'll need to get used to somebody else."

"I hate that you always make sense." The last thing he wanted to do was hold her back from her dream job. Garrett could hope the person hired efficient and kind as she was because things had been going smoothly. Other than Rufus's determination to use the sofa as his own personal cushion.

"It's the practical side of me. It's not always a good thing, but most of the time, it works."

An hour later, two thrilled kids and April left, all of them ready to take on the big-city stores like Saks and Macy's. Garrett shut the door and turned to face Sandy, who stood there eyeing him with curiosity, Rufus by her side.

"So, young lady, what are we going to do today?" What did one do with a three-year-old? April had already taken care of feeding her, which was both good and bad. One, he didn't have to do it, but two, it would have been an easy way to use up forty-five minutes. And he didn't have a tie on, so no worries there. He glanced at her toybox.

"Do you want to play with your toys? I'll be right here and can watch," he suggested, remembering the last time.

Sandy took him by the hand, led him over to the corner, and pulled him downward, indicating she wanted him to join her. Garrett sat on the floor, not quite successfully able to accomplish sitting cross-legged. He used the toybox as back support, drawing up his legs to get more comfortable.

She handed him a doll, and Garrett resigned himself to what came next. Sure enough, Sandy reached for her dishes, this time expecting him to play along. Every step of the way, she waited for him to copy her. Each sip and each bite, she expected him to follow her lead. He felt foolish, but at least no one was here to see him. As for Sandy, she was all giggles and smiles, her face full of expressions that kept him entertained.

The tea party lasted quite a while, Garrett doing all the talking. He resisted the urge to let her play on her own, remembering April's advice. Bond with the children. When Sandy grew bored with the tea party, she gathered her toys and tossed them in the toybox.

A kid after his own heart. Garrett struggled to his feet and moved to sit on the couch, relieved to be up off the hard floor. Sandy climbed into his lap and shoved a storybook in his hand, looking up at him expectantly.

"*Goldilocks and the Three Bears.* That's a fun story." It wasn't long until naptime, and this would be an interesting way to ease into it. He began to read the book, and little by little, he noticed her eyes begin to droop. Garrett stopped reading, but almost as if on cue, her eyes popped open, and she'd turn the page, pushing the book upward and urging him to continue.

Three times, they went through this process, until finally, Sandy nodded off just enough to allow him to put the book down. Now the trick was to get the sleeping child back to her bed without waking her.

Over the past few days, Sandy had grown more and more attached. Her falling asleep in his arms made him realize how much trust she'd put in him. It had started right from the beginning when he'd met her, but now it was obvious to anyone who cared to notice. When they were in the same room, she always managed to be close by, keeping an eye on him.

Garrett held her future in his hands, and it was a scary feeling. Instead of millions of dollars for a business client, his time was even more valuable spent molding the lives of the children entrusted to him. April was opening his eyes to a whole new way to see things, and Sandy was opening his heart.

"Hey, sleepyhead, let's put you down in your bed." Talking to a sleeping child. He had to be losing his mind. Garrett shook his head and carried Sandy down the hall, laying her on the bed and pulling up the covers. Unable to resist the urge, he leaned over and kissed her forehead.

Sandy's eyes opened, and wide blue pools of sweetness stared up at him as she gave him a sleepy smile. "Daddy." Sandy reached up and threw her arms around his neck, pulling him down to her.

Daddy. Her first word since her parents died. A word that had the power to touch his heart as no other word could have done.

"Sleep tight and sweet dreams, sweetheart." Garrett smiled as she drifted off to sleep. He stayed there for quite a while, just watching, before finally going back to the living room. He had work to do and the perfect opportunity to do it.

The dog followed him and jumped on the sofa. "Get off the couch, Rufus." The sofa wasn't his bed, but apparently, the fleecy dog cushion in the corner wasn't good enough. Only Italian designer leather seemed to satisfy the beast.

An hour passed, and so far, Garrett had managed to accomplish zero. The word *daddy* reverberated in his head. His morning with Sandy had gone fine, more than fine. But Garrett knew better than anyone else, fine was a fleeting thing. There were 364 other days in the year for problems. And problems led to arguments, and arguments led to divorce. But he wasn't even married.

It was a lot to think about for a man who'd been a bachelor a week ago, coming and going as he pleased, with no one to answer to. One simple word from Sandy, and he finally understood what was at stake. The little girl had looked at him with love shining in her eyes.

Garrett was beginning to see things in a new light, and he had April to thank for the revelations. Without her help, everything would have been a disaster. She'd been working day in and day out to help him and the kids, and she'd be gone next week. Tomorrow was the only opportunity to give her time off to show his appreciation for all she'd done and to explore the city.

There were two problems with the idea. One, April didn't know the city well enough to head out on her own, and two, Garrett wasn't sure he was ready to handle three kids, even if only for a few hours.

Jim and Bev.

Garrett hit the speed-dial button for Jim. "Hey there. Got a second?"

"Sure. You at the office? You need to get a life, you know." Jim had been after him for ages to date and find something other than the office life to pursue. But for Garrett, the office was his life and his love. It was something he could control, and therefore, maintain order.

"For your information, I'm not there. I'm at home watching Sandy while April's out shopping with the other two."

Jim whistled. "I'm impressed. What do you need from me? Instructions on how to change a dia-per?" The laughter in his voice irritated Garrett.

He wasn't a complete idiot with kids as everyone seem to expect.

"For your information, she's three and not in diapers. Laugh all you want, but so far, I've managed quite well."

"Give it time. It's early yet." Jim kept laughing. "Seriously, I'm just harassing you because I had to find out about the kids from Brooke. What is it you need from me?"

"April hasn't had a day off since she started taking care of the kids. I thought it would be nice to give her a free day tomorrow, and I could take her sightseeing as a way of saying thanks. And she leaves next weekend. I was hoping you and Bev could watch the kids."

"Say no more. Of, course we'll watch the kids. Bev will be ecstatic. This is a nice surprise turn of events—you and April on a date."

"It's not a date, just a thank-you outing." He didn't date. It was too complicated. And April had already made it clear that Hallbrook was her home. His efforts to change her mind had fallen short.

"Sure. Call it what you want, but yes, we'll swing by and pick them up at ten after church if that's okay with you."

"Perfect, that will work. And Jim, don't be getting any ideas. It's just a thank you." If Bev and Jim started matchmaking, he'd never hear the end of it. Best not to let them get started.

"That's the third time you've said that. Who are you trying to convince? Me or you." Jim taunted him before hanging up, cutting off any chance for a reply.

"Hey, Ted." April raised an arm to wave at the concierge, her hands full with bags overloaded with shopping goodies. Melanie and Bryan trailed behind her, each one carrying what they could to help.

"Here, let me get the elevator for you." Ted raced ahead of her and pushed the button.

"Thanks. Obviously, we had a successful day of shopping." They'd bought way more than April had first planned, but she couldn't say no. Well, there was one thing she'd rejected—the hot pink bra Melanie had tried to convince she needed. At seven. Not on her watch, and she'd seen no evidence to the contrary that it was necessary. Girls wanted to grow up so fast these days.

"I can see that." He chuckled. "Kids starting school soon?" They were supposed to be.

"Garrett's taking care of getting them enrolled. I think they start the Wednesday after Labor Day."

The elevator dinged, announcing its arrival.

"That'll be nice for them. Make new friends." Ted held the elevator door open. "Have a great day."

"Easy for the adults to say. You're not the one going to a strange school," Bryan muttered after the door closed and started for the top.

"It'll be okay. You'll see."

"But what if they don't like us?" Melanie's eyes were wide and wondering, filled with unease.

"Who wouldn't want to be friends with two great kids like you guys? Especially sporting your new cool clothes."

The elevator stopped, and they exited and headed down the hallway to Garrett's. April prayed the day had gone well for him. There hadn't been any emergency calls—which was a start. But as to what the place looked like...that might be another story entirely. April set the bags down and tried to locate the key card. Digging through the bottom of her purse, she finally found it and opened the door. The kids hurried inside, leaving April to follow.

"Mr. Garrett, look at what we bought." Melanie tossed her bag on the sofa. "I have new leggings, shirts, and shoes. The stores here are to die for. So much to choose from, unlike the stores of Hallbrook."

"I'm glad you had fun. What about you, young man?" Garrett asked Bryan.

"I got some clothes and a new pair of sneakers. But clothes are kind of a girl thing." Bryan scrunched his face.

Bryan could say what he wanted, but he'd had fun, and she knew it. She was guessing he was trying to act older, pulling a man-to-man bond with Garrett.

"I tend to agree. Glad I got to stay here. Why don't you show me what you bought?" Garrett was trying to find a way to share the experience and connect with the kids. Another excellent move on his part.

April glanced around, spotting Rufus sound asleep on the carpet next to his bed. She smiled and shook her head. "Where's Sandy?"

"She's still sleeping. I'm sure she'll wake up soon. It's been over an hour." Garrett appeared to have survived parenting 101 with flying colors.

"Kids, try on your new stuff to show Garrett, but be quiet so you don't wake your sister."

"You have to show him what you bought," Melanie spoke up. "You have just as much as we do."

"That I do. But Garrett doesn't want to see my new clothes." She hadn't been able to resist and had gone overboard. Knowing there were a few extra dollars going into her bank account had let the temptation genie out of the bottle.

Garrett looked surprised; one eyebrow raised in question.

"Don't worry, my charges won't show up on your bill. I used my own credit card," April said quickly, not wanting him to think she'd overstepped her boundry.

"I didn't think you did, although I wouldn't have minded. You've earned it." He grinned, the corners of his eyes crinkling. "And then some."

April was surprised at just how relaxed Garrett appeared to be. "You're paying me enough for me to afford my own purchases, so in a way, you're paying. How's that for compromise?" She smiled, turning back to watch the kids model their clothes.

"Your turn, Miss April," Melanie crossed the room and handed April the bags. "Fair's fair."

She was uncomfortable with Garrett watching, but she couldn't say no.

"Show him the dress. You gotta see this," Melanie told Garrett.

April wished Melanie had forgotten the dress, but no such luck. When she'd seen it on the rack, she'd fallen in love with it. The long-sleeve dress was made of gauze and lace, the deep-blue coloring almost the same as her eyes. Small wooden beads were sewn into the edge of the V-neckline in a scrolling pattern that matched the belt. The dress landed just above her knees, perfectly show-ing off the brown cowboy boots the salesgirl had her try on.

The minute she'd tried it on, she'd fallen in love with it. It hadn't come cheap, but then how often did you get to shop in New York City and splurge on yourself? The answer was never.

Her pulse ramped up a notch or two as she walked down the hall.

"Wow! Now that's what I call a dress."

April blushed under Garrett's intense gaze. "The saleswoman said they just got it in today, and when she showed it to me, I couldn't say no." His compliment had flustered her.

"I can understand why. I think you should wear it tomorrow."

She frowned. "Tomorrow?" Won't I be a bit over-dressed for taking care of the kids?"

"I'm giving you the day off if you want it. I've arranged for Jim and his wife, Bev, to watch the kids. I thought before you leave, I should take you sightseeing around the city."

April's jaw dropped, her mouth wide open. It took her a moment to recover. "Are you asking me on a date?" Holding her hand the other night had been awkward, but he'd been clear it was by way of thanks. This was an outing without the children—a real date. Like a man-and-woman-who-like-each-other date.

"No, not a date. It's a way to show my appreciation for everything you've done. A thank-you of sorts." For one brief second, April had let herself imagine. And just as quickly, tamped down her wayward thoughts. Maddison would have an opinion or two, which is exactly why she wouldn't mention it to her friend.

"It's still a date," Melanie chimed in.

Garrett shook his head. "You don't understand, but April does. Right?" He looked at her for confirmation. "She's going back to Hallbrook and we live here. A date would serve no purpose."

No purpose. Ouch. But she wouldn't let it ruin her chance to spend the day alone with Garrett. "He's right. And, yes, I'd love a tour of the city."

"What about us seeing stuff? When do we get to explore more?" Bryan asked, not at all caring about her and Garrett going somewhere together alone.

"We have the rest of today. After your sister wakes up, why don't we check out a few kid-friendly things to do. Maybe we could go to the Empire State Building and check out the observation deck where you can see for miles and miles, or we could rent bikes and ride around Central Park checking out more food vendors."

"Yay!" Both kids' smiling faces sealed the deal.

They were acting as though they were a real family. The closeness they shared was more than any bond she'd ever felt with any of her foster families while growing up. It was like looking through a window to see another side of life, one with hope and happiness.

For just a few moments, she let herself imagine what it would be like if they were her family. She loved the kids as if they were her own, and she admired Garrett for trying to make things right and accepting the conditions of his mother's will. But next weekend her part in it would all come to an end, making her more determined than ever to enjoy it now and make wonderful memories.

"Let me change out of this dress, and then I'll check on Sandy and get her ready." Apparently, Garrett had graduated to parenting 102.

Chapter Thirteen

♥

"**D**OES EVERYONE HAVE THEIR book bags packed and ready to go? Jim and Bev will be here any minute," Garrett asked the kids.

"I do." Bryan moved to stand next to him. "I wonder what kind of fun we're going to have to-day?"

"Jim told me one of his friend's sons is having a birthday party. They thought you two would enjoy meeting some kids your age. I think Trey, the young boy, is turning nine. And I'm sure Bev will love having Sandy to herself. The kid will be spoiled by the time we get her back." He shook his head, but truthfully, didn't mind in the slightest.

"I've got Sandy's stuff packed. Do they have kids of their own?" April asked, her gaze one of concern. "Taking on three kids is a lot of work."

"Tell me about it. But no, they don't have kids. They've been trying for years without success. I think that's why he thought it was ironic that I suddenly have three."

"Hopefully, there are girls at this party." Melanie tried to pull her hair back in a ponytail unsuccessfully.

"Here, let me get that." April fixed it for her, handed her the backpack and helped her to slide it over her shoulder, careful of her wrist.

"Thanks, April. I'm ready," Melanie announced.

Knock. Knock.

"That must be them now." Garrett opened the door for Jim and Bev. "Come in. Thanks for agreeing to watch the kids."

"Anytime. You have no idea how excited Bev's been since I told her." Jim winked.

"He's been just as excited. Don't let him make you think otherwise." They stepped inside.

"I'd like you both to meet April St. James, the kids' temporary nanny. April, this is Jim West, my partner at the firm and his wife, Bev."

April extended her hand in greeting, but instead of a shake, Jim took her hand, turned it over, and kissed the back of it. "You're perfect." His comment made no sense at all.

"Perfect for what?" April had to ask.

His eyes twinkled with merriment. "For Garrett. He's told me so much about you."

"You mean as his nanny?"

"Maybe." He shrugged.

"It's nice to meet you, dear. But enough chit chat, Jim likes to tease. Introduce us to these precious darlings." Bev stepped forward, cutting off April's opportunity to find out what Jim had meant. She reached out to pick up Sandy, who was eyeing her cautiously, half hiding behind April's leg, as she clung to her.

"It's okay, sweetheart. Bev's going to play with you today." April stroked the girl's hair, trying to reassure her.

The security hold loosened at first, and then Sandy let go, moving out from behind April.

"Aren't you a little sweetheart," Bev crooned, picking her up and hugging her close.

"That's Sandy. This is Melanie—" Garrett touched her shoulder, "—and this is Bryan."

"Can we go?" Bryan's impatience had reached its limit. "I'm tired of only having girls to play with." He rolled his eyes and headed for the door.

"I don't see why not, young man. Today will be so much fun. I say let's get the party started. We can leave these two old fogies to tour the city." Bev's hearty laughter rang out in the room, the woman bursting with energy for such an early morning hour.

April handed the diaper bag to Jim. "I know you have Garrett's number, but here's mine, just in case you can't reach him." She handed Jim a paper with her number on it. "Please don't hesitate to call for any reason. Sandy can sometimes be a bit anxious away from familiar things. Oh, and she doesn't like to talk, but don't let that fool you, she understands everything."

"Don't you worry about a thing, honey. She'll have so much fun with me she won't have time to think of anything else." Bev was confident of her abilities; sure of herself.

"Perfect. But promise you'll call if you need anything," April reiterated. She leaned forward to kiss Sandy on the top of the head.

"Of course. Have a wonderful time on your non-date date," Bev teased as she headed out the door behind the kids.

"You need to stop telling people your version of today's outing, Jim. Everyone will get the wrong idea, including the kids." Garrett shot his friend a pleading look, not that it would do any good. Jim clearly had his own ideas of what was going on, and nothing Garrett had to say would change that.

"Well, from where I'm standing, I'm thinking you two are the only ones with the wrong idea." Jim closed the door behind him, leaving them alone.

Garrett turned to April. "At least you and I are clear."

"Very clear." April nodded. "They seem to forget I'm leaving soon."

"Exactly. Shall we leave?" Garrett was pleased April had worn her new dress. Her raven hair cascaded down the sides of her face, gently moving as she walked toward him. He couldn't help the excitement he felt, the sensation vaguely reminiscent of the time when he was in twelfth grade and had a crush on Jenny Lou. But then everyone had a crush on Jenny Lou.

This feeling, however, was stronger than he remembered as a kid, whether because he was older or because it was April, he was uncertain. Either way, it was not something he wanted to dwell on. This was two friends on a tour of the city. Not a date. Although it certainly felt sort of date like, information he'd keep to himself.

"Where are we going first?" April asked, the excitement in her voice undeniable.

"It's a surprise." He'd stressed over what to do with only a limited amount of time available, finally deciding on a few special treats. Some a little more unique than others.

"Okay by me. I've always liked surprises." Something else he appreciated about her. Some women wanted all the details, but she wasn't one of them. An outing in the city cried for spontaneous, and he was more than willing to run with it.

"I just need to feed the dog. Wade is coming later this morning to take him out. Come on, Rufus, time for breakfast." Garrett filled the bowl while the dog sat and watched his every move. "You be a good dog while we're gone and stay off my couch." He grabbed a few pillows from the closet and laid them out in a row across the cushions, hoping they would deter the dog. He pointed at his bed. "That's your bed, use it."

"I think that's a lost cause, but it's fun to watch you try." April laughed.

"Maybe I should just give up and put the couch in my office, and then pick up some gaudy, cheap sofa he won't even look at twice."

"And neither will anyone else." She shook her head as if he'd lost his mind.

Maybe he had. "Shall we?"

He opened the door and let her pass, his hand landing on the small of her back. He led her to the elevator and guided her inside when it stopped at his floor. He liked the closeness. The elevator started down, seconds later jerking to a stop, and knocking April off balance into him. His arms

came around her protectively, and her hand landed on his chest. Face-to-face, neither one moved.

The urge to kiss her hit him like a baseball
bat. *Not a great idea.* "This happens sometimes.
Some glitch in the system they haven't worked out
yet, but it should be fine. Trust me."

"And if it's not?" she asked, her eyes never leaving his face. Her pink, glossy lips were tempting,
but still, he resisted. There was no going back if
he gave in.

"It's never stayed stuck. I've been after them to
fix it, but they seem to think it's caused by an
overload of the system when too many of the elevators are being operated at once, and they aren't
sure which elevator is causing the short yet." His
mouth provided the right answer, but only half
of his brain was doing the thinking, the rest was
focused on her lips. He lowered his mouth, inch by
inch, unable to stop the inevitable.

The elevator lurched again, breaking the moment as the doors opened and two more residents
joined them. "See. All better."

April stepped back out of his arms, and Garrett
found himself missing the closeness.

Once outside, he hailed a taxi to take them to the harbor. They slid in the backseat of the car, their legs and bodies touching increasing his awareness of her. Her lilac fragrance surrounded him, drawing him closer. The desire to connect with her was stronger than ever.

"Corner of 22nd and Jackson please," Garrett instructed the driver, trying to force his brain back into the friendship corner.

The fifteen-minute taxi ride seemed to take forever with the satiny skin of her legs uncovered and mere inches from his. He took her hand and led her down the sidewalk to the marina.

They stopped at one of the docks where a boat was anchored.

April glanced up at him, her eyes lit as though it was Christmas morning and she'd received a special gift. "A harbor cruise. What a wonderful surprise."

"Yes. I wanted to do a sunset one, but then we'd get back too late for the kids, so this was the next best." He still hadn't let go of her hand, and the warmth was nice.

"It's perfect. Not to mention, sunset cruises are date like, and we're trying to avoid that impression. Right?" Message received. Garrett stepped up to the counter and paid for the tickets. They climbed aboard to wait for the others and for the cruise to start.

"You can see the Statue of Liberty from here." He pointed in the direction of the famous lady. "They'll take us right by there. I've always loved this view of the city."

"It's exciting, not to mention different from anything I've seen. Even a bit overwhelming." April's excitement was a breath of fresh air.

They found a couple of seats near the front, and Garrett laid down his jacket to reserve them. With the sun, they wouldn't need the warmth, but one never knew this time of year what to expect in the way of a brisk breeze on the harbor, and so he'd made sure to bring something for her.

They headed to the railing and leaned against it, just as the deep bellow of the horn blew, signaling their departure.

"This is gorgeous. Can I ask you something?"

"Of course, you can ask me anything. We are living together, after all," he teased.

"Hilarious, wise guy. But in that case, I'm just curious why you're not married? Why did you choose business with such a single-minded passion? Your friend Jim does both."

He hadn't seen that coming. And it wasn't his favorite subject. "Why do you ask?"

"Because of the kids. I know this all came as a shock to you, this sudden change in your life. Sometimes I sense you resent it, as though you're struggling to relate. Have you never wanted children in your life? To have a family?" The intensity of her gaze made him uncomfortable, but mostly because she wouldn't like his answer.

"To be honest, no. I'm not married because I don't choose to be. As to a family, I never intended to have kids." The truth was best, and maybe even more important, considering he was having a hard time keeping away from her. April would steer clear of him now, making it easier to avoid the damage a short-term relationship with her would cause all the way around.

"Why? The average person in America grows up, gets married and has kids. What makes you different? I'm not saying it's wrong, I'm just curious." April turned her gaze out across the harbor, her hair flying in the breeze.

"It's a long story, and I'm sure you don't want to be bored." It was a story he didn't share with anyone. By choice.

"We've got time. We're cruising the harbor, taking in the sights. It's just you and me. I know it's none of my business, but I can't help but worry about the kids."

Now he understood why she was asking. For a minute, he'd wondered if she was trying to find out more about him and his thoughts on marriage and relationships for a more personal reason—like she was interested. Not that he wanted her to be interested, but it would've been flattering.

"You don't think I can do this, do you?" Garrett came right out and spoke the words, putting a name to the real problem.

"It doesn't matter what I think. Do *you* think you can?"

He let out a deep sigh. "At first, I didn't think so. But then something happened, and I'm starting to change my mind."

"Do you want to tell me? What happened that made you start to believe?"

Garrett couldn't tell her the whole truth because she was part of it. She was helping him change and see things differently. And he was starting to believe in himself, that he could do this. The parenting thing. It was scary, but it was a challenge he felt he was up to. "I was going to tell you this last night, but with everything going on, there wasn't a chance, and I didn't want to tell you in front of the kids. I'm not sure how the older two will take it."

April turned and glanced at him, the intensity of her gaze warming him like the sun. "Now I'm really curious."

"When I was putting Sandy down for her nap yesterday, I read her a bedtime story. *Goldilocks and the Three Bears*." The scene had replayed in his head over and over, and each time, his heart melted more. "She was half asleep, but then she opened her eyes, called me daddy, and reached up to give me one of those I-love-you hugs. The really tight kind. And then she fell asleep." It was a moment he would cherish forever.

April reached out and covered his hand with hers. "That's amazing. She hasn't spoken since her parents died. I could see she was growing attached to you, but this is incredible. She trusts you. It won't be long, and she'll be talking again. Thank you for sharing such a rare and special moment."

Garrett tried to find the words to express himself. "I think it's the first time I realized I'm a dad. You know, really felt it."

"And what exactly are you feeling? Having three kids, that is. Four, if you count the dog, and as huge as he is, he counts." April grinned.

"It makes me nervous." Last night, the call from Angelica put everything into perspective. She wouldn't be back for another couple of months, the deployment mission she was on considered critical. Any help he thought he'd get from her, was gone, and her unsolicited advice hit hard.

She was right though. Changes in his life were inevitable, and they started with selling the penthouse. It wasn't a place where the kids and the dog could run and play and well, be kids. The three of them were used to the country and being outdoors, but Sutton Hill was in a business district and not the kind of place you played outside.

And then he started to wonder when it would all blow up in his face like it had with his parents. Except when it happened, he wouldn't be able to divorce the kids and walk away from them the way his father had done. He was stuck.

"Are you worried about making mistakes? Or of not knowing what to do?" April laid her hand on his arm as if to encourage him to continue the soul-searching journey he'd started.

"No. Of them ruining my life. I know that sounds awful, and I've never told this to anyone before, but I watched it happen with my parents. It's the kids who lose, and I don't want to do that to them." Why was he telling her this? He didn't want her to delve into some psychoanalysis mumbo jumbo. He'd thought about it enough over the course of his life, always coming up with the same answer. Marriage and kids were trouble.

"Tell me what you remember," she urged, the tone of her voice direct and unrelenting.

It was clear she wouldn't rest until she heard the whole story.

"My parents argued all the time, and it always seemed to be about my sister and me. The arguments were awful, and I used to try to protect my sister by getting her out of the house so she wouldn't hear the angry words hurled back and forth. The last fight they had was my fault. I'd asked for a dog. My mother said yes, my dad disagreed. The two could never agree. It was the last thing they argued about, and it ended with him deciding it was time to divorce. My dad left, and that was the end of our family life. Pathetic right?" It was ironic that he'd wanted a dog when he was kid, and now he'd been saddled with one.

"But your mom and dad aren't you. There are plenty of parents who don't fight. A relationship is about love. Two people won't always see eye to eye. A marriage is more than that. It sounds to me as though your parents weren't in love. It's a shame they argued in front of you and made you feel responsible." The warmth of her hand intensified as she tightened her grip.

"I used to think kids ruined everything. But then these kids come along, and Sandy has me wrapped around her little finger. I can't imagine ever getting furious with her or anything she's done. She's just a child. It's all so confusing."

"I think you're on the right track now. You had a lifetime to hold on to a belief that molded you, and even though it's a misbelief, it's part of who you are. Give yourself time to accept that what you believed all these years, isn't the truth."

"But I don't know how to be a parent." He still remembered the first miserable night when he'd failed at everything. Followed by a miserable day that ended up in the emergency room.

"Someone once told me the trick is to let your heart guide you."

That was easy for her to say. She had a heart. He'd considered putting the older kids in boarding school and finding daycare for Sandy all because he didn't want to deal with them. Talk about selfish and heartless—that was more like his father than he wanted to admit and just as heartless.

But April's words gave him something else to consider. The question was, could he change?

"Look, there's a dolphin." April grabbed his shirt with one hand and pointed with the other. She pulled out her phone and started taking pictures.

Garrett was relieved for the opportunity to change the subject. A little too much soul searching for him, and he wanted this to be a fun day. "We have tons of them here. There are several cruises that come out each day just for tourists and locals to see them. There's something about the sleek creatures that call to people, bringing joy with each sighting."

"They are friendly and cute, what's not to love?" April leaned over the railing to get a better glimpse of the dolphins as they played in the water.

The boat cruised through the harbor, the captain pointing out various landmarks as they passed. The Statue of Liberty loomed just ahead. "We'll cruise right past the old lady so you can get some good pictures if you want."

"It's an amazing symbol of freedom and new life. Like you now, with your new life. Now all you need to do is find the freedom in it."

"Easier said than done." He'd never known anyone with such an upbeat approach to life. She was always looking for the best in people, a trait he enjoyed. And one he'd miss after she left.

Garrett regretted the cruise was over as they pulled alongside the dock. "You love the outdoors, don't you?"

"What gave it away?" She glanced up at him and nodded. "The outdoors is my freedom. I've got my share of past issues, and I don't enjoy constraints. It'sone of the things I love about Hallbrook. Everybody's friendly, but not in your face. In the city, it would be hard to find the freedom I need, although out here on the boat is a close second. There's space here, even in the middle of the concrete jungle."

Garrett chuckled. Unable to resist the temptation, he pulled her in his arms and leaned her back against his chest so she could watch as the cruise boat maneuvered its way back to the docks. "What kind of life do you want?"

"I want to be loved for me and not what I can do for others." Her words surprised him, and he sensed there was a story here—the key to April St. James. The question was, did he want to unlock her past? To bring himself closer toward knowing her, something that was usually a precursor to a relationship, something he wasn't ready for.

"You made me talk, now it's your turn." Garrett couldn't resist asking. He wanted to know her story. Wanted to understand the intensity of her statement. Who wouldn't love her for her? She was a loveable person, and if he were looking for a relationship, she'd be the kind of woman he'd want. Real. Honest. Trusting. Dedicated. Faithful. Sweet. The list was long.

She let out a deep breath and glanced up at him, then turned back to look out over the water. "Fine. Here's the ugly story of my life. It's called foster care. There are a lot of wonderful foster homes out there. I've seen them since I've been working with County Social Services. But for every ten good ones, there's one that slips through the cracks and should have their rights revoked. Somehow, those were the ones I seemed to end up in." Her voice was soft and low as she spoke, the breeze making it hard to hear, and he leaned forward to capture every word.

"You grew up in a foster home?"

"Homes. Plural. I'd stay at each one until I outgrew my usefulness, or the county figured out what was going on and shut them down." April shrugged, trying to act as though it meant nothing, but he sensed the truth. The system had let her down. *Badly.*

"What was going on?" Garrett was almost afraid to ask, but he wanted to know.

"Babysitting. Cooking. Cleaning. Yard work. Basically, I was free labor while they sat back and collected money for putting a roof over my head."

He'd heard the tales of bad foster homes but couldn't imagine April living in them. Her childhood must have been awful. At least he'd had his mother after the divorce, and she'd loved him and his sister without question. "I'm sorry. What happened to your parents?"

"I never knew my dad, and my mother died. Breast cancer. I was eight at the time. I went from a loving home to no home, no family, no relatives.

No nothing. And no one who cared what happened to me."

"You've come a long way." It was the truth. There was no evidence of the past she described echoing in the personality of the woman she was today.

"Well, it was either feel sorry for myself, or get it together and make a life. I moved to Hallbrook, and for the first time ever, I began to feel like a somebody. The people there genuinely seem to care about me. I love being a part of something bigger, a community."

"Thanks for telling me." Knowing her background, he felt her pain and wished he could make it all vanish. He rested his chin on her head. "You're an amazing woman, April. Anyone who knows you is lucky to have your sunshine in their life."

She turned to look up at him, her soft lips curved in a gentle smile. "Thank you. What a sweetly poetic thing to say."

The crew finished docking, and Garrett gathered their belongings. They made their way off the boat along with the other passengers who were eagerly waiting to move on to the next touristy thing.

"So, what's next?" April asked, closing the subject.

"See for yourself." He pointed at a luncheon table set up at the end of the dock, complete with white wine and flowers. "I arranged it with the owner and had them do a catered picnic for us."

"Watch out, I'm beginning to think you're a romantic. Are you sure this isn't a date?" She flushed with pleasure, the dimples on her cheeks deep with the grin she shot him.

"If it was, I'd have already done this." He leaned over and kissed her, letting his mouth linger seconds longer than a friend-to-friend kiss. When he pulled back, her fingers touched her lips, her gaze full of wonder.

"*Ummm*, you know this is crazy, right? It can't be a date. I'm leaving, and it will confuse everything."

"Tell me about it." He shook his head and shrugged. "I've wanted to do that for days. Raising his glass of wine to hers, he toasted. "To our mixed-up non-date. I hope you're enjoying the city."

"I am, thanks to you." April sipped from her glass, her gaze enchanting.

Their lifestyles were on opposite ends of the rainbow, but it didn't stop him from wishing things could be different. If only he could convince her to stay and see where this attraction between them led. He was tired of fighting it. The kids would love the idea, and he wouldn't need to hire anyone, because he'd already had the best nanny and housekeeper money could buy.

My life's aspiration isn't to be a nanny and housekeeper in some posh penthouse suite. April's exact words. Would it be different if he bought a house in Queens?

Chapter Fourteen

♥

"CAN WE DO SOMETHING fun today? I'm bored," Melanie whined.

"Think of all the fun you had yesterday." The kids had come back from Jim and Bev's worn out and ready for bed early. April, on the other hand, had a hard time sleeping, her day with Garrett extra special, a day she'd never forget. He'd only kissed her once, but oh, what a kiss.

"But this is supposed to be an adventure." Melanie's mood was a direct result of overstimulation yesterday, but nothing new to April when it came to dealing with kids. And the only way to deal with a sour mood was to perk them up again, just not on such a grand scale.

"I've got an idea. Why don't we take a before-school field trip this morning? Now that I'm more used to getting around, I think we can handle getting somewhere on our own. What do you think?" April bumped shoulders with Melanie playfully, trying to make her laugh.

"Where to?" she asked. Bryan stopped rolling around on the floor with Rufus long enough to hear her answer.

"*Hmmm.* Let me think. I've got it. What if we visit Garrett? It might be exciting to see what it's like to work as an executive here in the city. I'm sure he won't mind, and it'll be fun." At least, she hoped he wouldn't mind. After yesterday, her confidence in the suggestion had risen several notches. "We'll call it a bring-your-kid-to-work-day field trip."

And a bring-your-nanny-to-work field trip because she was just as delighted to see where he worked. She had no idea what the kiss meant, or if it meant anything at all, but April hadn't been able to stop thinking about it. Or him.

Their non-date had been a day of fun and exploring, and a chance to get to know one another. April couldn't help but treasure the time they spent together. She also realized that if Garrett would trust his instincts, he'd be a great dad. Both made it harder to walk away this weekend, but it was his kiss that made it darn near impossible. Originally, she assumed he and Brooke were an item, but now she wasn't so sure. Not unless he made a habit of kissing lots of women.

"Sounds okay." Melanie shrugged noncommittally. "Could be fun."

"Definitely more fun than watching more movies or reading," Bryan chimed in.

Sandy nodded, her eyes lighting up with excitement. Of course, at the mention of Garrett's name, she would agree to go anywhere.

"Then let's do this." April packed a few kid essentials, baby wipes, tissues, crayons, and paper. Be prepared was her motto. Bryan held Sandy's hand, leaving Melanie to carry her own car seat, and April to carry Sandy's car seat and the bag.

It wasn't long before they were downstairs, Ted holding the door open for them as they exited to the street. "Would you like me to get you a taxi?"

"No, thanks." She wanted to learn to assert herself, and this was an opportunity to try. "I've got this."

He chuckled but waited nearby just in case she failed.

"Taxi!" she hollered, raising her hand in the air. Several taxis passed by, but none stopped. "What did I do wrong?"

"You have to yell louder," Bryan interjected.

"No, she needs to wave her hand more, like a flag," Melanie insisted.

"No, she needs to step off the curb like she means business and call out exactly the same way she did." Ted's words of advice gave her the confidence to try again.

"Taxi!" she hollered, this time stepping off the curb, following Ted's instructions. *Be assertive.* A yellow taxi pulled over, mere inches from April. She jumped back, her arm out to keep the kids from moving forward until the vehicle came to a complete stop.

Ted opened the door, helping her get the kids inside and belted in. "Thanks, Ted." She waved and slid in the front seat. "Corner of Hampton and Spring Street, please. It's the Hampton East building."

The driver nodded, pushed the meter button, and pulled away from the curb. At each stoplight, the kids asked if they were there yet, letting on they were into way more into this field trip than acted.

The ride took less than twenty minutes, and soon they were pulling up in front of the building. So far, so good. Once inside, she looked for the Bradley& West name on the sign next to the elevator, checking for which floor they needed. Melanie pressed the button for the thirty-second floor. On the ride up, April realized she forgot to call Garrett to give him the heads-up. Her confidence faltered slightly.

He kissed you. April straightened. It would be okay.

The elevator doors opened, and the kids raced out, their eagerness to see where Garrett worked now unchecked.

"*Shhh*," April admonished. "It's a place of business, so we have to be quiet." The first thing she noticed was that the decor matched the same clean, contemporary lines of Garrett's house. Cold, impersonal, and dreadfully businesslike. Contemporary would never be her thing.

"May I help you?" the receptionist asked. She was a younger woman, but formidable both in her starchy business suit and her voice.

"Yes, I'm April St. James, and I'm here to see Mr. Bradley. Garrett Bradley," she amended in case there was more than one Bradley.

"Do you have an appointment?" The woman's chin rose a notch as she checked her computer and then looked back at April.

"No. I don't need one. These are his...children." It sounded strange when she uttered the words, but it didn't make them any less true.

"Mr. Bradley doesn't have any children." The woman's voice was now several degrees colder.

"I beg to differ with you." It wasn't up to April to explain. "Now, if you'll just buzz him, I'm sure he'll let us in." This was like getting past the gates at Fort Knox.

"Someone to see Mr. Bradley. I think she said her name was April St. James. She's here with three children and no appointment. Should I send her back or tell her to make an appointment?" The crisp voice sent chills down April's back. "Yes, Miss Taylor. Thank you." The woman looked up at April, disdain evident in her haughty expression. "You may proceed to the back. Just through those doors down the hall on the right. Miss Taylor will meet you there."

Apparently, there were two gatekeepers to get through to see the mighty and powerful Mr. Bradley. Luckily, the kids were staying close, and so far, behaving.

"Ms. St. James, what a pleasure to see you again. Is Mr. Bradley expecting you?" Brooke's voice made it clear she was less than pleased to see April and the kids, regardless of her words.

"No. It was a spur-of-the-moment decision to come here. I thought it would be fun for the kids to see where Garrett works." April felt guilty for the white lie, but Brooke didn't need to know that. Besides, she was getting tired of explaining herself.

The woman's eyebrows rose a notch at the use of Garrett's name. "This is a place of business. I'm not sure this is a great idea. In fact, I'm positive it's not." She let out a deep sigh, her gaze landing on the children. "He's busy with a new client. You should leave and find some other way to occupy your time. Isn't that what you're paid to do?" The catty tone of her voice set April on edge.

"I think we should let Mr. Bradley be the judge of that, don't you think? They are his children." April glared back at Brooke. She had no intention of backing down or leaving until they talked to Garrett.

Brooke glanced at the three children again, her upper lip curling slightly as if the thought of kids in her office was inconceivable. "Very well, if you insist. Follow me. Children, don't touch anything."

"As if," Bryan muttered.

His judgment of the woman was spot on, but it wouldn't do for her to allow him to vocalize those opinions. "Bryan, that's enough." April shook her head, sending him a clear message.

Brooke leaned in close as they walked side by side, the kids a few steps behind. "Don't think I don't know what you're up to. You're not the first woman to come up with some lame excuse to worm her way into Garrett's life, hoping to be Mrs. Bradley, and I'm sure you won't be the last. I'm surprised you'd even try though, considering you're leaving this coming weekend. Bit of a reach, don't you think?"

The woman had lowered her voice as if they were conspiring together—but that would be like being in cahoots with the wicked stepmother in Cinderella. "It's not what you think." It was easier to tell the woman what she wanted to hear in the hopes she'd back down. The kiss she'd shared with Garrett...well, that was for her lips only. And she wasn't a kiss-and-tell kind of girl.

"Please. It's exactly what I think. I've been with Garrett a long time and know him better than anyone. And fair warning, he doesn't like kids, and he doesn't like dogs, so you can just forget this whole family picture you're trying to paint. As soon as we get them accepted into boarding school and find a daycare for the little girl, this will be a non-issue."

Boarding school? And daycare? It was the first April had heard of the nonsense. He couldn't possibly be thinking seriously about either option. Neither was in the best interests of the children. She'd have to talk it over with him sometime when they were alone. However, with school just around the corner, she'd need to do it soon.

"He wouldn't do that to them." It was all she could think to say, her mind spinning. April hadn't missed the word *we* in the bomb Brooke dropped. The confirmation of the two of them as a couple was upsetting. The man had kissed her, and she hadn't been able to push aside her growing feelings. She might be leaving, but she'd also started to care for Garrett as more than the children's father. But it would seem Brooke did, too. And the miserable woman was making decisions with Garrett for the kids. Poor children.

The day had started out sunny but turned cloudy. If what Brooke told her was true, there was a storm brewing on the horizon. What she needed was a prospect for someone to help with the house and kids, or she didn't stand a chance of talking him out of such a disastrous decision. If she hadn't already registered for college and sent in her money, she might consider postponing leaving, but she couldn't stay in the city and couldn't pass up this opportunity. She had to find a replacement and convince Garrett sending the kids away was the wrong decision for all of them.

The secretary pushed open a massive wooden door and entered, leaving them to follow.

"Brooke, what is it—April? What are you all doing here? Garrett stood and started her way, meeting her halfway across the office. His smile was encouraging.

"She's here to visit. I told her you were working on a new file and extremely busy, but she insisted." The woman shook her head as if April were clueless.

Garrett glanced at Brooke. "That will be all, Brooke. I've got this. Close the door behind you." It was a clear invitation for the woman to leave, and April couldn't help but shoot her a satisfied smirk.

"Hey, kids. Hope you're behaving for Miss April today?" He lifted Sandy up in his arms and crossed the room toward the window as she gave him a tight hug around his neck.

"We are." Bryan was the first to answer.

Garrett pointed to a giant billboard on the side of a nearby office building. A dog picture illuminated the neon sign, and Sandy smiled. "I'm busy, but I can stop for a few minutes. What's going on?"

"We decided on a before-school field trip to do something different. More fun. We dubbed this take-your-kid-to-work day. I forgot to call you first. Sorry."

"This is a really cool office." Melanie beamed. "We won't touch anything, Garrett. We promise."

"Why won't you touch anything? All I ask is that you don't destroy the place." He chuckled. Kids came up with some of the silliest ideas.

"That lady who just left warned us not to touch." Bryan shrugged. Maybe not so silly after all. Brooke was a formidable woman.

"Don't worry about that. I'm the boss here, so she can't fire you or anything." *More proof Brooke was overstepping her bounds.*

"I've never been to somebody's office before. This is cool," Bryan said, moving to stand next to the window. "Wow, we are really high up."

Garrett tweaked Sandy's nose. "Are you being a good girl today?"

Sandy nodded; her eyes lit up with excitement.

Garrett loved her smile, and it warmed his heart. He headed back to his desk. "Let me tell Jim you're here. He's dropped in several times already this morning talking about the fun he had with you guys yesterday."

"Mr. Jim is here, too?" Bryan asked. "Cool."

"Sure is." Garrett buzzed the intercom. "Hey, Jim. My insta-family stopped in. You got a second?"

"Wouldn't miss it." Less than a minute later, the door opened, and Jim walked in, full of smiles and hugs for the kids. "Nice to see you again, April. I heard you had fun yesterday. Garrett told me some of what you did. Impressive." He nodded.

"It was amazing. Garrett's a wonderful tour guide." She couldn't keep the admiration out of her voice as she recounted the day, Brooke, or no Brooke.

Jim's intense gaze made her feel like a bug under a microscope. He turned to Garrett. "You need to find a way to keep this one."

"I'm trying, believe me. But she starts school right after Labor Day at Plymouth U."

April loved hearing that Garrett spoke of her kindly. She'd watched him evolve from bachelor to daddy, and it had shown her a side of him she hadn't expected but admired. A lot.

"I should run. The kids have tried out your desk, looked out the window, and scoped out the putt-putt golf thing you have over there in the corner. Next, we move to boredom. My cue to leave." April knew exactly how long a kid's attention span would last and the dangers of when it ran out. "Come on, kids. Time to let Mr. Garrett and Mr. Jim get some work done."

April took Sandy from Garrett, and they all said goodbye and headed for the door. She stopped and turned back to Garrett. "Dinner is at six., so try not to be late. I'm making Cajun Chicken pasta, my specialty."

"A man could get used to home-cooked meals every night." Garrett nodded; his eyes lit up with anticipation.

"I get home-cooked meals every night by having a wife. Comes with night-time privileges as well. You might want to try it sometime, Garrett." Jim was ready to burst with laughter at Garrett's sudden grimace. Okay, so marriage was not anywhere on Garrett's agenda. He'd told her that in the beginning.

"If you had a housekeeper or wife before now, you wouldn't have needed me, so I'm glad you didn't." She joined in the teasing, finding it easier to laugh off Jim's direct comment.

"True. I'm glad I didn't, either." Were they still talking about cooking meals, or was something else cooking behind the scenes?

Chapter Fifteen

♥

GARRETT'S ALARM SOUNDED OFF at five. He folded his blankets, topped the pile off with his pillow and placed them on the shelf in the hall closet. He filled an oversized thermos of the coffee April had set up to brew, not wanting to miss the robust taste of the coffee blend she'd perfected for him. He headed down the hall to his office where he'd hung fresh clothes and put his toiletries to make things easier with April occupying his room. He dressed and wasted no time heading out the front door. The last thing he wanted to do was wake the kids or the dog.

Garrett hailed a taxi, anxious to get to the office and double-check the merger stats and to do some extra market-analysis reviews for the oil industry.

Mr. Hamilton's late-night text with concerns over falling oil prices was valid but based purely on speculation. If they dropped, it would affect the bottom line of the deal and the closing, which in turn meant Hamilton's ability to merge with Baden Enterprises at a fair price. All current indices showed prices stabilizing, at least for the foreseeable future. But Garrett wanted to double and triple-check his information just to be on the safe side.

Garrett reviewed all updates on the market that were reported before the opening. Nothing changed. The prices had ticked up a little higher, but nothing that would be a deal breaker. Hours passed, but he didn't notice until Brooke came in, bringing him a much-needed cup of coffee. She set it on his desk as he stood and stretched.

"Morning, Garrett. I see you're hard at it already this morning. Is there anything I can do for you before I get started on my task list?" Brooke was organized to the T, which was probably why they worked well together. She was good at predicting his every need, which was handy when he wanted something in a hurry.

"Any chance you can get me one of those honey buns from the downstairs vending machine. I came straight here this morning and missed by breakfast stop at the café."

"No problem. You need to eat better than that. Let me know when you want lunch, and I'll order us something from the deli."

"Best idea I've heard all morning. Thanks." Garrett nodded, the idea of lunch already making him hungry.

He managed to get in another couple of hours before his stomach forced him to call it quits. He pressed the intercom button on the phone. "Brooke, if you're in a place you can stop and run to the corner deli for our lunch. I could use a sandwich. My treat."

"Of course. And I know just what you want. Smoked turkey, gouda cheese, heavy on the mustard, light on the mayo, and all on whole-grain bread." His secretary rattled off his regular request.

For every place he ate, he had a favorite. One day, he'd mix it up and surprise her, but not today.

Smoked turkey sounded perfect. "You know me too well. Maybe I'm too predictable."

She laughed. "Maybe, but it makes it easier for me to take care of you. Should I pick you up one of those dark chocolate and almond cookies you enjoy?"

"Why not. A sugar rush might be just what I need."

"I'll be back shortly, and we can have lunch together. It'll be a nice break."

That wasn't exactly what he'd intended. She'd be camped out in his office if he didn't find something else to do during that time. Garrett sat back in his chair, his thoughts drifting to last night and April.

He'd gone home at six just liked she'd requested. Dinner on the table. Family talk. Movies. Kid's bedtime. Alone time with April. There was something to be said for having someone to talk to when he arrived home at night, and he hadn't even minded a lot of *someones* while the kids were still awake.

Garrett smiled to himself as he pictured April's smiling face, her hair blowing gently in the wind.

He'd stopped himself from kissing her a second time, having already crossed the line once. But the warmth of her sunny face was hard to resist. He knew better than to travel down that road. His road was in the city, and hers was in the country, and the two had no chance of a collision. Their relationship was just a fender bender that had brought them together and made him think of possibilities.

Thinking of April made him want to hear her voice. See how her day was going. He stared at his cell phone for all of thirty seconds, debating whether to call. He picked up the phone and dialed, the decision made. It was just a phone call. Disappointment settled in hard when her voicemail clicked on. He hung up the phone without leaving a message. Garrett tried the house phone just in case her cell was dead. Again, no answer. Bryan or Melanie could answer the phone if April was tied up with Sandy or in the kitchen. Maybe they'd gone out exploring? Yes, that's probably what it was.

Five minutes later, he hadn't read a single word of the report he'd pulled up, his thoughts all on

April. It was easy enough to find out if she'd left the building, although he hated the idea of checking up on her. Just one phone call and no one would ever know. Garrett located the number and dialed.

"Sutton Hill, front desk, this is Ted." Garrett was relieved to hear Ted's voice. The other new guy who covered for Ted, Bill something or other, wasn't as easy to work with. Getting information from him was, at best, like digging a well to get to the water.

"Hey, it's Garrett. Do you know if April and the kids left the building? She's not answering the house phone or her cell. With her being in a new area, I worry." The excuse sounded plausible even to his own ears.

"No. She hasn't passed by my desk, and I've been here all morning. Probably just got her hands full." Ted's answer made him feel better. At least she wasn't out trying to manage the hustle and bustle of the city.

"That's what I was thinking. Thanks."

Fifteen minutes later, Garrett still hadn't read another word. He tapped his pencil against the desk and thought about trying to call April again. He reached for the phone just as Brooke entered the office, carrying several brown paper bags.

"Lunch is here. I'll set up a place to eat over by the window. Just give me a few minutes." Brooke took charge, just like she always did.

Except he didn't want to have lunch with his secretary. He wanted to have lunch with April. Or at least talk to her. Just to make sure she was okay. *Yeah right.*

"Don't unpack mine. I'm going to take my lunch on the run and catch a taxi back to the penthouse. I need to check on April and the kids." He pushed up from his chair and started across the room. Boss's privilege.

"But you never—"

"I realize that," he insisted, cutting her off. "Let Jim know he can reach me on my cell and that I'll be at the penthouse. Thanks." He took the bag from her and headed for the door.

"Will you be back this afternoon?" Brooke called out after him, clearly unhappy with the change in plans.

"No. I'll see you in the morning. Call me if you need anything." Suddenly, everything felt right. He hadn't blown off work in years, and he was long overdue.

"Okay. I have those boarding school information packets you asked me to get. I'll put them on your desk."

"Thanks." He closed the door, ending any further chance of conversation.

Garrett hailed a taxi and was back at Sutton Hill in less than twenty minutes. "Hey, Ted." He waved at the concierge on his way to the elevators.

"Mr. Bradley?" Is everything okay? I've never known you to come home in the middle of the afternoon on a workday." The man looked truly perplexed.

"I know, I know. But April's only here a few more days, and I feel terrible for dumping everything on her shoulders. It's my duty to help out."

"Sounds like a plan. She's a beautiful lady, and one could see why you would want to spend time with her." Ted winked.

"It's not like that." He wasn't sure what it was, but he did want to enjoy what was left of it. Jim's face would be priceless when he found out Garrett had left for the day.

The ride to the top floor didn't take long, and Garrett pulled out his key card and swiped it across the pad. He pushed open the door, bending to put his briefcase by the front door. "Hello, anybody home?"

Three faces stared back at him their eyes wide in shock.

"Wh...wh...what are you doing here?" April was the first to speak, but it was the terrified expression on her face that struck him the hardest.

Not exactly the greeting he'd hoped for. "Is that any way to greet someone? I wanted to come home and take you all somewhere to get out of the pent- house. I'm trying to be more hospitable." He glanced from one face to the other, not liking what he was seeing. *And why was she holding his DVD player?*

"We weren't expecting you. Maybe you should head back to the office." April's directive was seconded by Melanie and Bryan who stood close to her, one on each side.

If something doesn't seem right, it probably isn't. April's own words. His stomach clenched. He took a step forward. "What's going on?"

"N...nothing." She winced.

"April St. James, I haven't known you long, but long enough to know you're not telling me something. I demand you tell me what's going on. And why weren't you answering your phone? And what are you doing with my DVD player?" He fired off the questions, out of patience. All three of them seemed guilty about something, and he wanted to know why.

Even the dog was hunkered down in the corner, eyeballing the scene unfolding but staying out of the mix.

"Garrett, I'm sorry. This isn't a kid-friendly place. I was in the shower, and Sandy got a hold of the crayons again. When I came out and shouted at her to stop, Rufus got overly excited. And then the kids told me there was a problem with the DVD player. Everything's just a mess." She was on the verge of tears.

"Go back to the part about a crayon." Images flashed through his mind that she'd drawn on the floor or something, and he cringed. He had to see for himself. "Step aside."

The three of them looked at each other, and April nodded her head slightly. When they stepped back, he saw a nightmare come true.

His stomach plummeted and, in the void, anger took its place. "What happened here? This is insane. Are you serious?" If it had only been the floor, it might have been okay. But red and blue crayon drawings decorated his walls. His crystal floor lamp lay on its side, the glass globe shattered across the floor. Food crumbs were littered everywhere, and a purple stain next to the coffee table now colored the white rug like an abstract painting.

He shook his head, trying to dispel the image. His head was going to explode. Count to ten. April's words popped into his head, but he wasn't sure he was capable of counting.

Garrett tried to focus, closing his eyes to block out the war zone. *One. Two. Three. Four. Five. Six. Seven. Eight. Nine. Ten.* He opened his eyes. Nothing had changed. Not the destruction or his mood. There was only one thing left he could do.

"Don't wait up for me." Garrett turned, grabbed his briefcase, and headed out the door, slamming it hard behind him. The only place he wanted to be right now was back in his office. Work would drown out the images. Allow him to think of anything other than what he'd just seen. The man who controlled everything in his life suddenly couldn't control anything.

He'd always known kids were a problem, and this was proof. Why his mother had ever thought this could work for him, he'd never understand. If April couldn't control them, he didn't stand a chance. Boarding school was sounding more and more like a winner.

What happened to two adults having a grown-up conversation? April understood Garrett's reaction. His place had been destroyed. She'd have given anything to make it all disappear, but she couldn't, at least not in the short time that had passed since she'd first discovered the disaster.

Fifteen minutes. That's how long she'd been in the shower enjoying the luxury of Garrett's massage jets. The interviews this morning hadn't gone well and had been topped off with a healthy dose of guilt laid on by the kids unintentionally with their pleas for her to be their permanent nanny and housekeeper. She'd just wanted a few moments of peaceful bliss.

Fifteen minutes. That's all it took to realize she could kiss her bonus goodbye. She wasn't having any luck finding a replacement, but worse, when Garrett got home and took one look at the place, he'd fire her before she had the chance to interview the last couple of people.

And she wouldn't blame him. April glanced around the living room, still unable to comprehend the level of destruction.

She hadn't been sure whether to be mad as a hornet, crawl under a rock to hide like a bug, or cry like a baby. None of those options would have fixed the problem—neither one of them. The house or Garrett.

They'd just started to clean up when Garrett had shown up unexpectedly, blowing all her plans to have the place in tip-top shape by the time he returned. But at least he hadn't fired her—yet.

"All right, kids, let's get to it. He'll be back, and then he'll see it's not so awful." April tried to put on a cheerful face and rally the troops.

"What if he stays mad and doesn't want us? Will he send us away?" *The poor darlings*. April's heart was breaking, knowing what they were thinking.

Especially since she also knew Garrett had been thinking of sending them to a boarding school. Although that had nothing to do with anything the children did wrong, and everything to do with poor judgment on Garrett's part.

"It'll be fine. Trust me. Mr. Garrett will be back, and all will back to normal."

"I'm sorry, Miss April. I know you asked us to watch Sandy. We didn't do a good job, did we?" Sandy, the little termite, had turned into a Picasso, her artwork gracing the walls and the floor. The silver lining, if there was one, was that she'd left the sofa alone, just like April had told her. Bryan and Melanie had been too wrapped up in their tablets to notice their sister having her own kind of fun.

"Don't worry about it. Accidents happen. But next time I ask you to watch her, you'll know why it's important to do just that. It only takes minutes for everything to go wrong." Other than the lamp and DVD that needed fixing, the rest could be cleaned, provided the grape soda came out of the rug.

"Yes, ma'am," they answered in unison.

It wasn't their fault Garrett hadn't given her a chance to explain. He was probably back in his office, venting his woes to Brooke, who would be all too willing to comfort him. Fringe benefits with the job. Although April was pretty sure Brooke was looking for more than fringe benefits. That woman was after a ring.

Garrett needed to understand he had responsibilities, and he couldn't just walk away because he was angry. She got that he wasn't familiar with having kids around or anything to do with them, but she could've told him about one of the greatest inventions since the washing machine. Washable crayons.

April couldn't shake the guilt for her part in the fiasco. She replayed the scene in her head, still unable to believe what had happened. How was she to know that when she hollered for Sandy to stop coloring the walls, she would set off a chain of events that turned one mess into utter chaos?

Rufus had gone nuts and charged into the room, knocking into Bryan, spilling his drink, and sending popcorn flying everywhere. And then the dog knocked into the lamp and busted it as he tried to get away from the uproar and raced for the corner, his tail tucked between his legs.

It was a comedy of errors, made worse because of the penthouse suite's perfection. And if it hadn't been for Garrett's reaction, by now, April might be laughing.

She'd managed to order a replacement globe for the lamp that would be delivered in two days. And the DVD player was only jammed—a pair of tweezers and two minutes had it fixed. It wasn't as if this was the first time she played electronics repairman.

April had ignored Garrett's calls because she hadn't wanted him to sense anything wrong in her voice, but never in a million years had she expected him to come home. And to think he'd been ready to take the afternoon off and spend time with them. She'd been trying to make him understand that investing time in the kids would take him far. The kids would have loved another outing with Garrett.

Unfortunately, today's fiasco was three giant kid-sized steps backward in the bonding and relationship process, something she couldn't afford if she intended to fix Garrett's relationship with the kids before she left.

The children were working hard to help, cleaning the crayon off the walls and the floor. Even Sandy chipped in while April took care of the glass and vacuuming. It wasn't long before they had the place back to the way it was, except for the lampshade she had on order. Objects were replaceable, his relationship with the children wasn't, something Garrett needed to learn.

The question was, would he?

Garrett didn't come home for dinner. His absence was noticeable, and the kids were rather quiet. There wasn't much she could say to make things right. That would have to come from Garrett.

April stayed up, hoping for a chance to talk to Garrett and explain things when he was calmer and prepared to listen. Except that hours later, he still hadn't come home. She started to fall asleep on the sofa when her phone dinged, alerting her to a text.

Garrett: Working. Might not be home.

Working? Yeah, right. It was after eleven p.m. The only thing he'd be working on this late was his secretary. Seeds of jealousy sprouted out of nowhere. April headed for bed, but sleep evaded her. No matter how hard she tried, images of Garrett and Brooke drove her crazy.

It was none of her business who he dated, or who he married, for that matter, but she'd feel bad for the kids if they were stuck with a woman like Brooke, she-devil that she was.

The kids would be off to boarding school before seven sunsets had passed if he married Brooke. What April needed to do was find someone to replace her, someone that would do the job so well that Garrett wouldn't need Brooke, boarding school, or marriage. It was the perfect solution for the kids and her because they needed someone who cared about their well-being, and she needed to be able to leave knowing in good conscience they would all be okay.

April needed more candidates, because the two scheduled for tomorrow didn't sound ideal, and she held little hope one of them would work out. One was nineteen, and she worried about the older kids not respecting her authority since she was so young, and the other—well, she wasn't sure the woman could handle Rufus. From the picture in the file provided, it looked as though a strong wind could blow her over in a storm. Her petite build was no match for the dog.

She would put out several more calls in the morning and try to line up more qualified candidates. The biggest problem April kept running into was finding someone who would do everything he required. A lot of people were fine with some of the things, but not all of them. It was asking a lot of someone.

What he needed was a wife.
The right wife.

Chapter Sixteen

♥

GARRETT STILL COULDN'T BELIEVE he'd made a mistake that would cost Mr. Hamilton millions of dollars if he couldn't find a way to fix things. But how could he fix the price of oil when he had no control over it? After the incident in his penthouse suite, he'd returned to the office furious and silenced his phone, not wanting to talk to anyone. *Biggest mistake he ever made.*

Mr. Hamilton's sources had been right, or at least they appeared to be right. Garrett still wasn't convinced. Every indication pointed to a false drop but convincing his client before he fired him would be difficult. Garrett spent all afternoon and evening working on a new plan of action, one Mr. Hamilton would agree to.

"Go home, Brooke. Get some sleep. I'll keep working on this." Garrett let out a deep sigh.

"I can stay. I don't mind, and you know it. Stop beating yourself up over this. Kids are a distraction. You would have never missed the changing market price if you hadn't been provoked to outraged by the fiasco you described at your place. I can't imagine how you felt walking into such a mess." Brooke shook her head and rolled her eyes. "You're not to blame."

It wasn't that easy. Garrett was sure Jim wouldn't see it that way. Jim's personal life had never interfered with his ability to get a job done right.

"It doesn't matter what happened at home. I should have been monitoring the situation. I was aware Mr. Hamilton was concerned about oil prices, and it was my job to stay on top of the situation. I still don't get it though. All signs pointed to the fact this couldn't happen. I still can't believe oil prices tanked in the space of twenty-three minutes."

Two and a half million dollars divided by twenty-three minutes calculated out to over a hundred thousand dollars a minute lost to Mr. Hamilton's bottom line, because there was no way Baden Enterprises would merge for the same price they'd negotiated earlier.

Garrett ran his hands through his already ruffled hair. He'd have none left if he couldn't find a way out of the hole. His reputation and that of the firm depended on it.

"The sooner those kids are in boarding school and daycare, the sooner your life returns to normal." Brooke crossed the room to hand him the latest updates. "You'll get through this, you always do."

"I haven't made any decisions about the kids. I'm not sure about anything anymore. Go home," he reiterated, wanting time to think things through without Brooke's constant interruptions.

"If you insist. I'll be back in the morning. You're more than welcome to stay with me tonight if you need a place to stay. You know I'm five minutes away, and it's quiet there."

Garrett stopped to look up at Brooke as she picked up her purse and headed for the door. The idea of staying at Brooke's place was unacceptable, the mere suggestion probably crossing several ethics codes in the human resource manual he'd drafted when they started their business.

"Thanks, but that won't be necessary. I'll probably just stay here and keep working and sleep on the couch if needed."

She shrugged. "Offer stands if you change your mind." Brooke left, not looking pleased with his rejection.

Long into the night, Garrett checked over every inch of the tick sheet for the stock price of oil, noting every change from the days leading up to the drop and in the hours that had passed since then. He also researched the news coming out of the Middle East, hoping to find something that would point to a reason and give him an insight to the future prices and ultimately, the value of Hamilton's holdings. But none of it made sense, and there was nothing that would have tipped him off to the impending loss.

His gut told him to pull out of the merger altogether. Call Baden's bluff...his new low-ball offer not even close to the true value of Hamilton's company. But getting Mr. Hamilton to agree with him would be the problem, especially without proof of why he should listen and follow Garrett's advice. On the verge of bankruptcy, something no one else knew except for Hamilton's financial team of advisors and Garrett, the man would try to salvage some of his assets and his respect, and he would not be easy to convince.

Garrett stayed up through the night, and by morning, he'd barely managed two hours of sleep on an uncomfortable couch. And for his efforts, he had a stiff neck, a bad attitude, and he was no closer to solving the problem of how to convince Hamilton to hold off closing the deal.

Making his way to the coffeepot, Garrett poured himself some of the black drudge that was hours old. He thought of April as he took a sip but shoved all thoughts of her aside as Jim entered his office—earlier than he'd seen him at the office in years.

"Rough night?" Jim asked.

"You could say that? I guess you heard." Garrett shook his head, feeling as though he'd let not only a client down but his best friend as well.

"I did. Let's wait until the dust settles before we start packing our boxes." Jim's attempt at humor was lost on him, his brain unwilling to function in any than other than stress mode at the moment.

"Hamilton's already considering firing me. The reputation of Bradley & West is on the line. I'm sorry. I know the hours you've put in and the sacrifices you've made to build this place up. I honestly didn't see this coming. I screwed up. I let April and the kids distract me, and that's why this happened."

"Seriously? You're allowed a personal life and personal time. You can't be in work mode twenty-four-seven. I get that this doesn't look promising, but it's not over yet. And it's just one deal. We'll survive this."

"I don't know how you can be so sure."

"Because we excel at what we do, and most places are willing to overlook one blemish on a track record." Jim was willing to take it easy on him, but it was more than Garrett was willing to do for himself. It was his mistake, and that made it unacceptable. Everything he did needed to be right.

The same principle applied at home as it did at the office. Another mistake on his part he'd yet to deal with. Throughout the night, he'd had plenty of time to think.

He realized that kids could be a handful, and perhaps he'd dumped an impossible task on April. His place wasn't a kid-friendly home, and until he found them a new place, there would be problems. Money could fix everything they'd damaged, and he had plenty of that. But money couldn't take the hurt he'd seen in their eyes right before he left.

The one thing he hadn't done was act like a dad. Whether he'd wanted the role or not didn't matter, because he was one.

And he'd been wrong not to stay and listen. He should have stayed and helped her clean up. The only redemption in his reaction was that he had counted to ten. *Thank you, April.*

"Let's just hope you're right. Just so you know, I'm working on the home-front issue also. To make it better."

"Does that mean you're going to take April flowers, take the kids a couple of gifts, and apologize to them."

"Is that what you do when you screw up?"

"Yes." Jim smirked.

"Then that's what I'll do. But I also put in a call to the realtor. Angelica's right—I need to sell the penthouse. I'll buy a bigger place more suited to my new family. Something with a back yard."

"Sounds to me like you're on the right track, my friend. The only problem I see is April."

"What about her?"

"You're letting her leave. Big mistake. I can see you care about her. Bev thinks you love her."

"Bev's wrong. Of course, I care. She's a friend, and she was a great help, but she's going back to Hallbrook and starting college next week."

"College isn't forever. Marriage is if you put your heart and soul into it."

"You know I don't believe in all that."

"Well, maybe it's time you started believing."

After Jim left, Garrett hashed over his friends' words in between trying to solve his work crisis. He also managed to call his maintenance guy and arranged for the man to come to the penthouse later tonight to assess the damage and match the paint color. By the sounds of it, a toddler drawing on the walls wasn't an uncommon occurrence.

By five p.m., he was no closer to figuring out a new plan, one that would bring Hamilton and Baden Enterprises back to the table. His stomach rumbled, reminding him April would have dinner ready by six and would be expecting him. *And he wanted to be there.*

He shut off his computer and escaped the office, relieved to see Brooke had stepped away. No explanations required. This morning, he'd instructed her to hold all calls and no interruptions unless they were Mr. Hamilton or April. Although he'd had several from his client, there hadn't been one word from April.

Garrett hailed a taxi. "Sutton Hill," he told the taxi driver. "And stop at the flower shop on the corner of Abner and Dean."

The guy signaled his understanding and flipped on the meter. Twenty minutes later, they pulled up in front of the store, and Garrett jumped out. "Wait right here. Two stops to make."

He grabbed one of the colorful arrangements sitting outside the shop and shoved a twenty in the man's hand to pay for them. Garrett left the store and headed left, passing three stores before coming to the small toy store. He picked up a coloring book and then put it back down with a chuckle.

Say no to crayons was his new motto.

"May I help you?" the clerk asked. The kid looked to be in his early twenties, and Garrett figured he was his best chance at getting this right.

"Absolutely. I need something for a nine-year-old boy and a seven-year-old girl."

"Well, what sort of things do they enjoy?"

"I don't know." Garrett shrugged. "I just met them," he said by way explanation.

"Okay, then. You need to play it safe. Here." The man put a Tonka truck in his hands, presumably for Bryan.

"Are you sure about this? It seems kind of kid-dish." Garrett couldn't remember the last time he'd played with a truck.

"Are you kidding? Boys of all ages love these things." The kid seemed sure of himself.

"I'll take your word for it." They walked three aisles over into what could only be described as the pink aisle. Everything a girl could imagine was here in every shade of pink possible.

The clerk handed him a giant doll. It was almost as tall as Sandy, but he couldn't imagine Melanie playing with it. She had her sister, the real thing instead.

"All girls play with dolls." It was as if he could see the indecision in Garrett's face. At least if he was wrong, Sandy would have a new playmate. "I'll take it."

"And for the youngest? She's three."

"Stuffed animals are always a safe bet. Unless you love noise, then a kid's drum set is fun. It's just plastic."

"No. No drums. I'll take the oversized mouse. Minnie, right?"

The clerk shook his head and laughed. "Yes, Minnie." He followed the guy to the register, paid, and headed back to the waiting taxi. They drove down the street a bit and pulled up in front of Sutton Hill. Garrett paid the taxi driver, tipping him extra for waiting. He grabbed his briefcase and tried to find the best way to hang on to the bulky pack- ages and not crush the flowers.

"Here, let me get that for you, Mr. Bradley." Ted ran down the steps to help.

"Thanks. If you just let me rearrange this, I should be fine." Pressing the briefcase up under one arm and holding it tight against his side with his elbow, he grasped the other three bags by the plastic handles, keeping the flowers safe in the other hand. "I've got it now. Thanks."

"Have a nice night." Ted waved.

The ride to the top was nerve-wracking. Garrett was unsure of what to expect when he showed up. He slid the key card across the pad and pushed open the door. When he entered the suite, the first thing he noticed was April talking with the maintenance guy.

"Glad you're here, Morgan. I didn't expect you this early. Give me a second to put these down." He put the toys on the kitchen table and returned to the living room. Rufus bounded toward him and started to jump up, trying to get to the flowers. "Down boy." Garrett turned away and raised the flowers up over his head and out of the dog's reach. Rufus surprised him when he sat, his tail wagging.

"Would you look at that, the dog is obeying you." Morgan smiled.

"It's a first." Garrett handed April the flowers and then reached down and patted the dog's head.

April smiled at him, her soft gaze full of forgiveness. *Before I even asked for it.* She was an amazing woman. "I'm sorry. We'll talk about it in a minute. I just need to give Morgan the heads-up as to what we need to be done to fix everything."

"Garrett, I'm not sure what you need me to do. I've been here talking to April, and it seems that she has everything under control."

"What do you mean?" He stepped back, steeling himself to look at the wall and not react. "You already fixed it?"

"He didn't, I did. They're called washable crayons, and if you'd stuck around, I would've told you about the greatest development in kids' toys since we were babies."

Now he really felt like a fool. He'd never heard of such a thing, but the name spoke for itself.

"Guess I'll be leaving. You all have a nice night." Morgan headed for the door, but not before Garrett noticed his all-knowing grin. "Glad it all worked out."

"Goodnight, and thanks anyway." After the door closed, the awkward silence grew.

"Thanks for the flowers. You didn't need to do this." April's voice was soft and without judgment.

"Yes, I did. I overreacted, and I'm sorry." If anything, her attitude made him feel worse.

"It's not that you overreacted, it's that you left. The kids need reassurance from you that you're not mad at them." Ouch. That hurt because it was the truth.

"Where are they now?"

"They're watching a movie in Bryan's room. And they've promised to be gentle with your DVD player. It had a DVD stuck in it, and they panicked." Her gaze beseeched him to understand as she reached out to lay her hand on his, her touch gentle.

"I've got something for the kids." Garrett swallowed hard, the lump of shame in his throat making it difficult.

"You don't need to buy things for them. They just need you to be here. They need a connection with you." April was right. She was always right.

"Now you tell me about buying things. I've got a Tonka truck and a giant baby doll that I'm almost positive aren't the older two kid's age bracket, but the guy insisted they'd love them. And a stuffed animal for Sandy."

"A Tonka truck for Bryan? Doubtful, but I could be wrong. The doll for Melanie, not so much. She's got her sister for that, and she's more into art. Like Sandy." She grinned. "And stuffed animals are always fun." April's laugh was a wonderful sound that gave him hope things could return to normal.

"Sounds as though my efforts were an epic fail. At least I overrode the guy on the drum set for Sandy."

April grinned. "Good call. You can give the doll and truck to Sandy," she suggested.

"Won't the other two feel left out? I wanted to apologize to you and the kids."

"It was a nice idea, but I think they just want to spend time with you." The genuine warmth in her smile touched his heart.

"By the way, how did the interviews go this morning? You haven't said anything." Garrett still wasn't sold completely on the idea of replacing April, but he understood it was for the best.

"Not so hot. There's one other agency I'll call tomorrow. I'm sorry." She shrugged and let out a huge sigh.

"We'll figure it out together." Garrett tried to reassure her, knowing she was the kind of person who would want to make sure the kids were taken care of before she left.

"Did you remember to enroll them in school? They need to start soon."

"I haven't. But thanks for the reminder. I need to make some decisions about their schooling."

"You're not still considering boarding school, are you? That would be awful, and they are already worried you want to send them away because of yesterday's mess." April wasn't pulling any punches, her comment a direct hit knowing he was considering exactly that.

Her opinion meant far more than Brooke's when it involved the children or anything else for that matter. But he still wasn't sure how it would work if he didn't send them. "Whatever gave them that idea? I've not made any decisions. Right now, I'm dealing with work issues that have become a top priority. Stop worrying. Whatever I do, I'll make sure they're taken care of. I promised." It was a promise he intended to keep.

"Okay, just remember they need you." She looked up at him, the light of hope in her eyes.

"I'm not so sure after my reaction to the mess. I still can't believe the crayon just wiped right off the walls. That's remarkable."

"By the way, I found the exact match to your lampshade and ordered it online. It'll be here in tomorrow." The relief was evident in her voice.

"You didn't have to do that."

"But I wanted to. I felt like it was only right."

"What's right is you here helping me with the kids. That's what's most important." He meant every word. Somehow, he had to convince her to stay. She was the perfect nanny for him.

His overreaction had caused the problems at work, not the kids—proof he was no good at parenting and family.

Chapter Seventeen

♥

A PRIL FIXED THE KIDS breakfast and got ready for this morning's interview candidate, all while going over the events of the previous evening. Garrett had done his best to interact with the kids and get past the awkwardness. But when he sat down in the armchair after the kids were in bed and not next to her on the sofa when they watched a movie, she realized something was wrong. Her attempts to find out what, however, were met with a denial of anything other than work stuff.

She wanted to believe him, but he'd shut her out, making it hard to know what was going on. At least peace and harmony had been restored to the Bradley residence. Now the only thing she needed to do was find a nanny, and not dwell on thoughts of Garrett and Brooke spending the night together, because it was none of her business. She had a job to do. End of story.

Time was running out, and she could only hope this candidate turned out better than yesterdays. One by one, the kids strolled into the kitchen, Melanie awkwardly carrying Sandy on one hip while trying to keep her injured wrist from getting bumped.

"Good morning, kids. You're all on the same schedule this morning. That helps."

"Good morning, Miss April," they answered in unison.

"Your breakfast is ready. Here, let me take Sandy, and I'll feed her." She reached for the little girl who lifted her arms up, ready to be carried. April buckled her in her seat and sat down to feed her. Rufus had followed the kids into the kitchen, sitting close by, hoping for food to drop on the floor. It was all extremely homey and comfortable.

Sandy didn't seem to be hungry this morning, so rushing her was useless. "You still full after last night, honey?" She brushed back the blonde curls from Sandy's face.

"Why do you ask her questions you know she won't answer?" Bryan asked.

"Because I believe she understands, and one of these times, she's going to answer me."

"If you say so. Seems silly to me." Bryan went back to filling his face, bite after bite, as though he hadn't eaten in days. Endless pit.

"Bryan and Melanie, can you keep an eye on Sandy while I jump in the shower?"

"Sure. And I promise not to take my eyes off her this time. No more mistakes, not like last time." Bryan was nine going on fifteen, the weight of the world on his shoulders.

"Honey, you're not to blame. There was no way to know Sandy would get into Melanie's crayons when you were in the bathroom. Don't take it too hard, kiddo." Bryan had decided he was the man of the family, and he took his responsibility seriously most of the time. April would prefer him to just be a boy and enjoy his childhood. She hated that he felt responsible for something that could be termed as nothing more than an accident. Where there are kids, there are accidents.

The kids April oversaw had gotten into trouble hundreds of times, and she'd done everything she could to keep that from happening. It had just never seemed to be enough. She understood how it felt to be blamed for something out of her control. It was important for Bryan not to blame himself.

"But Mr. Garrett was so mad, and it ruined our night. I just can't help but feel responsible." Bryan let out a sigh.

"Honey, Mr. Garrett was upset because he's not used to children and the chaos that comes with them. He's still getting used to the change. For him, it's like going swimming for the first time and jumping in the deep end of the pool."

"That makes sense." Bryan shrugged.

"Besides, it's in the past. We had a nice dinner last night, and all is back to normal. Families have ups and downs. It goes with the territory."

"It was fun last night," Melanie piped up to put in her two cents.

April hesitated to head for the shower. It was one thing to act like she wasn't worried for Bryan's sake, quite another not to be worried. This would be one of those in and out, five-minute showers. No more luxury for her, no matter how hard it was to turn off the water with the massage jets blasting hot streams across her shoulder.

She barely had time to get dressed and fix her hair before the doorbell rang. April opened the door to meet the woman who had been highly recommended by the new agency.

"Hi, come on in. I'm April St. James."

"Hi, thank you. I am Corinne Carruthers." The woman entered, glancing around the place. "This is an amazing apartment. It's unlike anything I've seen here in the city. What does Mr. Bradley do?"

"He's a partner at Bradley & West, a law firm here in the city."

"Must be a successful attorney to have a place as nice as this. Where are the children? I'd love to meet them. I want to hear all about them. I'll tell you about myself, and then we can compare notes and see where we stand."

A take-charge woman—exactly the type of person Garrett would prefer. April couldn't help but admire Corinne's open and direct attitude.

"Follow me." She led her to the kitchen. "This is Melanie, and she's seven." She placed a hand on her shoulder. "And that's Bryan, who's nine." She pointed in his direction. "They start school next Wednesday. Mr. Bradley is enrolling them here. They are both excellent students."

"It's nice to meet you, kids. My name is Corinne. I also loved school and did well. I promise I'll help you in any way I can if I end up working as your nanny."

Bryan grimaced. "I'm a straight-A student, so there's not much I don't figure out on my own. But thanks."

Melanie shot him a look of disbelief. "Yeah, right. You're just trying to get on the babysitter's good side."

"Am not. You don't know anything about me and my schoolwork. Mind your own business." Bryan's chin rose an inch.

"I know you got a C on one of your papers last year because Mom had to sign a note."

Bryan raised the corner of his lip and mocked Melanie.

"That's not a nice gesture, young man. I would hate it for anyone to do that to you. It's disrespectful." Corinne took charge, and April didn't mind at all. It was refreshing to see the woman in action, her approach to correction the same as April's. Talk to the kids and explain things. Most of the time, that's all that was needed.

"I guess." He shrugged. "Sorry, sis," he added as an afterthought.

This woman's skills at diverting issues between the children were remarkable. Not only had she stopped a back-and-forth battle instantly, but she'd managed to add in a lesson and produce an apology. April was practically sold by the time they left the kitchen.

There had to be something wrong with this woman, or could it be that she was just lucky enough to have finally found the perfect candidate. Other than the fact she was young and attractive, which shouldn't matter. The rest of the interview continued exactly as expected, and they sat down to discuss the specific terms to work out hours and the schedules.

"I've spoken with Garrett, and he's agreed to give you off Wednesdays and Sundays, but otherwise, you would be expected to be here full-time. He's planning on buying a bigger place, one where the children will each have their own room, and of course, there will be one for you. Until then, there's not enough room here. He's hoping you can arrive by six and stay until after the children are in bed and he's home." April tried not to let her excitement run away with her.

"That's not a schedule I can work with. I'm available Monday through Friday from seven to six. I consider this a regular job, and I take it seriously, but it's not my entire life. I can be everything he's looking for, but on my terms when it comes to scheduling. I think what I'm offering is more than reasonable. The choice is up to the both of you." And there was the catch. April should have known something wouldn't line up.

"I see. I'm afraid this won't work then. He was quite specific about wanting a live-in person, at least after he finds a new place. You see, he just gained guardianship of the children, and he's not all that accustomed to raising kids and the demands that may occur. I think he prefers to have somebody else on hand to handle things." Garrett was capable, he just didn't trust his own judgment. In time, it would happen.

"I'm sorry. I'm sure it must be difficult for him. He needs to trust his instincts." Corinne spoke with the same wisdom April tried to impart to Garrett.

"That's what I've been trying to tell him, but he doesn't consider himself a natural. If you change your mind, please be sure to call me. I think you'd be perfect for the job if we could work this out." She hated to let the woman leave, but there was no choice.

"The problem is, at six, I head over to the nursing center and spend time with my mother. And as much as I think this job also sounds perfect, my mother and her failing health are more important to me. I really am sorry."

Another *almost-perfect* candidate. What a letdown.

Corinne left, and April couldn't help the disappointment washing over her. She didn't want to leave Garrett in a lurch, and she wanted what was best for the children, but she'd already paid for the semester at college. She simply couldn't stay. But no nanny meant no bonus, and she'd have to find a part-time job.

April went to check on the kids in the kitchen.

"Did she leave?" Melanie asked.

"Yes. She can't work the hours Garrett's asking for. I'm sorry it won't work out."

"That stinks. I like her the most out of everyone we've met." Melanie shrugged.

"Me, too," Bryan added.

Maybe April should talk to Garrett about the hours, get him to agree to a different game plan. Corinne seemed too good to let walk away without trying harder.

Sandy wandered into the kitchen and tugged at her shirt.

"You hungry now, sweetie?" April picked her up.

Sandy nodded her head.

"How about a peanut butter and jelly sandwich?" She nodded again, but then April already knew it was one of her favorites. She handed Sandy the sandwich and poured her some milk in her sippy cup.

The doorbell buzzed, surprising April. She wasn't expecting anyone else.

She glanced through the peephole, shocked to see Brooke standing there. The woman wasn't high on April's list of people to deal with today.

"Come in, Brooke. What can I do for you?"

Brooke sailed in as if she owned the place. "Garrett asked me to stop in and pick up a file he left here. I grabbed the mail from downstairs while I was at it."

"Here, I can take those and see that he gets them." She held out her hand, but Brooke ignored the gesture.

"That's okay, I'll leave them on his desk. That is what he prefers." Her message was clear. She'd done this before, and it was a routine. Being face-to-face with Brooke knowing she and Garrett had spent the night together recently made her presence all that much worse.

April's stomach clenched as she tried not to picture them together. The woman's cool haughtiness was a look April could never achieve.

"Must be nice to have you to run errands for him. I can't imagine why he didn't come to get the file himself." Jealousy prompted the snotty retort, but she didn't regret it.

Brooke's eyes narrowed. "He's busy at the office still trying to clean up the mess from the other day that happened because of you and the kids. He's stressed out, and I'm trying to help him any way I can to get through this." Her razor-sharp voice delivered the dig.

I just bet you are. "Yes. He said there were some things going on at the office. I'd hoped he'd work it out." April tried to be nice, not wanting to get into an argument with Garrett's assistant.

"Work it out? Losing a client millions of dollars doesn't get worked out easily. But you wouldn't understand. It's a good thing you're leaving this weekend and the kids will be starting boarding school next week. I'm not sure the firm's bottom line can take Garrett being distracted much longer."

April blanched.

Millions of dollars. Ouch. She understood his stress now more than ever. But boarding school? Next week. It wasn't possible.

Garrett had told her he had to think about his options but hadn't mentioned having made any decisions. There was no way he would lie to her. "There must be some mistake. Garrett said nothing about boarding school."

"There's no mistake. We even found a daycare for Sandy. As soon as we have everything worked out, the only thing he'll need is a part-time nanny and cleaning lady. I spent all night helping him work through this, trust me. I know what's best for Garrett."

April just bet she was helping him. The question was, doing what? "I don't believe you."

Brooke eyed the pack of mail in her hands, a sudden evil grin on her face. "The school called me last night, but here's your proof. See for yourself." Brooke handed her a large manila envelope addressed to Garrett. The return address was stamped Livingston Boarding School in Connecticut.

He hadn't even bothered to try to keep the kids close by. *How could he*? April could feel the tension rising as she tried to assimilate this new piece of information.

Brooke dropped the rest of the mail on his desk, picked up a file, and with one last grin, sashayed out of the office and out of the suite without so much as a word.

April glanced down at the envelope she held, still unable to believe it was true. Maybe Garrett had just inquired about boarding school. She'd known he was getting information. Yes. That's all this was. Information about the school. Brooke was wrong. She trusted Garrett, and he wouldn't do this. He wouldn't have lied.

She dropped the envelope on his desk and started down the hall. *Open it*. After a few seconds hesitation, she turned and headed back into his office. April picked up the letter opener and slit the end before she could change her mind.

It was just information on the school. Who cared if she read it? It wasn't private. If it was the acceptance letter like Brooke indicated, then that was entirely different, but it didn't change the fact she wanted the truth.

Dear Mr. Garrett Bradley,

We are pleased to inform you that Melanie and Bryan Williams have been accepted into the Livingston Boarding School beginning the Wednesday after Labor Day. We look forward to getting to know you and the children as they grow and learn. Enclosed is a list of what you need to provide for them to help make their adjustment to the dorms successful.

April scanned the document, still unable to believe what she was reading. Brooke had told the truth.

Garrett was a liar.

So much for trusting in him. So much for thinking he was on the right track and that she was making a difference. Clearly, his mind had been made up. Was he ever going to tell her the truth? Or was he just going to let her leave and believe he would rise to the challenge of parenthood?

Anger ripped through her like salt on a wound. She reached for her phone and dialed Maddison's number. She needed a voice of reason to help her calm down, not wanting the kids to see her like this. It was heartbreaking, and the thought of facing them knowing what she realized was in store, would tear her to pieces. April knew all too well what it felt like not to be wanted. How could she not fall to pieces in front of the kids?

Some kids attended boarding school as a choice and as a life experience, but this wasn't the case. If given a choice, these kids would never agree. This was about Garrett, and about what Garrett wanted for his life.

"Maddison, thank goodness you answered."

"What's wrong? You sound terrible." Just hearing her friend's voice helped rein in the emotional wall threatening to break.

"I am. You won't believe this, but I just found out Garrett's sending the kids to boarding school. He lied to me. He flat out told me yesterday he was still just considering it. This is beyond considering...I saw the acceptance letter."

"Calm down. I'm sorry. I know how much you care about those kids. But, April, it's just a job, honey. You needed to find somebody to take care of them. Do your job and come home. You've got to try to keep your personal feelings out of this. Think of it as one of your cases. I know you care about every one of the kids who cross your path, but you've always been able to distance yourself. Maybe taking this job was too much for you, with your background and all."

"It doesn't matter. What's done is done, and I can't change how I feel." April drew in a deep breath, trying to calm her racing heart.

"Then pick one of the candidates you've interviewed and hire them. Come home. It's time." Maddison was the voice of reason she needed to hear.

"Maybe you're right." She let out a heavy sigh. "I don't want to be here when he tells the children. I won't be able to stand by and watch him break their hearts." April fought back against the tears threatening to fall.

"Were any of the candidates viable options?"

"The one today was phenomenal. Other than the fact she's gorgeous and has to be done by six every night."

"What does gorgeous have to do with it?" Leave it to Maddison to zero in on the slip.

"I don't know. I shouldn't have said that." April didn't want to care about Garrett, but she did. Enough to make her jealous of Brooke, Corinne, and every other woman who gazed at him with appreciation in their eyes.

"Do you have feelings for Garrett?"

"No. Not like that. It's just, I like him. Liked him. Past tense," she lied. "Don't get me wrong. But I thought I was helping him, and maybe I've let it get in the way of a business deal. Things have become more personal. I thought we were friends. Until now, that is." It didn't matter what she was feeling, it wouldn't work. They were totally different people, not to mention he had Brooke.

"By the sounds of it, it's a good thing you're getting out of there. Call the woman back, make it work, get your bonus, and come home." Her friend had always been the voice of reason, and this time was no exception.

The only thing April didn't tell Maddy was that she'd hidden the envelope, hoping the spots would get filled and the children couldn't attend. It was petty, but if it slowed down the inevitable, or better still, stopped it, then it was worth tampering with his mail.

"Yes, you're right. And I know exactly what to do. Thanks, Maddy."

"See you this weekend, kiddo."

"Sure thing." *Or sooner.* April closed her eyes, trying to work out the details of what she needed to do. Corinne was the right person for the job, and Garrett would just need to adjust his hours. And if the kids were at boarding school, that would just leave Sandy to take care of, unless she was at daycare. It was all so confusing, but it would be between Garrett and Corinne. Her part in this would be over.

She dialed the woman's number. "Corinne, this is April St. James. We spoke this morning."

"Yes, April, of course, I remember you," Corinne reassured her.

"Do you still want the job?" April decided to get right to the point.

"But I thought you said—"

"I changed my mind. Mr. Bradley needs your services, and I think you're perfect for the job. The kids liked you and were disappointed when

I told them you wouldn't be coming back. If you want the job, it's yours. Monday through Friday from seven to six, just as you wanted." April rushed headlong into the offer. She was desperate for Corinne to agree.

"But I thought my schedule wouldn't work with his hours?"

"I'll take care of that part. I think under the circumstances Mr. Bradley will be more than glad to accept your terms. I, on the other hand, have one condition for this arrangement."

"Which is?" Corinne asked, her voice hesitant.

"You return to the apartment now and start immediately. Mr. Bradley will be home at six, so it's only a couple of hours today. I can go over some of the details you'll need to know and introduce you to Mr. Bradley." She held her breathe, waiting to hear Corinne's answer, praying she'd say yes.

"Wow, I don't know what to say. I enjoyed the kids and would love to take care of them. I accept. Thank you for considering me so highly." Corinne seemed genuinely pleased, and it made April feel a whole lot better. She had accomplished everything she'd been hired to do. The kids had a nanny they liked, and April trusted her. Garrett was the one not getting what he wanted, but tough. He could figure out the rest on his own.

"You're welcome. See you shortly. I'll let the kids know you're coming." And let them know she was leaving. That would be the hard part.

"April, is everything all right? You sound different than you did this morning."

"I'm fine. Or I will be. I just need to get back to Hallbrook. I start school soon and I'm nowhere near ready. Thank you for accepting the position."

"Okay. See you in a bit." Corinne hung up, and April let out a deep, cleansing breath.

Now for the text to Garrett before she lost the nerve.

"Hired new nanny. Starting immediately. Her hours are Monday through Friday 7 to 6 and off on weekends. Highly recommended by her agency and the kids like her a lot. Adjust your schedule, it's the best I can do."

She was surprised to get an almost immediate response.

"Great news. I will work with those hours if she comes with those high recommendations. I look forward to meeting her. Hope she can cook. You've spoiled us. See you tonight."

His response was amiable and accommodating, not at all what she'd expected.

"Hey, kids, good news." April dug deep to pull a smile from out of nowhere in order to make this right for the children.

"What's going on?" Melanie asked.

"Corinne's agreed to watch you guys. She'll be your new nanny."

"I wish you would stay, but I know you've got school." Bryan's dejected look was that of a young boy trying to be brave.

"You'll be in school just like us," Melanie added. "But why can't you go to school here? I don't want you to leave." Her voice had taken on a slight whine, tugging at April's heartstrings.

"I'm enrolled at Plymouth University, and my home is in Hallbrook. But remember, no matter where we are at school, we always need to do our best, right?" She wanted to encourage the children to put their best efforts forth in all that they did in life. It was a motto that had stood her in good stead throughout a not-so-happy childhood. "I asked Corinne to come back today because I've got so much to do to get ready for school. Since she's available, I figured it would be better this way. I can tell her what she needs to know, and I'm hoping the two of you will help her out with anything else she needs."

"When are you leaving?" Bryan asked.

"I've arranged for a shuttle service to get me to the airport later tonight. Corinne will be here at seven in the morning on weekdays to help you get breakfast and get ready for school. And then she'll take care of Sandy."

It was the easiest way April knew to avoid a scene. "But you two can call me anytime you want. Here, I'll give you both my number." She jotted the number down at the top of their notebooks. "And I've got something special for you." She handed them each a photograph from when they'd stopped at one of the photo booths on the street and taken pictures. Just silly pictures, but they were special to April.

"I still hate that you're leaving," Melanie said, a pout on her face.

Even Sandy seemed to sense what was going on and came to stand beside her, arms held up high. April picked up the little girl and hugged her tight.

"I should start packing, and Corinne will be here soon. I love all three of you. Don't ever forget that."

"We love you, too," both kids responded.

Melanie got down from her chair and hurried to April's side, giving her a big hug. Bryan was right behind her, and the four of them had a group hug that would leave an imprint on April's heart forever.

Chapter Eighteen

♥

APRIL'S MESSAGE ABOUT FINDING a woman to take care of the kids should have been met with relief, but that's not what he was feeling. Over the past two weeks, he'd gotten to know and appreciate April, and not just as a nanny.

From the moment he'd kissed her, he'd found himself wanting to spend more time with her, and now she was leaving. It was always the plan, and he understood she had to return to Hallbrook and start her classes, but he'd also thought maybe they could see each other.

Hallbrook wasn't that far away. But ever since he'd overreacted to the destruction of his penthouse, she'd been more on edge, and Garrett sensed she was pulling away, preparing for Sunday's departure.

It was up to him to convince her they needed to see each other again. The idea of her simply vanishing from his life was unsettling. Garrett scanned his key card and entered the penthouse, bracing himself for the chaos he'd come to expect. Instead, he found the exact opposite.

The older kids were sitting quietly at the table coloring. Sandy played nearby on the floor with her dolls. He could hear April from down the hall; presumably, she was talking to the new nanny.

"Hey, kids. Why the long faces?" They all looked up, not having noticed him before.

"Miss April's leaving," Melanie whined, her eyes tearing up. "We don't want her to leave."

"We all knew this was for two weeks. Sunday is still a few days away, and I'm sure we can find some fun stuff to do with her before then."

"No. She's leaving tonight," Bryan spoke up.

"What? Why?" That wasn't their deal. *Until you find a replacement.* And she'd found one.

She'd upheld her end of the bargain. It still didn't explain why she felt the need to rush off.

"She's got stuff to do," Bryan answered. "That lady from your office came, and I think it made her mad."

"Brooke?" That made even less sense. He'd sent his secretary to pick up a file, not to harass April. He shook his head. Understanding women would take a lifetime.

"Let me talk to her and find out what's going on. Maybe there's a way to convince her to stay a few more days." Garrett was surprised how much the knowledge she was leaving tonight made him feel as though he was losing someone special. He walked down the hall, following the sound of her voice.

"The girls are in here together, and Bryan has his own room." April was explaining the setup as he joined them.

"Hey there. I left a bit early, hoping to get more of a chance to talk with you." He directed his comment to the new nanny, extending his hand in welcome, and noting the sudden tension in April. "I'm Garrett Bradley." The new nanny was an attractive young woman in her mid-twenties, but Garrett only had eyes for April. Her sudden departure was concerning.

"Hi. I'm Corinne Carruthers." She shook his hand. "I love your place. It's so upscale designer." Her enthusiasm was appreciated considering once upon a time, he used to consider the place perfection.

"Thank you. The kids add a lived-in touch, but the core of the place still exists, at least for the time being." He grinned, realizing the lived-in look was growing on him. It felt...homey.

"Well, I'll try to keep it intact for you." Corinne winked, the more personal gesture startling him. With April leaving, he needed this woman to help with the kids, but if she imagined he was part of the package, she needed to guess again.

"I appreciate that. It sounds as though April's providing you with all the details you'll need. She says you come highly recommended. We appreciate your agreeing to start work on such short notice." He kept his tone businesslike, making sure they were on the same page.

"It's hard to pass up an opportunity such as this one." Corinne's reply left him unsettled, knowing it was a done deal. The idea of April leaving hit him hard.

"April, the kids tell me you're leaving tonight. Is that true? I thought you were staying until Sunday. I had plans for this weekend." He didn't, but he would make some if she stayed.

"We agreed I'd stay until I found someone, and with Corinne here tomorrow, you don't need two of us. The longer I stay, the harder it will be on the kids when I leave. Besides, I need to get ready for school."

It sounded like a well-rehearsed line. She was withdrawn, more reserved, almost as if she'd already checked out mentally. "I see. You know best when it comes to the kids." Bryan was right, April intended to leave tonight. He'd have to wait until later when they were alone if he had any hope of understanding the cold briskness he heard in her voice. It was one thing to notice she was pulling away, but this...this was something else entirely.

April took a step toward the door. "Now, if you'll excuse me, I'll let you two work out any remaining details. Corinne must leave every night on time to visit her mother in the nursing home, so you can't keep her here late. I'll be in my room packing. Thank you again, Corinne. You're a lifesaver. Don't forget, you can call me if you need to know anything." The two women hugged, and April headed down the hall to his room.

"If you'll follow me to my office, we can finish our discussion there."

"Sounds great." Corinne followed him into his office, and within ten minutes, they'd finalized the terms and hours. Corinne was quick to exit promptly at six, promising to return at seven tomorrow morning.

Garrett thumbed through the mail Brooke must have picked up from downstairs and left for him. There was nothing but junk and a statement from the bank he'd review later. Pulling open the top drawer to toss the letter in, he spotted the boarding school brochure. He unfolded it, reading over the information yet again. The school offered everything the kids would need, and it would be an amazing experience if the brochure was to be believed.

The question was, would the kids agree? The news of coming to New York hadn't gone over well, and Garrett sensed they would embrace boarding school with even less enthusiasm. He slid the brochure back in the drawer and closed it. Time to check on the kids, and with any luck, find out what was going on with April.

"Who wants pizza for dinner? I can have it delivered." Their long faces reflected how he was feeling, but it was worth a shot to try and cheer the group up.

"I do," the kids answered at the same time. Sandy nodded and smiled.

He headed down the hall to his room and knocked on the slightly open door before entering. April glanced at him, quickly looking back down as she folded the shirt she was packing. The blue dress hanging on the closest door brought back memories of Sunday and the special day they'd shared. Especially the kiss. He couldn't let her leave tonight.

"What time's your flight? We were going to order pizza, and we're hoping you'd be able to join us." Garrett wanted to ease into the conversation.

If there was anything he'd learned, slow and easy worked better when it involved April, versus cut and dried like at the office. There was no room for bulldozing this conversation.

"I'm sorry, I can't. It's at nine-fifteen. I need to be there two hours early." April's voice was still crisp, her actions as she folded the clothes jerky. Agitated.

"I could charter the helicopter for you tomorrow," Garrett offered, hoping to entice her. He could practically have her home in the same amount of time she'd wait at the airport.

"No, thanks. I've already got a flight booked."

He was failing miserably at trying to draw her out and find out what was going on. "Can I take you there?"

"That would be harder on the kids. It's okay. When in New York, I'll be a New Yorker and hail a cab."

He reached out for her hand, stopping her from the folding process. "What's going on?" Subtle wasn't getting him anywhere, and he was getting desperate.

She pulled her hand back and shook her head. "Nothing. I told you, it's time to go home."

"Can I see you again?"

April stopped and stared at him, confusion clouding her eyes. "I don't think that's a good idea."

The only thing left was to be direct and to bulldoze through the issues. "Why not? We've had fun together. And then there was the kiss. I want to explore the attraction I think we're both feeling."

"You've got your hands full already, and it would never work out, so there's no sense exploring anything. We are two very different people. End of story."

"What's wrong?" He took a step closer, lifting her chin to force her to make eye contact.

April took a step back. "Nothing. Just let me go home. It's where I need to be."

Garrett wasn't going to beg. Women were impossible to understand at times, and this was one of them. "Okay. I need to order pizza. I'm hoping to cheer them up." Garrett hated to leave things this way, but she wasn't giving him much choice. If she wasn't interested in pursuing what was between them, it was time to retreat. He wasn't an expert on relationships, but the last time he checked, it took two people.

Monday morning took forever, and when Corinne arrived, Garrett was relieved to head for the office. It wasn't that the kids had done anything wrong, it was simply without April's guidance and peace-keeping abilities, finding things to do, and keeping Bryan and Melanie from their constant bickering wasn't easy. Her abrupt departure and stiff hug in front of the kids left him unsettled. As for the kids, they missed her, plain and simple, and nothing he did, it seemed, made it better. He missed her as much as they did, although he made a point of trying not to show it.

By Wednesday, he was exhausted. Work all day. Kids all night. Corinne was working out fine during the day, but it left him zero time for himself after she left. His appreciation for working parents rose a thousand percent.

Garrett pressed the intercom button. "Brooke, can you get me a printout on the Aygen Oil and

Compton Energy Sources financial statements for the past three years please?"

"I'll get right on it. Anything special I'm after?" "No. But I've got a possible angle to the price gouging I want to check out." Maybe he had exhaustion to thank for the insight, but after the kids had gone to bed and he had a chance to breathe in the golden sound of silence, the idea had come out of nowhere.

If he was right, it was a powerplay between oil conglomerates—one that would soon right itself. Baden was trying to take advantage of Hamilton, and Garrett wasn't about to let it happen. Oil prices would surge again, and Baden would be right back in the game. They needed Hamilton's company.

Brooke entered his office and dropped off the printouts.

"Thanks, that will be all." He was trying hard to reestablish the office boundaries that needed to be in place. Brooke seemed as though she wanted to say something, but thankfully, she turned and left. *Message received, but not welcome.*

Garrett perused the files, and with each passing hour, he grew more and more certain he was right.

He pushed the button for Jim's office, wanting his opinion before he made the call to Mr. Hamilton. "Jim, can I see you a minute? I've got something I want you to hear. Get a second opinion."

"I'll be right there." True to his word, Jim walked in minutes later. "What's up?"

"The Baden-Hamilton merger. I think I know what's going on, and it isn't good." Garrett filled his partner in on his findings, citing all the reasons that proved his theory.

"Excellent research. But what are you going to do? Doesn't Hamilton lose either way?" Jim asked, sitting back in his chair as he pondered the information.

"Only if the price doesn't come back up soon. But I believe it will. This is just temporary. I want to call Baden's bluff." To wait out this price-fixing war was risky, but not to wait would ruin his client, something Garrett couldn't accept.

"Hmmm. Great idea, and it might even work." Jim nodded. "I trusted you'd figure something out. You come out looking like a hero if you're right. If you're wrong, it could be the complete downfall of Bradley & West."

"I'm right, and you know it. I know what it means to our business and to your family, but I have no choice—I need to help Mr. Hamilton. I'm hoping you'll support my decision."

"I get it. You feel responsible for his losses. As far as I'm concerned, do what you need to do. I'll support your decision. We started this business together, and together we can weather anything."

"Thanks, Jim. You won't be sorry." Jim rose. "I can only hope you're right." He let out a deep breath and left.

Next up, the call to Mr. Hamilton himself. Getting him to agree would be harder. Jim trusted him, Mr. Hamilton...not so much at the moment.

By the time he hung up the phone, he was mentally drained. In the end, Mr. Hamilton had finally succumbed and agreed to the plan. Garrett sat back and stretched, giving himself a few minutes to regroup before drawing up the documents for a powerplay against Baden Enterprises.

It took him an hour to finalize the document. He checked it over himself, not wanting anyone, not even Brooke to know what he was doing. He was counting on a knee-jerk reaction from Baden.

Garrett headed for Jim's office and knowing he didn't have a client in with him, entered without knocking. He crossed the room to stand in front of the window. "It's done. Mr. Hamilton was on board after a bit of convincing. Now we wait."

"Stock markets open in the morning, but we should start to see news updates before that. Maybe get wind of what's in store."

"Yes. Let's just hope I'm right." He glanced at his watch. Five-fifteen. He needed to leave soon. He'd need every bit of the ride home to mentally switch gears.

"What else is going on? How's it working out with Corinne and the kids? You've been in a funk lately, and I can't help thinking it's gotten worse since April left."

"If I am, it's because the kids aren't happy, and I don't know what to do about it. School starts next week, but they are bored. The house is too small. The realtor called and still doesn't have anything that matches what we need, and the kids miss

April." He stared out across the expanse of the city, trying to make sense of the chaos in his life.

"By the looks of it, you're missing April just as much as they are, if not more. You may have single- handedly saved the Baden-Hamilton deal and Hamilton, and you should be ecstatic. Instead, you're in my office looking as though you lost your best friend. And I'm sitting right here, so it must be her." Jim leaned back in his chair and chuckled.

"Of course, I miss her. She was nice, and we had fun together. But she made it clear she's not interested in anything else."

"And why is that?" Jim persisted.

"Because we are two different people. Very different. Her words. Not mine." Although she hadn't been far off the mark. They were different, but he'd been willing to put aside some of those differences to be with her. She clearly wasn't interested in doing the same.

"She has a point. You're city. She's country. You never wanted children, but you have three. She adores children and has none. I'm sure would love kids of her own one day. She'll make a wonderful mother."

"What's your point?" Garrett frowned.

"The point is, the differences are fixable. I think you love her, and you're refusing to see the truth." He'd been thinking the same thing, the fixable part anyway.

But love? He wasn't there yet, or at least he didn't think he was. Jim might be closer to the truth than he wanted to admit. If it was true though, it was better that he stay away. It would only end in disaster. "I'm not cut out for love and marriage. You know that."

"You are not your father, and the two of you aren't your parents. Couples can get married and love one another. The kids aren't the problem between you and April. They are the solution."

Jim was crazy.

Wasn't he? "Since you're into psychoanalysis, what do you suggest I do?"

"Labor Day weekend is coming up, and the office is closed on Monday. Take the kids home for the long weekend. Let them visit friends and be back on home turf. See what happens. Get your life in order. And while you're there, talk to April. Tell her how you feel. Or better yet, show her." Jim stood.

"I'll think about it." *Show her*. He might just have to do that.

Chapter Nineteen

♥

A PRIL ARRIVED AT THE Labor Day festival early, her promise to deliver the cookies she'd baked all night to the Hallbrook volunteer rescue squad booth driving her from bed this morning at four a.m. Her fingers were stained with red and blue from the icing she'd used to color the flags this morning.

When she'd run into Captain James and his wife, the pair had been quick to ask for her help, and April, with too much time on her hands and little to do, had been quick to agree. The past week had gone by slowly without the kids, and she welcomed the chance to do something helpful.

The rescue squad was always short on funds but in high demand.

The annual craft festival was the perfect way to attract people to the area. Garrett's mother normally coordinated the food and craft booths, but this year the task had fallen to Mary Ellen Hutchins. Mary Ellen had done an excellent job taking over, but she'd made a few changes. Now, the food and craft booths were in different areas.

April spotted a couple of young girls about Melanie's age doing cartwheels, and one girl hanging off to the side to watch, a cast on her wrist. *Melanie?*

She squinted to get a better view. Melanie was in New York. Her brain was playing tricks on her. She took a few steps closer.

"Miss April!" the girl squealed and ran toward her.

April's eyes misted over. *Melanie.* But what was she doing here? April wrapped her arms around the girl and hugged her close, dropping a kiss on her head.

"What are you doing here? And where are Garrett and the others?"

Melanie looked up and smiled. "I'm so glad to see you. Mr. Garrett brought us here 'cause we were homesick. And we wanted to see you."

"How's your arm?"

"It stinks. I'm stuck with the cast and can't do lots of things. And it itches." Melanie held up her arm for April to see. "But I got lots of people to sign it."

"That's cool. So where is Garrett?" April searched the crowd, trying to spot him. She couldn't believe they were all there. It was sweet of Garrett to bring them back, but she worried it would make it harder for them to leave again. Another rookie mistake on his part, but he'd learn.

"He took Sandy to get her face painted, and I get to play with Lacey and Teresa, a couple of friends from school. Bryan's off with his friends doing stupid boy stuff. Last I saw him, they were playing down by the creek."

"It's so good to see you, sweetie. I miss all three of you."

"Do you miss Garrett, too?"

"Of course, but shouldn't it be Mr. Garrett to you? We discussed the whole respect thing once before." She did miss Garrett, but the last thing she wanted to do was discuss it with a seven-year-old, especially one who might run back and repeat everything to the man himself.

"No. Garrett told us it was too formal for our special relationship." She shrugged.

Wow. Some things must have seriously changed since she'd left. "I've got to drop off these cookies. I'll find you when I'm done."

"Yay. Can I have one? I miss your cookies," Melanie begged, a pleading look in her eyes that April could never resist.

"Yes. I'll make a donation for you. How's that sound?"

Melanie took a bite. "*Hmmm.* I love these. Miss Corinne's cooking is okay, but I love yours best."

"Thank you. Corinne will get better as she learns what you enjoy." April left the girls playing and headed for the booth, keeping an eye out for Garrett. Melanie hadn't mentioned anything about boarding school and didn't seem concerned about leaving her friends. Garrett must not have broken the news to them yet. He was running out of time, and April wouldn't want to be in his shoes when he made it known.

She approached the booth. "Here's my cookies. Ten dozen sugar cookie flags, just as I promised."

"They look delicious. Bless your heart for making these." The captain took the load of stacked boxes from her, placed one on the table and the rest on a spare table at the back of the booth.

"It was fun. There's ten dozen minus one." April dug in her purse for some money. "Here's a dollar. I bumped into Melanie Williams and let her have the first one."

"These will sell fast. They almost look too good to eat, except I've tasted your cookies, and saying no isn't an option." Captain James chuckled.

"Thank you. I'm glad you love them." She grinned. "I'm going to walk around, but I'll try to stop back by later." April waved and wandered off in search of some great finds at the craft booths. Almost an hour passed, and she was ready to leave, but she refused to go home without seeing Sandy and Bryan. She followed the row of booths, going around the final one, closest to the creek.

Several blankets were laid out for family picnics, the kids running around nearby. She spotted Bryan, Melanie, and Sandy. Garrett was nowhere in sight. She frowned.

"Looking for someone?" Garrett's deep, gravelly voice asked from behind.

"Yes. No. Why aren't you with the kids?" She hadn't meant it to sound like a reprimand, but she was embarrassed to be caught peering around the corner like a stalker.

"I spotted you coming this way and wanted to talk to you. I would have found you earlier, but I've got my hands full with the kids." That was a nice way of putting her in her place.

"Sorry, I didn't mean it that way." April felt awful. He was at the festival with the kids in Hallbrook, and all she could do was insult the man. The truth was she was thrilled to see Garrett again and didn't want to spoil the moment. After she'd left New York, she'd wished a million times she'd confronted him about the boarding school, even though she realized it was none of her business. What she thought was right for others, didn't make it so.

"Yes, you did. Your vote of confidence in my parenting skills has never been flattering." He grinned and shook his head. "Don't dare to deny it."

"We both know your parenting skills measured a zero on your first night. Burnt spaghetti was on the menu if my memory is right?" She shook her head, fighting back the laughter.

"Maybe, but I'm getting better at it."

"I'd have to see it to believe it." It sounded great, and she wanted it to be true. He was here at the festival with the kids, which was definitely a step in the right direction. She couldn't help but wonder how it had all come about and though tempted to ask, bit back the question.

"Then stick around." Garrett winked.

"I might just do that. For the kids."

"I expected nothing less, but I can hope you'll stick around for me also."

Was he flirting with her? April remembered the kiss. And Brooke. "So is Brooke with you?" Not what she wanted to ask.

"Why would she be with me? I'm not working."

His eyes narrowed in confusion.

"You two are together, right? In and out of the office." She hated herself for going down that road, but she couldn't resist. After a week of torturing herself about it, she wanted the truth.

"Just in the office. I don't mix business and personal. Whatever gave you that idea?" Garrett seemed perplexed, and his answer sounded genuine. Hope surged, but she quickly tamped it down.

"Doesn't matter. Something Brooke said, maybe I misunderstood." But she hadn't misunderstood the fact they'd spent the night together. So, what if he did his mixing at the office, it was still mixing. She should feel sorry for Brooke but couldn't quite bring herself to go that far. If the woman was pinning after Garrett, she was hanging her heart and her hopes on the wrong man, if Garrett was to be believed.

And therein lay the problem. He'd lied to her about boarding school, so why wouldn't he lie about having a relationship with Brooke? When would she quit trying to make him into something he wasn't?

Maybe when I fall out of love with him.

Bryan spotted her and came over. "Hey, Miss April. It's cool to see you again."

"Oh, come here. You're not too old to hug me in public, young man. You can tell your friends I made you do it." She pulled him into a bear hug.

He glanced around before hugging her back. "That would work."

She wrapped her arm around his shoulders, and they headed for the blanket. Sandy looked up from her doll, her baby blues lit with pleasure when they landed on April. She stood and flung herself forward as April scooped her up and hugged her tightly.

"Hey, baby girl." She kissed her on the cheek and ran her hand over her pigtails. "I adore your braids and bows. Did Melanie fix them for you?"

Sandy shook her head and pointed at Garrett. April was shocked, looking at him for confirmation.

"It's true. Melanie taught me how to do it. It's quite easy once you get the hang of it." He shrugged as if it was no big deal. But Garrett Bradley braiding Sandy's hair was a huge deal. An incredibly jumbo-sized deal.

"I'm surprised. Impressed, but surprised.' She glanced down at the blanket, noting several bags full of purchases. "Looks as if you're planning to live off festival food for the next few weeks."

"He bought—"

"Food." Melanie had started to speak, but Garrett cut her off. "Different things that looked good."

Melanie frowned but didn't say another word.

Bryan grinned, the whole cat and cream scenario coming to mind.

"Would you care to join us?" Garrett asked, indicating for her to sit.

"I'd love that. I just need to run and check on something. I'll be right back." April wanted to get the kids some of her cookies before they sold out, and maybe even one or two for the grown-up kid. He'd earned at least two with the pigtails.

Back at the booth, she scanned the table. "Where are the cookies I brought? I need to buy a few for some friends of mine."

Captain James shook his head and laughed.

"They're gone."

"What do you mean gone? Ten dozen cookies sold in under an hour?" It wasn't possible. Captain James was always one for a joke or two, and this was a huge one.

"Yes. Some guy bought the lot of them."

"Quit teasing. There's no way."

"Honest. Scout's honor." He crossed his heart.

April frowned. "Well, that stinks."

The captain laughed. "Not the way I see it. He paid double for the lot of them. I told you they would sell quickly once word got out you baked them."

"What does that have to do with it? How did he know?"

"Because the man asked which cookies you made and bought them all." Captain James turned away to assist another customer, and April left.

They spent the rest of the afternoon together, and April couldn't remember a time when she'd been so carefree and relaxed. She steered clear of the whole boarding school issue, preferring to focus on making memories. April couldn't help but admire Garrett's newfound ability to manage the kids, enough that she realized she was jealous of the bond they all now seemed to share.

They were growing into a family. *One that didn't include her.*

Chapter Twenty

♥

GARRETT HAD COME TO town for the holiday weekend but running into April yesterday solidified some of the things he'd previously been unwilling to identify. He realized Jim's advice had been rock solid.

First and foremost, he loved the kids.

Somehow over the past weeks, they'd edged their way into his heart to a point his life was richer for having them in it.

Yesterday, he'd truly been a part of a family, the kids looking to him for everything. His mother had known all along when she chose him as their guardian that he needed them. She hadn't known she would die, but she had known once Garrett met the children, they would eventually wrap themselves around his heart and squeeze life in the cold depths where previously only numbers and business could reside.

Second, he loved April.

Not as a nanny for his children, but as a woman.

It was the only explanation for why his heart did a somersault the minute Melanie had mentioned seeing her at the festival. He'd meant to call her over the weekend but hadn't gotten up the nerve.

Instead, he'd played with the kids, all while keeping watch for April out of the corner of his eye, practicing what he should say. And of course, he'd bought her cookies. Every last one of them to the tune of $250. Melanie had almost spilled the beans, or the cookies, in this case. Garrett inwardly laughed, wondering what she would say if she knew the truth.

He didn't want to send the wrong message. He wanted more than her cooking, or her housekeeping, or childcare services. Not that he didn't love those qualities about her, but it was more than that. Proving it to her after he'd just bought ten dozen of her cookies would be next to impossible.

The third thing he'd realized was that the kids were happier right here in Hallbrook. More so than they'd ever been in the city. This was their home. And even Rufus was a part of that.

Seeing them run around and play with their friends, the sound of their carefree laughter touching a place deep in his heart. It's not that they were unhappy in the city, but here, they were filled with joy. A joy that he didn't remember having as a child their age. These kids had lost their parents and their new grams, and they still managed to find happiness. There was a lesson in their childlike innocence, and one he didn't want to close his eyes too.

The answer hit him like a bolt of lightning illuminated in the sky. They needed to move back to Hallbrook.

He called Jim to run a couple of ideas past him, hoping he'd agree and was ready for the challenge of the partnership taking on a third person. Garrett spent the night working out the details after his partner agreed to the plan whole-heartedly. Of course, Jim was also convinced Garrett needed to patch things up with April.

Garrett had been quick to point out he was doing it for the kids, not bothering to mention they'd run into her at the festival and that he was about to do just that. Some things were better left between him and April. She was the missing piece in his life, and he wouldn't let her walk away without a fight.

He waited for the kids to wake up, his renewed spirit and energy toward life something he hadn't felt in a long time. Not even when oil prices had shot up last Thursday, fully recovering from the secret dealings of the oil conglomerates, had he felt this good.

By the time all three were up and wanting breakfast, Garrett had ironed out the tiniest of details and managed to fix breakfast. Eggs and sausage and toast. And other than the toast being a little dark, he'd done a fair job. He even poured the juice in their glasses, remembering how April used to do that for the kids.

"Good morning. Now that everyone is at the table, it's time we had a family discussion."

"Morning," Bryan mumbled, rubbing the sleep from his eyes.

"Morning. What are we going to talk about?"

Melanie covered her mouth as she yawned.

Sandy crossed the kitchen to his side. "Morning, Daddy."

Words he'd never grow tired of hearing. It was the first time she'd spoken in front of the others, reserving her use of words for him alone at night when he tucked her in. He glanced at the other kids to see how they would react to her use of the word daddy.

They stopped what they were doing and stared, then looked at each other. Bryan shrugged.

"Sorry, guys. I hope it doesn't upset you. She started saying it a couple of weeks ago."

"It's okay, I guess. I mean, you can have the job. I thought I wanted it, but after Melanie started begging for a bra and you had to buy her one, I decided the job wasn't for me. I'll stick to hanging with my friends," Bryan said, a grimace on his face.

Garrett had to laugh. Melanie had insisted she'd needed a bra their first morning back in Hallbrook. It hadn't been one of their finer moments, but it had been one of the most hysterical. Luckily,

Sharon, the saleswoman at the small five and dime department store in Hallbrook had helped him decide which bra was suitable for a seven-year-old, even if she hadn't been able to keep from laughing while she did it.

Melanie turned red in the face. "It's none of your business anyway." She stuck her tongue out at Bryan.

"Melanie, that's enough." Garrett was quick to put out the fire, knowing what was in store if he didn't.

"So, what's the family discussion?" Bryan asked.

"One of the reasons I'm successful at work is that I always create a plan of action. And that's what I did last night. It starts with one simple question for you three. How would you feel about moving back to Hallbrook and living here? You'd start back to school on Wednesday with your friends."

"Really? You mean it?" Melanie jumped up and hugged him.

"I say awesome." Bryan nodded, his boyish grin back in place. "But what about New York and your job?"

"I've talked to Jim, and we've agreed that it's for the best. I'm going to put a satellite office here. Work from home and fly there when needed."

"What's a satellite office?" Melanie asked.

"It's when two offices are connected and operate as one from different locations." Garrett wasn't sure she understood, and he tried to think of another way to explain it.

"This is the best day. Thanks, Garrett." Bryan nodded.

"Thanks, Da—Garrett." Garrett's heart did a somersault. For one second, Melanie almost called him dad. One day it might happen, but for now, he was loving *Da-Garrett.*

"Since you're in agreement, here's the plan I worked out last night. I want to call it Operation April. I love her, and I'm almost positive you all do too. We need to prove to her we got this family thing figured out, and that we want her to be a part of the family not for what she can do for us, but for what we can do together as a family." The kids didn't even seem remotely shocked.

"We know that. We're not blind. But how do we get her to come back?" Bryan asked.

"Excellent question. I figure we've got enough cookies in the freezer to last a month, which gives us a month to get everything perfect, and then we invite her to dinner to show her what we can do. Maybe we'll even get lucky and see her in town, that way she doesn't forget us. And her cookies will help remind us of what's at stake.

We need to learn to cook and clean and get organized with your school- work and cleaning your rooms. I'm going to have the house remodeled to make it bigger so April can have her own quiet place to prepare her school lessons when she's teaching. What do you both think? Will it work? Are you in?" He'd never pictured himself negotiating and planning with children what could turn out to be the biggest deal of his life.

"Sure, it'll work. Girls love that kind of stuff." Bryan conspiratorial tones were as if the two of them were collaborating on a secret mission.

"They do, buddy. At least, that's what I'm hoping anyway."

"I think it's sweet. Of course, it'll work. She loves us," Melanie chimed in.

"She does at that. All we need to do is get everything done and then invite her over. To show her we want her, not need her. Deal?"

"Deal," Bryan and Melanie answered in unison.

"Deal," Sandy spoke up, making everyone laugh.

"Okay, then, while I try to find a sitter for Sandy while I'm working, can you two clean up the kitchen and watch her. I still know lots of people here, and I'm going to find someone local to help us out."

"Jessica might know someone," Bryan pipped out.

"Amazing idea." Garrett ruffled the boy's hair, and Bryan beamed under the praise.

Life was chaotic with the kids but in a good way. And they weren't the cause of issues between adults. Garrett realized that love could conquer all if two people were willing to work together and learn to compromise, and he looked forward to the chance to prove it to April.

Chapter Twenty-One

THREE WEEKS INTO CLASSES, April was overwhelmed with the workload. Between her class schedule at Plymouth University and her teacher's assistant position three times a week over in Conway, free time was a commodity as valuable as gold.

Now, more than ever, she was grateful for Garrett's offer and bonus, although she still felt guilty for cutting out early. Without the money from her time in New York, it would have been tough to handle her classes, the homework, and the internship, all while holding down a full-time job.

She hadn't heard from Garrett or the kids since the Labor Day festival, and she missed them. All of them. She'd reached for her phone at least a dozen times wanting to call but held back. The kids would be in school by now, and who knew if they were allowed cell phones in boarding school. As for Garrett, nothing had changed, and it was still better if she protected her heart, which meant no calling.

April was intent on treating herself after she found out she aced her morning exam, and her afternoon class had been canceled. She called Maddison, hoping she could meet her at Sally's, but her friend was working. That was the problem with being off in the afternoon. Everyone she knew had regular jobs and were either sleeping to work the third shift, or they were at work. After she parked, she crossed Main Street and entered the diner.

A young server approached her; one April didn't recognize. The girl sported purple hair and an earring in her eyebrow, which would be unforgettable by themselves, but the snake tattoo on her right arm was even more shocking. Christina—the girl's name tag identifying the newcomer. Sooner or later, April would get the scoop on how the girl had ended up working at the diner because news in town usually made its way around eventually.

"What can I get you?" the girl asked, neither a smile nor frown on her face.

"Peach pie à la mode." Sally's pie was the best in the county, and although not so hot on the sweet calorie counter, having it as an occasional treat wasn't so bad on the waistline. She'd jog a mile later to make up for it.

"Anything to drink?"

"Sure, a cup of coffee, please. With cream, no sugar."

The girl walked away without another word. She wasn't rude, just not what one expected here in Hallbrook.

April shrugged and glanced around, looking to see if she recognized anyone. Old Mr. Peterson sat in the corner with pie à la mode. The man had one of the largest dairy farms in the area and made some of the best ice cream, of which Sally bought and sold, but Mr. Peterson still came here to eat it. April wondered if he was sweet on the peach pie or Sally.

The bell on the door jingled, and Mrs. Jenkins entered. She glanced around as if looking for someone, and then shook her head. The elderly woman had manned the library for the past thirty-plus years, refusing to give up her position as head librarian. And she knew everyone in town. Her gaze returned to April, the older woman smiling as she crossed the diner and sat down to join her. Invited or otherwise.

"Don't see much of you lately. Glad you're finally finishing your schooling, young lady. I'm just waiting for someone, so don't worry, I'm not here to stay."

"It's fine. Maddison couldn't make it, so I'm on my own."

Christina delivered her pie. "Anything else?"

"No, thanks. Mrs. Jenkins, would you like something?"

"No, thank you. I'll order when my friend arrives." The server turned and left.

"That girl looks like trouble, mark my words. Don't know why Sally would think her granddaughter would fit in here."

The urge to defend Christina was strong. "She's unique and expressing her own identity. It doesn't make her trouble." She didn't have to know the girl to understand there was a story.

"Girl got sent here by her mother from the city because she couldn't handle her. That's what I hear anyway." Another example of a child who didn't seem to be coping well with life. Maybe she had no one to reach out to. It made April want to help her.

"Sally knows what she's doing. Hallbrook might be just the place for the girl. We have lots of country air to refresh a person's soul."

"You always did have a good head on your shoulders and a big heart. Do you ever stop in to see the Williams kids anymore? I know how close you got to them. My, my, that little Sandy is a charmer. And she's talking now. What a blessing."

April sighed. "She is? I hadn't heard. That's wonderful. And, no, I haven't seen them lately, not since the Labor Day festival. With my schedule, I just don't have time to travel to New York to see them." The idea had crossed her mind though, lots of times.

"Why would you go to New York to keep in touch when they're right here in Hallbrook? Didn't you know Garrett Bradley moved them all back here?"

What? Garrett and the kids were here? It wasn't possible. No one had said a word to her. "No, I didn't." April couldn't believe it. They were here. The kids. And Garrett. Things had changed more than she could have ever imagined.

"Oh, I kind of had the idea that you two were sweet on each other, nanny or not." Mrs. Jenkins was in information-seeking mode.

April shook her head. "No. I just worked for him."

Except for the kiss after his thank-you date.

"Sandy goes to preschool now, and Taylor Milner is watching her and the older kids after school. That's Frank and Mary Watkin's granddaughter. They are kind and generous people. Still work at the hardware store, even though their kids practically run the place. Mary says Taylor sings the praises of those kids and Garrett, too. Seems like that boy got his act together coming back to town and doing the right thing by those kids."

The woman didn't stop talking, and April didn't want her to stop. She wanted all the updates on Garrett and the kids.

"I don't like the boy Taylor's dating. Doesn't have much respect for his library books and getting them back on time. You know I don't forget anything, and if you can't respect a book, how can you respect your elders? Boy's got some maturing to do if you ask me." Mrs. Jenkins had always been a stickler for the rules when it involved her precious books.

"I'm sure you're right." And just like that, she was off on another topic. April still couldn't believe it. Garrett and the kids were right here in Hallbrook. They hadn't left after the festival, according to Mrs. Jenkins. This was the first she'd heard about it. Her school and work had kept her busy and out of circulation apparently.

The bell jingled again, and Mr. Hadley, the town's most eccentric octogenarian, walked in. Mrs. Jenkins looked up, her face softening a bit as she watched him approach. She stood. "There's my date. Late, but I'll forgive him if he treats me to lunch." She winked and turned to leave, taking the older man's arm as he escorted her to a booth.

April let out a long sigh. It was the sweetest thing to watch two people in love, especially at their age. She finished her pie and glanced at her watch. School would be letting out soon, and April was determined to see the kids, even if from a distance. She wasn't sure what Garrett's reaction would be if she dropped in unannounced. It rankled he hadn't even bothered to call her.

It didn't take her long to drive to the outskirts of town to the Bradley estate. She pulled off to the side of the road to wait for the school bus, anxiously trying to confirm everything she'd heard from Mrs. Jenkins.

Ten minutes later, her proof exited the bus in the form of Bryan and Melanie. The two kids paused, looked in both directions, and then crossed the street to the driveway before breaking into a run for the house. It was true. But the glimpse she'd gotten wasn't near enough for her to put the car in drive and ride away.

She let out a deep breath, gathered her courage, and turned into the driveway. The kids stopped to see who'd come to visit. Their shocked but joyful expressions as they recognized her car and ran toward her, filled her heart to overflowing. This was what she'd come for.

April exited the car and met them with open arms. "Look at you two. You've grown so much." She hugged them tightly, tears of joy filling her eyes.

"Miss April, you're here. You came. I knew you would." Melanie smiled, hugging her again.

"Shut up, Mel. You'll blow it all." Bryan's rude comment caught her by surprise.

"Will not," Melanie whined.

"Will too," Bryan insisted.

Just like old times. She shook her head, ready to step in and put a halt to it. "What's going on? And, Bryan, saying shut up is not nice." It felt like she'd come home.

Bryan frowned. "Sorry, Mel."

Wait. What? "Apology accepted." The two of them glanced at her and then back at each other. As if by magic, they shrugged and then hugged. There was something odd going on.

"Hey, you two. What's going? April..." Garrett's voice came from the front porch, and all three of them turned to face him.

"She just showed up. Isn't that awesome?" Bryan asked, grinning.

"It is. Would you like to come in? My sitter is sick today, so I need to keep an eye on Sandy. Kids, your afterschool snacks are on the table when you're ready." Garrett took control as though he was a parenting pro.

"Yay. I didn't like the school lunch today. It was a nasty lasagna, so I only ate the salad part, and I'm hungry." Melanie grimaced.

"I'd love to come in. I don't want to intrude, but I wanted to see everyone again if that's okay." April was still trying to process what she was seeing and hearing.

"Of course, it's okay. I hope I'm included in the everyone you want to see." He gazed at her and winked, leaving her speechless.

They all headed inside, April fully expecting the house to be destroyed without someone there to clean up today. Twenty-four hours was more than enough time to make a mess, especially for a three-year-old and two older kids who weren't the greatest at picking up behind themselves. What she noticed, however, made her stop and take a deeper look.

The house was lived in, but clean. They made their way to the kitchen, Garrett scooping up Sandy on the way. She peered over his shoulder and held her arms out to April, clenching her fingers.

"Hold me." It was the first time April had heard her talk, and it was sweet music to her ears. Garrett had done wonders to bring the girl back around to feeling loved and protected. April was more than ecstatic to snuggle Sandy, and Garrett seemed more than happy to let her.

"Have a seat, and I'll get you a snack." Garrett was far more relaxed than she'd ever seen him. He moved toward the refrigerator, giving April a clear view of the table. The kids sat down, placed napkins in their laps, and then picked up their snacks. *My flag decorated cookies.*

"Are those my cookies? From the festival. How did you get these?" *Why* was a better question?

Melanie and Bryan grinned.

"He bought them right after I told him you donated cookies," Melanie had a satisfied expression on her face.

"All of them?" April asked.

"All of them," Bryan confirmed.

"All ten dozen minus one." Garrett chucked Melanie on the chin affectionately.

"Well, that explains why they were sold out when I returned to buy some for the kids. But it doesn't explain why you would want ten dozen." April stared at Garrett, waiting for an answer.

"We froze them. The kids and I are hooked on your cooking, and it was a way to keep things together, as if you were still here. It was a silly idea, but it worked."

"We've had one a day after school to make them last," Bryan chimed in.

She shook her head. "And what was going to happen once you ate them all?"

"We were coming to find you," Melanie said, her mouth coated in red and blue frosting.

"You were going to come and ask me to make more cookies?" April was confused, and a bit hurt. They wanted her for her cookies. Not her. She tried not to dwell on it. The kids wouldn't understand.

"Something like that," Garrett admitted with a grin. "You'll understand soon enough."

The kids talked nonstop, telling her about school and their friends and everything in between.

"What prompted the move here? I thought you couldn't leave the city and the kids had started boarding school last month."

"Boarding school? Isn't that a school where kids live?" Bryan asked. "Why would Garrett do that? He likes having us around, don't you?" The boy looked to Garrett for confirmation.

"Yes, son, I do." He ruffled his hair. Son.

"But Brooke said—"

"Anything Brooke said was Brooke's doing. I asked her to investigate the schools, and she took it upon herself to apply. Yes, I know all about that. I found an opened envelope stuffed in one of the bottom drawers of my desk when I cleaned out my office. Not sure how it got there." He smirked, knowing perfectly well she was the one who had put it there.

"Brooke overstepped her boundaries, and we've since parted ways. I didn't need a secretary in New York after moving here. I've cut back my workload and handle the cases I want to work on from the satellite office I set up at the house. It's best for the kids...and me." Garrett kept surprising her every step of the way.

"I'm impressed. I still can't believe you're here. In Hallbrook." She shook her head, taking it all in. If they lived here, and he hadn't put the kids in boarding school, what did that mean for her and Garrett?

"Well, believe it. The kids, Rufus, and I come as a package deal. And we are all hoping you'll give us a second chance. Me, mainly. I know you love the kids, and some things never change."

Her heart thumped loudly in her chest. From not a single call to asking for a second chance was a giant leap. Did Garrett need a nanny and a house- keeper? Because she was done with that job title. "I'm busy at school, and I'm not sure how it would work. I'm sorry."

The kids' crestfallen faces nearly broke her heart. It's not as though she wouldn't come to visit them. She just didn't want to work for Garrett.

"April, can I talk to you alone for a minute. Please," he asked, one eyebrow cocked upward, daring her to refuse his simple request.

She stood. "Sure."

"Kids, we'll be right back. I think I should explain things to Miss April in private."

April followed him out of the kitchen and into the living room. "There's nothing to discuss. I'm not looking for a job, no matter how much I love the kids. Those days are behind me. You know I want to finish school and then teach."

"I never said we need you to cook and clean and babysit. I can handle all that by myself just fine. Look around. Well, the cooking part is coming along slowly." He chuckled.

"Then what do you need?" she asked.

"You." Garrett leaned down and kissed her with more passion than she remembered. It was a kiss that made her think of love. And sugar cookies, the flavor still on his lips.

She kissed him back, unable to stop the flood of emotions. This is where she belonged. In his arms. This was like coming home. She pulled back. "Me?" she asked, wondering what he meant.

"Yes, you. You see, I can do everything I need to do to be a dad and a business partner, but the one thing I can't do is marry the woman I love unless you say yes."

Tears welled up in her eyes. A noise caught her attention from the hallway, and she turned to find three faces and a dog watching and waiting.

She turned back just as Garrett drop to one knee. "April St. James, will you marry us? Please say you'll agree to be my wife, not for anything you can do for us, but because we all love you and we hope you love us, too."

The kids surrounded them, and Garrett picked up Sandy.

The little girl held out a black box to April. "Will you be my new mommy?"

April couldn't see through the haze of tears falling unchecked down her face. She'd stopped in to visit the kids and wound up with a family.

A family of her own to love her, not because they needed her, but because they wanted her.

"Yes. Yes. Yes. Yes. And, yes." She dropped a kiss on each of the children's heads, and then one on Rufus, finishing with Garrett. "I love you, too."

The children cheered and danced around them as Garrett pulled her tightly into his arms.

April was home.

What to read next...

Love & Family
A small-town doctor, a woman determined to find answers, and the power of family. Will the truth finally bring peace to these troubled hearts?

If you enjoyed this sweet and charming romance, be sure to check out the ALSO BY ELSIE DAVIS section on the next page for more clean and wholesome romance.

BONUS READ

Want to keep in touch with new releases and what's happening in the world of Elsie Davis? Sign up for the monthly newsletter at Elsie Davis HEA (Happily-Ever-After) and enjoy DIGGING THE DRIVER (A Celebrity Corgi Romance) as a FREE BOOK!

The greatest compliment you could give an author is to leave a review in order to help other readers discover the same great stories you enjoyed. Amazon/Bookbub/Goodreads are all great places. Many thanks!!!

Another great way to keep in touch - *Follow Elsie Davis on FaceBook*

Also By Elsie Davis

Sweet, Clean and Wholesome Stories...with a Happily-Ever-After Guarantee!

Holidays in Hallbrook
(Sweet Romance Series for Holidays Throughout the Year)
Welcome to Hallbrook, New Hampshire. A small-town filled with the unexpected, lots of love, and of course, a beloved dog to ramp up the excitement.
Love & Order (Labor Day)
Love & Family (Thanksgiving)
Love & Peace (Christmas)
Love & Chocolate (Valentine's Day)

Love & Hope (Mother's Day)
Love & Liberty (Independence Day)
Love & Honor (Veteran's Day)
Love & Joy (Easter)
Love & Adventure (Father's Day)

Great Smoky Mountain Getaways
(Christian Inspirational – Women's Fiction Romances)
Juliet's Journey to Love
Poppy's Path to Love
Rachel's Road to Love

Crossroads Creek Cowboys
(Christian Inspirational Romances)
The Heart of a Cowboy
The Help of a Cowboy
The Return of a Cowboy
Coming Soon – The Care of a Cowboy

Crestfield Inn Romances

If you like special kinds of soulmates, a splash of the supernatural, and wholesome relationships, you'll adore this sweet bit of fun filled with romance and mystery.
Turning Back Time
Turning Up Roses
Turning Down Pie

Celebrity Corgi Romance
(Standalone Sweet Romance)
If you like light mystery mixed in with your happily-ever-after, you'll enjoy this second-chance romance and the race to save an adorable Corgi.
Digging the Driver

Gold Coast Retrievers
(Sweet Romance)
Special Golden Retrievers help their humans solve mysteries, save lives, and even find love...
Defending Dakota

Trinity River
(Sweet Western Romance)
Ranchers and farmers depend on the Trinity River for water, but when a secret conglomerate starts buying up property by fair means or foul, it's time for the landowners of Tumble County to fight back—Texas style. But what they don't count on, is finding love in the process.
Back in the Rancher's Arms
Small Town, Big Secrets

Coming Soon! (2023-2024)

Sundancer's Legacy – 9 Book series

Sundancer's Star
Sundancer's Joy
Sundancer's Heart
Sundancer's Majesty
Sundancer's Miracle
Sundancer's Glory
Sundancer's Kiss

ELSIE DAVIS

Sundancer's Moon
Sundancer's Splendor

About The Author

Elsie Davis is a *USA Today and International Bestselling Author* of over 25 sweet, clean, and wholesome romances, and a member of the ACFW. She discovered the world of Happily-Ever-After romance at the age of twelve when she began avidly reading Barbara Cartland, the Queen of Romance, and has been hooked ever since. After building her dream log home on top of a small mountain, she turned her attention to do what she loves most, writing. Elsie writes sweet Contemporary Romance and Contemporary Christian Romance from her heart...hoping to share a little love in a big world.

When she's not writing, she can be found birding, kayaking, camping, fishing, playing disc golf, and taking nature walks—hoping to spot wildlife. Basically, she loves all things outdoors, EXCEPT cold weather. She and her husband are avid Caribbean cruisers, but Elsie's favorite vacation was their cruise to Alaska. (In spite of the cold!) Indoors, she enjoys a toasty fire, and of course, a great romance with a guaranteed Happily-Ever-After.

https://www.elsiedavishea.com

9 781959 401902